WARRIOR WOLF WOMEN OF THE WASTELAND

Also by **Carlton Mellick III**

Satan Burger
Electric Jesus Corpse
Sunset With a Beard (stories)
Razor Wire Pubic Hair
Teeth and Tongue Landscape
The Steel Breakfast Era
The Baby Jesus Butt Plug
Fishy-fleshed
The Menstruating Mall
Ocean of Lard (with Kevin L. Donihe)
Punk Land
Sex and Death in Television Town
Sea of the Patchwork Cats
The Haunted Vagina
Cancer-cute (Avant Punk Army Exclusive)
War Slut
Sausagey Santa
Ugly Heaven, Beautiful Hell (with Jeffrey Thomas)
Adolf in Wonderland
Ultra Fuckers
Cybernetrix
The Egg Man
Apeshit
The Faggiest Vampire
The Cannibals of Candyland

WARRIOR WOLF WOMEN OF THE WASTELAND

CARLTON MELLICK III

AVANT PUNK

AVANT PUNK

AN IMPRINT OF ERASERHEAD PRESS

ERASERHEAD PRESS
205 NE BRYANT
PORTLAND, OR 97211

WWW.ERASERHEADPRESS.COM

ISBN: 1-933929-92-8

AUTHOR'S NOTE

Twelve seconds after completing Warrior Wolf Women of the Wasteland I said to myself, "Did I just write a fucking *Furry* book?" It wasn't supposed to be my Furry book. It was supposed to be my werewolf book. But I guess werewolves can be considered furries. They were probably the *original* furries.

I never thought I would write a werewolf book. But over the past few years several publishers kept asking me to write something with werewolves in it. I knew that if I was going to do it I would have to do my own werewolf mythology. I never cared for the whole full moon transformation thing. I wanted to do something more interesting. I also knew that I wanted the story to take place in a post-apocalyptic wasteland. I wanted it to be kind of like Road Warrior, but starring a bunch of werewolves instead of Mel Gibson. It ended up more like a Road Warrior Furry book than a Road Warrior with werewolves book, but I think it's better this way.

I have to admit that I like how there has been more of a focus on female werewolves in books and movies over the past decade. In the subtext, werewolf stories have always been about sexuality and releasing those animalistic desires that we are taught to repress by our civilized culture. Because of this, it's just more interesting when the werewolves are women rather than men. Though I guess hermaphrodite werewolves would be even more interesting than female werewolves.

This book was originally going to be called "Wolves of the Wasteland." When I told this to Rose, owner of Eraserhead Press, she said, "You can't call it that. It's not a Carlton Mellick III book title." I said, "What's a Carlton Mellick III book title?" And she said, "You know, like The Haunted Vagina, Baby Jesus Butt Plug, Razor Wire Pubic Hair. Wolves of the Wasteland is cliche." So I came up with a goofier title, one that seems like it could have come out of the Troma film catalog.

This is probably my longest book since Satan Burger. It was also one of the funnest writing experiences I've ever had. I wrote it in three weeks, in my office in Northwest Portland. By three weeks, I mean that I did nothing but write every waking hour for three weeks straight until I finished it. After a while, I pretty much forgot all about the real world and it felt as though I was living with these wolf girls as I was writing about them. And after I finished the book, I still couldn't get this world out of my head and started drawing pictures of the characters. I also have the urge to write a sequel or turn it into a series, which is something that never happens to me.

If I did turn it into a series I think I'd make it kind of like that Logan's Run television series, where each episode Logan finds a different culture that evolved in a weird way after the apocalypse. But for my series, there would be fuzzy biker chicks instead of that British dude. And they may or may not obtain a gentleman robot companion during their travels. If I don't go with the robot, I might go with a couple of pink ninjas or a leprechaun with a mohawk.

In any case, I hope you enjoy this book.

- Carlton Mellick III, 10/05/09 4:15 am

WARRIOR WOLF WOMEN
OF THE WASTELAND

Chapter 1

Daniel Togg

The wolves are howling outside of the three-hundred-foot-high steel walls surrounding McDonaldland. The wolves always howl at this time of day, around the time the sun goes down. I sit on my apartment windowsill, drinking some homemade ketchup wine from a styrofoam cup, listening to the wolves, and staring down at my toes wiggling in the frosty air.

Smoke is billowing out of the factories in the distance. Smoke is always billowing out of everything in this part of the country. Although, I don't like to call this country a *country*. It isn't as much of a country as it is a city, or maybe *kingdom* would be the most accurate term. The McDonald's Kingdom.

After the economic apocalypse, McDonald's took over. There wasn't anyone left to stop them. The government had collapsed. The military was disbanded. The rich had become poor and the poor had become violent. Then the Christian extremists got a hold of the missiles and took out every city they felt was the enemy of their god, which happened to be all of them.

The Blessed McDonald's Corporation brought order to the chaos. Surviving the economic disaster and the nuclear attacks, they were the most powerful organization left on the planet. They gathered the surviving Americans together and developed a new country the size of Chicago, a peaceful civilization that they could nurture and protect. They called it *McDonaldland.*

That was nearly twelve decades ago. Long before I was born. The citizens of McDonaldland don't live as

9

long as people used to, only about 50 odd years if they're lucky, so it has been a couple generations since the original McDonaldlandians died off.

The great wall was built around the city. It wasn't made of steel, not originally, nor was it three hundred feet high. That upgrade came a little later. The Blessed McDonald's Corporation said that the wall would keep out the unruly outcasts that lived in the wasteland surrounding their country, but the citizens of McDonaldland soon realized that the walls weren't designed to keep people out. They were designed to keep people in.

There isn't anything alive outside the walls anymore, except for the wolves. There aren't any people. Not that I would know for sure, because McDonaldlandians haven't ventured outside the country into the wasteland in a hundred years. But there have been no sounds of civilization. No airplanes flying over head. No voices. No horns honking. Just howling and occasionally scratching on the other side of the barricade, sometimes reverberating through the metal so loudly that I can hear it from several neighborhoods away.

My name is Daniel Togg. That was also my dad's name, when he was still alive. I live in the slums of McDonaldland, in the southernmost region of the *kingdom*. The walls cast such enormous shadows in this area that not a drop of light ever reaches my home no matter what time of day it is. It always seems like night. If it weren't for the wolves howling, I wouldn't even know that the sun is setting.

Although most McDonaldlandians consider this side of town gloomy and depressing, I really don't mind the darkness. All the buildings in McDonaldland are painted bright yellow and red—the colors of the McDonaldland flag. In the sunny areas of the city, I find these colors incredibly irritating to look at. The streets are yellow, the sidewalks are red, the walls are yellow, the roofs are red, the buses are yellow, the cars are red. Even when not wearing their work uniforms, the people wear red and yellow clothing to show their patriotism. The Blessed McDonald's Corporation says that these colors are designed to make you happy, but they do not make me happy. They make me very, very stressed. It is like the city is constantly yelling at my eyes. I am perfectly happy living on the dark side of town, where the bright colors are dulled by shadows.

Outside my window, I try to keep my second pair of arms hidden beneath a rubber yellow blanket, but sometimes they have a mind of their own and straighten themselves out when they are supposed to be bent. If I wiggle my fingers on all four hands at the same time, I'm usually able to get the new arms under control. But not always. Not many people are walking around on the shadowed street below, so I believe I'll be safe even if one of the extra limbs are revealed for a moment or two.

I'm lying in a hammock that serves as a makeshift balcony, although it's only a balcony for one man lying down. I made it out of burger wrappers and napkins. If twisted up properly you can make some pretty strong rope out of just about any paper, even toilet paper, as long as you don't let the rain get to it.

I like to make things. That's my hobby. I'll make just about anything I can think of, using all the items McDonaldland has to offer. After I relax away today's stress, I think I'll make a new batch of ketchup wine. Of all the things I make, I am most skilled as a brewer of beers, wines, and alcohols.

Being a brewer in McDonaldland is a terrible crime. It is considered heresy. The citizens of this country are only allowed to consume the items available on the McDonald's menu. All other food and drink is forbidden. You are not allowed to make your own food and you are certainly not allowed to sell it. Since alcoholic drinks are not on the menu, I have to make it myself, breaking one of McDonaldland's strictest laws. Even worse, I also sell it to people in my neighborhood, which The Blessed McDonald's Corporation believes cuts into their coffee and soda profits.

If they found out they'd probably force me to work a third shift with no pay for a year or two. Or maybe they'd just throw me out of the kingdom, into the wasteland, to be eaten by wolves. But whatever. I don't care. I'm willing to risk anything in order to make my own things.

I have yet to risk cooking my own food, but if I could get my hands on some raw ingredients (besides potatoes) I would sure as hell try.

The wolf howls can still be heard within the tiny kitchen section of my one room 10' x 10' apartment. Of course, McDonaldland apartments do not come with kitchens, because of the anti-cooking laws. But they do come with sinks, so I built a tiny kitchen around the sink for brewing purposes. I believe building your own kitchen is also against the law.

I learned how to brew from my grandfather. He tried to teach everyone how to brew their own beer and make their own things, but everyone else in our family (especially my dad and my older brother) had no intention of ever breaking the law. He also made his own food, because he worked in the warehouse district and had access to all of the raw ingredients he wanted. Because he made his own food, he lived much longer than all McDonaldlandians born in his year.

I really liked my grandpa, even though he was only around until I was eleven. He brewed beer, made wine, wrote books, and made some nice sculptures of boats and airplanes out of straws. I still have one of his straw airplanes. I've seen pictures of airplanes before in history class, and the sculpture was quite accurate, despite the materials from which it was created. Though it couldn't fly.

I can only make my alcohol out of the foods available on the McDonald's menu. The factories and farms that produce the raw ingredients have strict security measures to prevent someone like me from getting a hold of them (unless you had a job like my grandpa's). Things like wheat, flour, yeast, and barley are all unattainable, so I have to be creative.

Although I do work in the fry-chopping plant and have access to raw potatoes, I don't use them. I once stole enough potatoes to make some homemade potato vodka, but it was a pain in the ass and stealing from work is a risky business, so I don't do that anymore.

The first and most important ingredient to brewing is the yeast. Since I can't get yeast from McDonald's, I have to cultivate wild yeast myself. For this, I take apples from the apple dippers, the fruit and yogurt parfait, and the hot apple pies. I soak a hamburger bun in warm sugar water for an hour, then remove the bun and put in the apples. Then everything goes into an airtight container. Every day I open the container and add some more sugar. Yeast will grow and thrive in this mixture. After several days, I remove the apples and then I have my starter that lasts for years if properly maintained.

To make alcohol, all you really need is yeast, sugar,

and water. The yeast eats the sugar and excretes alcohol. It also produces carbon dioxide which will carbonate beverages. So I go to any of the McDonald's restaurants—there is one in each neighborhood—and buy any item that is high in sugar. Though some of the best items are free: ketchup, sugar, sweet and sour sauce, and jelly. Other good ingredients: fruit juices, orange drink, strawberry sauce, tomatoes, hotcake syrup, cookies, and fruit from the fruit and yogurt parfait.

My favorite, because it's so cheap and easy, is ketchup wine. I just get some tomatoes, ketchup packets, a little syrup, some apple juice, some of the yeast, and a lot of sugar. This mixture goes into a plastic container with warm water and a straw in it to release the carbon dioxide (otherwise it would explode). Once it stops bubbling, after a week or so, it's ready to drink.

If put into an airtight container with a little more sugar, the drink carbonates. I call that drink ketchup champagne.

My grandpa used to brew some really good beers, because he was able to get his hands on all of the raw ingredients he needed. He had to grow his own hops, which must have been the hardest part. I know they grow easily in this region of the world, but I wouldn't have the guts to grow my own ingredients.

Everyone in his neighborhood would buy his beer, and everyone on that side of town was really happy for a while. Then he was caught and taken away. Other brewers had only been fined and sentenced to work extra shifts, but they made an example of Grandpa. Nobody ever heard from him ever again.

After I'm done mixing together the ketchup wine, I get ready

14

for my next shift. It's shift after shift for me. Every lower class McDonaldlandian works at least two shifts a day. The pay is just too low and the cost of living is just too high. But that's the way The Blessed McDonald's Corporation has created it. Since every citizen of this country is employed by The Blessed McDonald's Corporation (apart from children, it's the law) and every citizen rents their home from The Blessed McDonald's Corporation, then McDonald's only has to lower pay and raise rent in order to get more hours out of their employees. But they only do this to the lower class workers, of course.

I tie my extra pair of arms around my waist tightly so that they don't move around, and keep them hidden beneath my work uniform. The worst possible thing that could happen to me would be for someone to discover my new arms. Anybody with deformities is instantly taken away without question, because The Blessed McDonald's Corporation doesn't want any of its citizens to think the deformities were caused by the chemicals that are put into the food ... which, of course, they are.

On my way out of the apartment, I run into the woman who lives across the hall. Like most women who are out in public, she is clothed from head to toe, covering her face and hair. Her outfit is similar to an Arab woman's burka, only instead of black the clothing is red and yellow. The only thing I can see is her demonic yellow eyes staring at me from behind the clothes.

"I smell things," she says to me. That's what she always says to me.

I'm not allowed to talk to her, look at her, or get too close to her unless she speaks to me first. Unfortunately, she always speaks to me.

"I forgot to take the garbage out again," I say. "Sorry."

"If you're cooking food in there you'll be exiled," she says. "They'll feed you to the wolves."

I try to respect her as much as possible, so I do not call her a bitch.

"I'm not cooking food," I say.

Not all women are clothed in this manner or need to be treated in this respectful way—only the women who have mothered children. It is a big part of McDonaldlandian culture.

"If you cook food I will tell," she says. "I will tell them to feed you to the wolves."

I just nod until she goes back into her apartment and closes the door.

I decide it would be best to be late for work. Everyone else is always early for work, so there's got to be at least one person late so that Landon, my boss, has someone to yell at. If Landon didn't have me to yell at then he probably wouldn't have much of anything to do.

Forget the bus, I'll just walk to work. A long walk would do me some good. The majority of McDonaldlandians are either obese or morbidly obese, because of their high fat diet. Not me. I exercise. I don't eat so much. Just like my grandpa taught me. We are required to buy at least three meals a day, but I use much of the food I purchase to create my alcoholic drinks.

As I walk down the darkened red sidewalk, I peek in at the obese families gathering for dinner in their apartments, unwrapping their to-go burgers and dripping secret sauce all over their double chins. It is no wonder most McDonaldlandians don't make it into their sixties.

16

I take the long route to work, on the edge of the farmlands. This section of the city is off-limits to all except the farmers, but I can look through the fence at the fields of wheat. There are a herd of cows grazing in the field, leaving trails of slime behind them. The lifeless mooing reverberates through the wheat field.

Cows of the past do not look like the cows we have now. They used to have four legs, a tail, and a head ... almost like an enormous dog. They used to be able to eat, poop, think, moo, and sleep without the need for a computer chip implanted into their brain. Cows these days are more like large mounds of meat with black and white spots. Their mouths are underneath them, so they consume food in the way that slugs consume food, by sliming on top of decaying matter and slurping on it. The computer chip controls their eating. They are not really alive.

These *nu-cows*, as they were originally called, also have small speakers implanted into their backs that give off a pre-programmed mooing noise whenever people come near. This is so that people will still think of them as living creatures instead of programmed slabs of meat. There are also *nu-chickens* on the other side of the farm.

Although the creation of these nu-cows was a bit disturbing to most people, there was a race of humans called vegans who were mostly happy about the creation of nu-cows because it ended the suffering of old cows.

Vegans lived a long time ago, before the formation of McDonaldland. They were people who believed that all living things are created equal and should be respected rather than utilized, so they refused to eat meat or harm animals in any way. They also tried to stop other people from eating meat or harming animals. This was a problem because other people did not believe that all living things were created equal, and they believed that man was on top of the food chain so they could do whatever they wanted with lesser species.

Another problem was that the Christians, which made up a good portion of the population, believed that animals do not have souls and were put on this planet by their god so that they can be eaten by Christians. Both vegans and Christians were adamant about their beliefs, and there was no way that one group could change the mind of the other's. That's the way beliefs work.

It seemed like the perfect solution for both groups was to create nu-cows. It provided meat, and at the same time ended animal suffering. However, neither group seemed completely satisfied with this solution. That's usually the way compromise works.

Veganism was outlawed by The Blessed McDonald's Corporation a couple of years after the creation of nu-cows.

The prayer bell rings. It rings five times a day and all citizens are expected to pray to The Blessed McDonald's Corporation when the bell goes off. It rings before dawn, at noon, at midday, after dusk, and at night. This is the after dusk prayer bell.

Nobody is here to see me, so I decide not to kneel down and pray on the spot as I'm supposed to. I avoid praying as much as I can.

The Blessed McDonald's Corporation created their own religion about 9 decades ago. They thought it would be best to do away with all the old world religions and create a new one that was more relevant to modern society. That is why I don't pray. I know the McDonald's religion is completely fabricated and borrowed from other religions that no longer exist. My grandpa told me that The Blessed McDonald's Corporation just combined all existing world religions into one with a McDonald's theme, and called it their own religion. The messiah, Ronald McDonald, was based on a character named Jesus, which the Christians believed in, as well as the Islamic prophet Muhammad. Mayor McCheese was based on gods called Yahweh and Allah. The Fry Guys were based on angels. The Hamburglar was based on the Christian devil, Lucifer. I forget who Grimace was based on. I think it was Jesus's friend Peter, although I don't think Peter was purple or retarded.

Even though the folklore of the McDonaldland faith is more closely associated with Christianity, the practice of the faith more closely resembles the old Islamic religion. Praying five times a day is one example of this. Another is the way that women dress. Of course, it is only the women who have had children who must dress in this way.

I realize that my knees are too clean today. In McDonaldland, it is important to keep your knees dirty. This shows other people that you pray long and hard when the prayer bell rings. Clean knees means you're a sinner and probably a heretic. You can get into a lot of trouble and quickly outcast if you are always seen with clean knees.

I do what I always do after I skip a pray time: I rub dirt on my knees. Not too much. Just enough to make it look like I pray with conviction.

Somebody comes around a corner and sees me rubbing dirt

WARRIOR WOLF WOMEN OF THE WASTELAND

on my knees. I pray that it is not a Fry Guy.
The man is wearing a furry blue suit.
Shit, it *is* a Fry Guy.

Fry Guys are not only the angels of the McDonaldlandian faith, they are also a term used to describe the authorities of McDonaldland who enforce the laws. Long ago, these people would have been called policemen, security guards, Federales, or maybe even Gestapo. They are called Fry Guys because they are the saving angels of McDonaldland.

In the official Bible of The Blessed McDonald's Corporation (which is available in vending machines at every McDonald's restaurant), the Fry Guys look like fuzzy blue, red, and yellow balls of fur with legs and googley eyes. In McDonaldland, the Fry Guys are ordinary humans, but they wear fuzzy suits like military uniforms. Some wear red, some wear yellow, some wear blue. The color indicates rank. The yellow rank is the lowest, the blue rank is the highest.

The man walking toward me is wearing blue, so he must be a Fry Guy Lieutenant.

"Rubbing dirt on your knees again, eh Daniel?" says the Fry Guy.

I recognize his gruff, monotone voice. It's my damned brother. Of all the Fry Guys, it had to be him.

"Hey, Guy," I say to him.

His name is really Guy. Guy the Fry Guy. How stupid is that?

"You have to stop doing that," he says, grunting and rubbing his enormous blond mustache. He always grunts and rubs his enormous blond mustache. "If it were anybody else who saw you you'd be getting ticketed a pretty steep fine right now."

I'd rather pay the fine.

"I know," I tell him, and try to move on.

"Hold on, little brother." He gets into my path. When he puts his large brick wall of a body in front of you, there's no getting around. "I haven't seen you in almost a year. Where have you been hiding?"

"It's been a year? I didn't realize."

Of course I realized. I was avoiding him on purpose.

"I'm the only family you have left," he says. "I'm surprised you wouldn't want to see me more often, especially during McDonaldmas."

McDonaldmas is based on a Christian holiday that hasn't been celebrated in a hundred years called Christmas.

"I was sick last McDonaldmas."

"Same as the one before that?" Guy says.

I shrug at him.

Guy the Fry Guy insists that I come home with him for dinner. He's stubborn and when he insists there is no way he'll let you change his mind. He remembered that I had yet to see his new baby who was born four months ago. Not coming to visit his newborn son was an error that I must rectify immediately, so he said. I didn't like meeting his last kid, or the one before that, so I didn't care to meet another one.

I tell him that I am late for work. He tells me that he will give me a note of excuse. Fry Guy Lieutenants have the power to do that.

As we walk, I notice the wolves are still howling. Sometimes

21

they howl all night. Even though he is a large burly man who rarely expresses any emotion, my brother still gets a chill every time he hears a howl. It was like that ever since he was a kid, but it seems to have gotten worse now that he's an adult.

I try to keep my extra limbs as still as possible. They were just baby arms when they started growing a couple years ago. I didn't have problems hiding them when I visited my brother back then, but now they are fully grown and much more difficult to hide. Perhaps that is one of the reasons why I avoid my brother. Out of fear of embarrassment among his coworkers, it's not likely that Guy would turn me in for having this deformity, but there's a good chance that he would find a doctor friend to cut them off. For some reason, I don't want to get them cut off. Even though they're not supposed to be there, I hate the thought of losing limbs. Plus, this deformity makes me unique and I try to treasure everything that's unique about me. That's what my grandpa always said: "whatever makes you strange is what makes you special."

My brother does not believe that whatever makes you strange is what makes you special. He believes that whatever makes you strange is what is wrong with you. As a Fry Guy, he works hard to maintain conformity amongst the McDonaldland citizens.

The only thing unique about my brother that I can think of is his big blond mustache. He is the only person in all of McDonaldland with such a large manly mustache. Because most McDonaldlandians work around food, they are not allowed to grow large mustaches. Most people have tiny wimpy mustaches.

Guy is very proud of his mustache. He grooms it

obsessively and stares at it for hours in the mirror while flexing his bulky muscles. His mustache is where he gets his confidence and strength, which he uses to be a good authority figure. I always wanted to shave off his mustache just to see what would happen. He treats the thing as if it contains all of his manly power, and he would become weak and helpless if he were ever to lose it.

Although Guy always acts like he is against individuality, I know that the reason he treasures his mustache so highly is because it is the one thing that makes him unique. It makes him stand out as someone special, someone privileged. He would never admit it—he probably doesn't even realize it— but Guy treasures his individuality more than anybody else in McDonaldland.

We pick up some burgers when we get to Guy's neighborhood. He gets extra hot apple pies, because he thinks I like hot apple pies. I did when I was a kid, but Guy is the type of person who doesn't take into consideration that someone's taste might change.

"You must get lonely in that tiny apartment of yours," Guy says through his puffy mustache. "Do you ever socialize with anyone?"

"I hang out with people from time to time."

To sell them my homebrew.

"Whatever happened to your friends, Frank and Robby? Are you still playing cards with them?"

I shake my head. "I lost contact with Frank last year. He just stopped calling. Robby disappeared some months ago. I guess he moved to another part of town. I went to see him at work a while ago but he must have changed jobs."

Guy looks down at the red sidewalk and switches the subject.

"You're going to love my new boy," he says, not in an excited parent's voice but in a mechanical matter-of-fact voice. "He's the cutest thing you'll ever see."

When we get to his luxurious apartment on the good side of town—that is so far from the McDonaldland walls that the howls coming from the wasteland cannot be heard—he immediately shows me his new baby boy to prove just how cute he really is.

I do not hold it. I just say, "Yeah, he sure is the cutest." Really, the baby looks just like every other baby. Small, chubby, and bald.

Guy grunts and nods in approval, then puts the baby down on the floor. He seems to treat it more like a trophy than a newborn human being.

"Molly, we have company," Guy shouts to the other room.

When Molly turns the corner, she has a wide happy smile on her face. But when she sees me, she doesn't seem to recognize me. Her smile fades and she exposes her fangs. A slight growl comes out of her throat.

Then she recognizes who she is growling at and composes herself.

"Oh, hi Daniel," she says.

Molly is looking bigger and hairier than ever. Beneath her red house dress, her entire body is covered in thick brown fur. Last time I saw her she still had some skin showing, but now it is completely coated.

She wags her tail as she approaches me and shakes my hand. I try not to stare into her yellow beastly eyes as her

24

claws dig into my wrist.

"Sorry," she says, when she sees the white scratches on my hand. "I'm still getting used to them."

The claws are also a new addition. As is her long muzzle.

Molly is turning into a wolf. This happens to all women, once they begin to have children. Some women become less wolf-like than others. I haven't seen a woman as wolf-like as Molly since my mother was pregnant with her third kid a long time ago.

It is a disease that came about in the early days of McDonaldland. They call the disease lycanthropy, which was named after a fictional disease of the same name that turned people into werewolves. But there is a big difference between this version of lycanthropy and the fictional one. For starters, only women are affected by this disease. It doesn't affect men. Secondly, the disease isn't spread from a werewolf bite. All McDonaldlandian women are born with this disease. Thirdly, the changes are not caused by a full moon. The changes occur only during the act of having sex. Fourthly, once the transformation occurs, the women do not return to human form as werewolves would the next morning. The mutation is permanent. Fifthly, the transformation doesn't happen all at once. The changes happen a little at a time, each time the female engages in sexual activity, including masturbation.

It is believed that these changes occur during sex because the mutation is a result of the virus reacting to endorphins released in the brain during sexual stimulation and especially orgasm. This is a shaky theory, however, because endorphins are released in the brain for more reasons than just sex.

Because sex is the cause of these lycanthropic

changes, sex has become illegal in McDonaldland. You can only partake in sexual activity if you obtain a permit from the board of directors. And you can only get a permit if you are married and only have sex to procreate. The permit is good for only five days and you are only allowed to have sex once per day. It doesn't matter if the pregnancy is a success or not after the five days are up. If the new wolf-like features are not too serious, then you can apply for another permit to have a second kid in the future. The upper class, of which Guy is a part, is usually allowed to get a third permit. This is why Molly is now almost more wolf than human. Most women are not allowed to mutate this much.

The burkas that McDonaldlandian mothers wear in public, that cover their skin from head to toe, are designed to hide their wolf-like features. But some women, the younger more liberal-minded ones, don't wear these outfits. They usually aren't able to get away with this unless their wolf-features are very subtle. Every once in a while you will run into a girl with fangs, whiskers, and glowing yellow eyes, but this is rare. It is considered low class.

Molly is ferocious when Guy gives her the burgers. She rips open the wrappers on three Double Cheeseburgers at once and tears into them with her slobbery black jaws. After the first bite, she realizes what she is doing and composes herself. She sits her two daughters at the table into their chairs and gives them their meals. Then she sits herself down and continues eating in a more civilized manner.

Women who are as wolf-like as Molly often have problems controlling their instinctual urges. They become more wild and unruly. Molly has probably transformed so much that Guy isn't allowed to let her out of the house. That is the law with some women who have been granted three sex permits.

If she becomes any more beast-like, the Fry Guys will have to capture her and release her into the wasteland outside of the walls. The only reason she hasn't been taken out of town already is probably because of Guy's status.

Even if they are not yet unruly, any woman who has sex without a permit is sent into the wasteland. It is not just against the law, it is considered heresy. It is McDonaldland's strictest law. There is no leniency toward any woman. Even the Chief of the Fry Guys had to send his own daughter into the wasteland, because she had sex a single time without a permit. I know that story all too well.

This is why there are so many wolves in the wasteland outside of McDonaldland. They are not real wolves. Real wolves have been extinct for a very long time. The wolves in the wasteland are the women who have been outcast from McDonaldland. They were once human, but now they are animals, howling outside the walls as if begging to be let back in.

I take a burger and a hot apple pie from the pile of burgers and apple pies. There is also a large bowl full of fries centering the table that the entire family is supposed to share. It's a dinner tradition that Guy took from our parents. This tradition always bothered me, because I don't like eating fries from the same bowl as everyone else. I especially don't like to eat them when there's a wolf woman like Molly digging her paws into the bowl every few minutes, leaving dozens of brown hairs on top of the food.

"How's work?" Guy asks me.

"Shitty," I say.

Molly growls at me. I assume it is for using foul language around her kids.

I ignore her and say, "I have to work two shifts seven days a week and my rent keeps going up. Even with two shifts, I have no money for recreation and for food I can only eat items from the value menu."

"You know," Guy says, I already know what he's going to say, "You should really come join the Fry Guy Force."

"So you always tell me."

"We could really use a guy like you. You're in better shape than half the guys on the force. You'd have better hours, better pay, more respect. You could move out of the slums into a good neighborhood. Get a wife. Have kids."

I want to tell him off, tell him I'd never become a Fry Guy, tell him I hate everything they stand for. But my extra arms begin to twitch. Whenever I'm overexcited, they always twitch. So I have to calm myself and be more civil with him.

"I really don't think I'm cut out to be a Fry Guy," I tell him.

"Physically, you're perfectly cut out for it," he says. "That's usually the hard part for new applicants. You just need an attitude adjustment. You just need to grow up."

I just smile and nod at him.

"They have great programs now to fix that," he says. "They're working on psychological reconstruction. There are even drugs that are being developed that can help you think more like a Fry Guy. Like me."

"I don't know about that," I say.

He waves his Big Mac at me. "I'm telling you, this is what you should do. You would be much happier."

28

Judging by Guy's monotone voice, being a Fry Guy hasn't made him much happier.

"Maybe some day," I tell him, to shut him up.

Molly glares at me with her bloodthirsty yellow eyes. She can see right through me. She knows I have no intention of ever considering joining the Fry Guy Force. She can tell that I despise everything that her husband stands for.

"Maybe some day you will stop being such a loser," she says, baring her fangs at me.

"Molly," Guy gently squeezes the scruff of her neck, which is what he does to anyone who embarrasses him. "Please."

"No," she says, tossing her husband's arm away. "You have just offered him an opportunity that could improve his life and he just throws it back into your face."

"I'm sorry," I say, lowering my head in submission. You have to do this with wolf women or else they might rip your throat out.

I stand up to leave before things get out of control, but Guy puts me back into my seat.

"She's just a bit snappy these days," Guy says.

Women are snappy most of the time, due to sexual frustration. The more wolf-like a woman becomes the more her sexual drive increases, and the more sexually frustrated she'll get.

"I'm sorry." Molly composes herself and tries to be cordial. She changes the subject.

"Are you seeing anyone?" she asks me, with a condescending false smile.

"No," I say.

"I think a woman is what you really need. Somebody who can clean you up and set you on the right path. If you had

WARRIOR WOLF WOMEN OF THE WASTELAND

a wife and maybe some kids you would know the importance of getting a good job and living in a good neighborhood."

Guy gives her a look and she backs off.

"She has a point, Daniel," Guy says, rubbing special sauce from his mustache. "Meeting Molly was the best thing that ever happened to me. You should find a woman to settle down with."

I shrug. "I'm just not interested in any women around here."

He shakes his head. "It isn't because of Nova?"

I take a big bite of apple pie.

"I see it is," Guy says. "It's been years. You should have moved on by now."

"She was the only girl I've ever been attracted to," I say.

"She was your girlfriend when you were a teenager," he says. "You're nearly thirty now."

"We were still dating in our early twenties," I said. "I probably would have married her by now."

"You've got to get over that," he says. "She's gone. She's never coming back."

I finish my food as quickly as possible and stand up.

"I think I better go," I say. "I'm already two hours late for my job."

November, who went by Nova for short, was the daughter of the Chief of the Fry Guys. He's one of the main reasons I hate the Fry Guys so much. He's the man who took Nova away from me.

In school, teenagers are usually plump. I'm not really attracted to plump girls, even though that is the desired figure of most McDonaldlandians. When I met November, she was as thin as me. She liked sports and exercise. She didn't like eating greasy food. We liked the way we looked.

It wasn't long before we became good friends. I would call her my *Novey*, as a pet name. She thought it was cute. She didn't like making things, as I did, but she liked doing things, which I decided I liked, too. She liked to climb trees, throw rocks at the nu-cows, steal burgers from fat men who didn't have the energy to chase after us, and look under the dresses of veiled mothers to see their hairy legs. She had less interest in maturity than I did, though that might have been because she was two years younger. She liked getting into trouble.

Her father didn't like her behavior. With his busy job and without a mother to keep her in line, she didn't have anybody to discipline her when she was doing things she wasn't allowed to do. So she did whatever she pleased.

When she had sex illegally, her father was forced to kick her out of town. She didn't have sex with me. Although we were very close, we never were very intimate. Everyone thought she was my girlfriend, we even kissed a few times to see what it would feel like, and we showed each other our naked bodies out of curiosity, but we didn't have that kind of relationship. I loved my Novey. I'm not sure, but I think she might have loved me back.

After her twenty-first birthday, on her way to work in the apple orchard, November was raped at gunpoint by a man in a yellow mask. Rape is very common in McDonaldland. Men are able to masturbate, so most men are able to sexually relieve themselves without the need for sex with women. But there are some men who need more than that. They don't care if it is against the law. They don't care about the women, or what it does to them.

If a woman is raped she is considered guilty of having

illegal sex, even though it was against her will. Some women do not have enough sexual stimulation for any changes to occur. These lucky few only have to keep silent about the sexual assault and nothing will happen to them. But the majority of the women who are raped are banished from McDonaldland and sent into the wasteland. This is what happened to November. The man who raped her got away, and she was the one to be punished for his crime.

It is believed that the wolves outside the walls are cannibals. If a woman is not developed enough as a predator she will be hunted down and eaten by the more wolf-like women. It is believed that none of the rape victims survive long in the wasteland. After only having sex once, they are hardly wolves at all. Just normal girls with slightly sharper teeth and slightly yellowed eyes.

Everyone told me that there was no way Nova would survive out there. She has to be dead. But I know November. She's a survivor. If it is survival of the fittest out there, I bet she found a hole to hide in and then masturbated over and over again day and night until she transformed into the biggest, toughest wolf in the wasteland.

Sometimes, when I hear the howls outside the walls, I like to think one of those wolves is her, causing trouble in the wild.

Guy the Fry Guy gives me a ride to work in his red Fry Guy McCar, that is shaped like a red package of fries with a yellow "M" on top. Cars used to be fueled by something called gasoline, but McCars are solar-powered. Almost everything in McDonaldland is solar powered.

I don't speak to him during the trip, but he speaks to me.

"If dad were still alive he'd have been pretty disappointed in you," he says.

"He was always disappointed in me," I say.

"That's because you reminded him of his dad," he says. "Grandpa didn't know how to fit in. He was a silly old fool. He committed crimes just for the sake of committing them. If he wasn't so insistent on going against the flow he wouldn't have been such a miserable man. I don't want to see you going down that same path."

I definitely want to go down that path.

"Yeah, I hear you," I tell him. "I'll try to get my act together."

Then we get to my work. A faded yellow building with no windows and only a couple doors.

"I hope you do," he says. "Now I want you to come visit me on a weekly basis, so that my children come to think of you as a normal uncle. Sundays would be best. Perhaps we can even attend church together.

"I'm not allowed in your church," I tell him. "I don't live in your neighborhood."

"If you arrive with me you will be let in," he says. "Just make sure to look your best."

"I'll see if I can get out of work," I tell him.

I have no intention of seeing if I can get out of work.

"It's important," Guy says.

I nod at him and get out of the car quickly before he makes me promise to meet him before church this Sunday. But, as I'm trying to get out as quickly as possible, one of my extra arms breaks free of its binding and slips out of my shirt.

He's looking right at me as I pull it back into my uniform. He doesn't say anything, just stares at me with a surprised face.

"See you later," I say, and walk away, pretending nothing happened.

Chapter 2

Guy the Fry Guy

My dad died when he fell into a giant fryilator. He was deep fried alive in a vat of boiling oil. Following in the old man's footsteps, I now work in the exact same factory that he worked at, above the exact same fryilator that he was killed in.

Guy forgot to give me the note of excuse, even though it was the only reason I let him convince me to go back to his house with him (he always does that kind of stuff to me), so when I arrive to work my boss, Landon, is more pissed than I have ever seen him.

"You know, I could get you arrested for ditching work like this," Landon says to me, wearing his tiny little yellow manager hat. "Do you know how many fries are consumed each day? Do you know what would happen if production went down by just ten percent?"

I'm not sure if it is a rhetorical question.

"I'd have to announce a fry shortage alert," he says to me. "And that's going to freak the Hamburglar out of everybody."

I stare at him for a minute, then say, "Sorry," and walk to my work station.

"Sorry?" Landon says. "Sorry?"

I get back to work.

"Get back to work!" he yells at me, even though I have already gotten back to work, and then goes to his office.

My job is to work the potato-chopping machine. I basically just dump boxes of potatoes into a machine that washes them, peels them, and then cuts them into fries. All I have to do is carry boxes around and push buttons on a machine.

I'm not the only one who works this machine. It is usually a two-man job. I work with a fat guy named Pete. Well, calling Pete *fat* doesn't really cut it, because pretty much everyone in McDonaldland is fat. But Pete is special. He is the fattest guy I know. It's because he eats a lot of salads, which are actually more fattening than Big Macs, and McGriddles, which are the most fattening thing on the McDonald's menu.

When I see Pete, he is sweating out of every pore in his body. I wasn't here, so he had to do the job of two people. Because Pete is so out of shape and so hopelessly lazy, he's used to me doing most of the work for him. I do the work of two people and he just tries to get out of my way. But Pete would have trouble doing the job of just one person, let alone two, so he is struggling to keep up with the machine.

When he sees me, he nearly collapses with exhaustion and relief.

"Thank Ronald you're here," he says, his voice cracking between rapid breaths. "I thought I was going to die."

"Sorry about that," I say.

Wiping wet hair out of his eyes, he says, "I don't care. Just take over for me."

I take over for him.

As I work, Pete collapses onto a bag of potatoes and gasps for breath.

"Never do that to me again," he says. "I nearly had a heart attack. And it didn't help to have Landon yelling at me the whole time."

"Landon's an asshole," I say.

"Of course he is," he says, wheezing, "but there's no need to swear."

I see Pete more than anyone else these days, because we work so closely together. But Pete is too much of a goody-goody for me to call him a friend. He's too patriotic, too conservative. Still, he's not a bad guy. Better than people like Landon or my brother.

While lounging on the potato pile, Pete pulls a cheeseburger out of his pocket. He takes a bite of the burger and blows his nose into the wrapper.

Pete doesn't even stand up for the next hour as I do both of our jobs. Usually, he at least pretends to be working. Landon must have really pushed him hard while I was gone.

After he gets back up, I notice something strange about Pete. Something is moving inside of his pants. At first, I thought it was just an erection. Since sex is illegal, a lot of guys get erections at inconvenient times. And with Pete being such a conservative religious man, I can see him avoiding masturbation as much as possible. But it isn't an erection, unless he has a penis the size of an elephant's trunk.

The bulge starts at his waist and goes all the way down his left pant leg ending a little past his knee. Once I see the bulge moving, I know exactly what it is. He's got the same deformity as I have. He has an extra limb.

While Pete pretends to work, the appendage kicks

37

and twitches in his pants. He tries to hold it still, but it thrashes around, probably because he overexerted himself while moving so many potatoes double-time.

After twenty minutes of it, the thrashing only gets worse. I can't ignore it anymore. I have to do something about it.

"Come with me," I say quietly behind his shoulder.

He looks at me like I'm mad. "What?"

I look down at his squirming pants, then look him in the eyes.

"I can help you," I say.

He still pretends that he doesn't know what I'm talking about.

I lean in closer and whisper, "You have to restrain it or else somebody is going to notice."

He reluctantly gives in and follows me into the corner, behind a mountain of potato crates. I untie a couple of potato bags and remove the twine.

"Pull down your pants," I say.

"But neither of us are working the machine…" he says.

I notice that he is sweating again.

"Then we have to hurry," I say.

When he pulls down his pants, I see a long skinny leg growing out of his crotch, between his dick and the plump of his upper thigh. It is not fully developed yet. It is the leg of a ten-year-old boy.

Pulling the twine around both legs, I realize that I underestimated the thickness of Pete's thighs. I have to knot two pieces of twine together for it to be long enough to tie down the new limb.

I get two more pieces of twine and tie the ankle of the new leg to Pete's knee. The new limb is still twitching.

"It's not enough," Pete says.

I think for a minute.

"If we had a bandage we'd be able to wrap it up against your leg, encasing it like a mummy. That's the only way we'll be able to restrain it completely."

"What's a mummy?"

"Corpses that were encased in bandages," I say.

"Oh," he says.

"If we can rip some cloth into strips that will probably work fine."

Before we can put my plan into action, Landon finds us behind the crates. He sees Pete with his pants down. At first, he thinks some kind of homosexual activity is going on.

Although homosexual activity is considered immoral in the McDonaldland religion, it is not illegal, so it is not uncommon for men to have sex with other men to relieve their sexual needs. However, this kind of activity is definitely not allowed in the workplace. It is an arrest-worthy offence.

Then Landon sees the extra leg I'm holding against Pete's thigh.

"What in the Hamburglar?" Landon says, staring at the extra leg.

Pete pulls up his pants as quickly as he can. I separate myself from him.

"We were just getting back to work," I tell Landon.

Landon is too shocked to say anything. He just goes back to his office and closes the door.

Back at the machine, I move potato bags as quickly as I can.

"Shit, Daniel!" Pete says to me.

"I know," I say.

"He saw it," he says. "I'm dead. He's going to tell the Fry Guys for sure."

I now see that Pete's obedience has always been motivated by fear, rather than conviction. If he were truly loyal to The Blessed McDonald's Corporation he would have reported his deformity to the Fry Guys at the first sign of his condition.

"Don't worry about it," I tell him. "Landon can't afford to turn in his workers. If he doesn't meet his quota it will be his ass on the fire. He's not the type to follow the rules at the expense of his own hide."

This calms Pete down a little bit. Unfortunately, Landon knows that Pete is next to worthless at his job. If he had the fat man arrested he knows that I could do the job for both of us and meet his quota every day until a replacement was found. But, at the same time, Landon does not like the idea of drawing attention to himself.

"Just work as hard as you can," I tell Pete. "If you show him that you're a useful worker he'll probably just pretend he never saw anything."

"Probably?" he says.

"It's the best assurance I can give you."

After the shift ends, Pete is able to relax.

"You were right," he says.

I shake my head.

"If Landon was to turn you in it wouldn't have

been during the shift," I say. "He has to meet his quota, remember?"

That nervous look comes back on Pete's face.

"Then when would he call them?"

"If he planned to today, he would have done it about ten minutes ago so that the Fry Guys wouldn't get you until your shift was over. He would have told them to wait for you in the parking lot."

"What?" he says, almost ready to cry.

"Don't worry about it," I say. "I really don't think he would risk drawing attention to himself. Tomorrow we'll go into his office and tell him that if he reports your deformity, we will report him for having failed to report you the instant he witnessed your deformity."

In McDonaldland, failing to report a crime is the same as committing the crime. However, there is not a written law against deformities, so I'm not sure if that would work in this case. Regardless, the Fry Guys would probably arrest Landon as well, because nobody is supposed to know that these deformities exist.

"Would that really work?" he asks.

"Of course it will work. Landon's an idiot."

That made Pete feel a lot better. He takes a deep breath and his stress begins to vanish.

When we leave the building, five Fry Guys are coming toward us. One in red, one in blue, and three in yellow. I'm as surprised as Pete is to see them. Once they reach us, Pete panics. He pulls down his pants and grabs his extra limb.

"It's just one leg," he cries. "You can cut it off. Nobody will ever know."

The yellow Fry Guys go for him and take him by the arms.

"Bring him to the truck," the blue Fry Guy says.

It's my brother.

"There's just more and more of them every day," says the red Fry Guy. The sergeant.

Pete looks at me.

"You said Landon wouldn't turn me in," Pete cries.

"He didn't," I say. "You just turned yourself in."

My brother points at me and the sergeant lifts my shirt. The red Fry Guy turns me around and shows my brother the two limbs strapped to my back.

When they turn me back around, I tell Pete, "They were here for me."

My brother just stares me in the eyes, unapologetically. He has a cold expression on his face, the same one he always has when he's ashamed of me.

"It's for the best," he says.

He's full of shit.

They bring us to the red windowless Fry Guy McVan. Whenever they take people away for good, this is the type of van they use.

After they put Pete into the van, I say to my brother, "Where the hell are you taking us?"

I always use the word *hell* instead of *Hamburglar*. It confuses most people.

"Into the wasteland," he says.

He won't explain any more than that.

Pete and I aren't the only people that are being taken away. In the back of the van, there are three more men. All of them with the same deformity as I, only they are in even worse condition. There is a short dark-skinned man with a third arm and two extra pairs of legs. Another man has at least seven fully grown extra arms and a few smaller ones budding on his torso. The third man is about my age. He wears a white suit, black gloves, and has a shaved head. He doesn't seem to have any extra limbs.

Nobody says anything until the van begins to move, then Pete says, "What's going on? Where are they taking us?"

"They're getting rid of us," the short man tells him. "They're going to drop us off in the middle of the wasteland and leave us for the wolves."

"They're not even going to do that," says the man with too many arms. "They're just going to take us out and shoot us."

The man in the white suit says nothing, but he watches the rest of us, examining us one at a time.

"How did this happen?" Pete begins to panic. When he panics, he talks a lot. "Why did this happen to all of us? I thought I was the only one with this condition. I thought I was becoming a freak. At first, it was just a lump. Then it kept growing and growing. Then it formed toes and a foot. I thought I was going crazy."

"It's got to be some kind of experimental hormone in the food," I tell him. "That's why they need to keep it a secret and take us out of town. There are probably a lot more people who have had the same deformities."

"A lot more," says the man in the white suit, breaking his silence. "Hundreds."

The rest of us look at him, but he doesn't say anything else.

Chapter 3

Pete

There aren't any windows in the back of the van, but through the front windshield I can see the large city gates ahead of us. I've never seen the McDonaldland exit before. It's always been hidden. It is in a walled area behind Fry Guy headquarters. You have to go through five different security gates in order to reach it.

We stop in a parking lot in front of the gate. The lot is filled with several types of automobiles I have never seen before. The vehicles are not yellow or red, they are black with razor sharp spikes on the roof and sides. And they are armed to the teeth with machine guns, flame throwers, and harpoon guns.

When the gate opens, one of the armed vehicles leads us into the wasteland. Another armed vehicle follows. In the front seat of the van, my brother looks back at me. His face is serious, almost angry with me.

Dawn breaks.

The road outside of McDonaldland is not yellow. It is black and crumbling. As far as the eye can see, the wasteland doesn't appear to be much of a wasteland. It is a lush forest. I have never seen so much green in all my life. It is not the miserable ruins they had made it out to be. It is the most beautiful scenery I have ever seen in my life.

As we are escorted through the badlands, I move up to the

45

chain-linked screen that divides the front seat with the back of the van so that I can speak to my brother.

"What exactly are you going to do with us?" I ask him.

He looks at me but he doesn't respond.

"Are you going to leave us in the middle of the wasteland to fend for ourselves?"

He says nothing, straightening out his mustache with a little comb.

"Are you going to execute us?"

He doesn't speak.

"Tell me something," I say. "Anything."

He doesn't say a word until he is finished with his mustache.

"You're getting a new job," he says. "Outside of the city."

"How much does it pay?" I ask, trying to crack a joke.

"It doesn't pay anything," he says.

"That sucks," I say.

"You've been drafted into a secret army. Outside of receiving supplies, this army has no connection with McDonaldland civilization. You will never be able to return. After this trip, you will never see me again."

"Can I refuse?"

"Yes," he says, "but it would mean your death."

"Then I guess I'll take the job."

He doesn't like my lighthearted tone of voice, but I guess I would feel the same way if I were him. It can't be easy when your asshole fascist Fry Guy job description calls for you to banish your brother into the wasteland, and your brother decides not to take your final moments together very seriously.

But my brother believes that everything should be taken very seriously all the time. There is no room for goofing around in his world. He's just like my dad. Every year, during McDonaldmas, my grandpa and I used to make fun of them from the other side of the room. It was supposed to be a holiday of fun and joy, but the two of them would always take it so seriously. The golden arches at the top of the red plastic tree had to be centered just perfectly. The Ronald McDonald nativity diorama had to be created just right. Even though they were trying to be such serious people, my grandpa and I thought they were completely ridiculous.

"So, what will I be doing in this secret army?" I ask my brother.

He gives me a very serious look. It is the same serious look he would use when decorating the McDonaldmas tree when he was a little kid.

"Hunting wolves, mostly," he tells me.

After a couple of miles down the road, I begin to understand why they call it a wasteland. Although the forests are lovely, the ruins out here are not. We pass small deserted towns that resemble junkyards. The buildings are rotten, burned down, and collapsed. The rusted skeletons of cars line the road. The bones of animals, perhaps human, dangle from the trees.

"Does anyone live out here?" I ask my brother.

He says, "I don't know. But I can tell you that besides those from McDonaldland, there hasn't been a living soul in this area of the world for over a hundred years."

Several more miles of wasteland and then we hit a dirt road. It isn't really a dirt road, but the old road has crumbled into such disrepair that it has basically become dirt. It is slow moving from here out. The solar powered cars normally move at sixty miles per hour max. Now they are moving at about twenty.

"How much longer?"

"Get back in your seat," he tells me. "This is the most dangerous part of the drive."

As soon as he says that, both front tires of the van pop. The vehicle comes to a stop.

"No, no," says the red Fry Guy in the driver seat. "Not here. Anywhere but here."

I don't sit back in my seat.

"What's wrong with *here*?" I ask.

"Just get back," Guy says.

The armed vehicle in the front of the caravan doesn't stop for us. It keeps driving.

"Where do they think they're going?" Guy says.

"They're ditching us!" says the sergeant. "Those fuckers!"

The black vehicle becomes smaller and smaller in the distance. Then we see a dark cloud rise from the horizon beyond the vehicle.

"Shit," Guy says, as he sees the black cloud.

"What?" I ask him.

It is too far away to see exactly what is going on, but the vehicle fires its machine guns for one short burst before it is flipped over backwards.

"Shit, shit," Guy says again.

"What?" I say again.

Then I see it, in the distance. The black cloud is some kind of enormous beast. It comes around the side of the car, now flipped onto its back. The thing looks like a big black dog, but it's huge, bigger than a McDonaldland city bus. It raises its muzzle into the air and howls. Then it bites through the passenger side of the armed vehicle, its teeth tearing through the metal as easily as you could through a burger still in its wrapper. It's too far away to hear the man's screams as he is bitten in half and chewed in the giant wolf's jaws along with most of the passenger side door.

Then we hear the howls coming from the forest. Maybe a dozen of them, from behind us, in front of us, on all sides. They close in on us within seconds.

Growling and snarling sounds race up behind us. With no windows back here we can't see it coming. We hear shouting and machine gun fire from the armed vehicle behind us, then we hear the driver slamming on the gas and the tires peeling out.

The peeling out sound continues, but the car doesn't sound like it's going anywhere. The wheels squeal in higher and higher pitches, but the growls in that direction are louder still. Then we hear the squealing tires move forward, one inch at a time, along the side of the van.

Once the vehicle moves up far enough so that we can see it through the front windshield, we see dust and smoke pouring out from beneath the tires. Then, as the back of the car comes into view, we notice what is wrong. Something is attached to the car. My first thought is that a tree trunk had fallen on the back of the vehicle, but once I see the eye on the side, I realize that it's not a tree.

We can only see part of its head, but it is an enormous blonde wolf with the vehicle's trunk in its jaws. Its muzzle snarls and tugs at the vehicle, like a dog who won't let go of her chew toy. The vehicle is able to pull ahead a few inches, but the wolf pulls it back, then it drives a few inches farther, then the wolf pulls it back.

The man standing through the roof of the vehicle at the machine gun is missing his head and part of his shoulders, blood gushes out of what was once his neck. The yellow Fry Guy in the passenger seat is trying to remove the body so that he can take his place at the gun.

"Drive," Guy says to the sergeant.

The sergeant can't take his eyes off of the other vehicle.

"Drive," Guy says, smacking him out of it.

The sergeant yells back at his superior, "We don't have any fucking wheels!"

"I said drive," Guy said, "so drive."

Once the yellow Fry Guy in the vehicle next to us gets his hand on the machine gun, he fires a few rounds into the beast's nose. The wolf barks a whimper and releases the vehicle from its mouth. Once freed, the car shoots forward at full speed. The driver quickly loses control, and swerves off the road, crashing head-on into a tree.

The blonde wolf wiggles off its bee sting of a wound and charges the vehicle. It snatches up the Fry Guy sticking out of the roof by his uniform. We see the man dangling in the wolf's mouth, screaming and flailing his arms, as the creature runs across our path to the other side of the road, disappearing into the woods.

Another wolf with reddish-brown fur emerges from the forest and pounces onto the armed vehicle. The driver inside screams in the direction of my brother as the weight of the creature crushes the roof of his vehicle, trapping him inside.

The sergeant finally hits the gas and the van moves forward, though very slowly on the flat tires. It seems like a hopeless endeavor, but I would probably do the same thing.

In the distance, the black wolf hears the van moving and turns away from the overturned vehicle. It charges us. Running down the road with its powerful legs, the beast moves twice as fast as any vehicle in McDonaldland. The closer it comes, the more enormous I realize it is. This one is even larger than the blonde wolf. Perhaps twice its size.

The creature doesn't stop running when it reaches us, it lowers its forehead and rams its face into the front of the van. I get a good look into its golden yellow eyes as it flips the vehicle over with its muzzle.

I tumble over Pete and would have slammed my head hard into the door if the man with nine arms wasn't there to catch me. The van on its side, all the mutants in the back are piled together. I look into the front seat to see my brother trying to get out of his seatbelt. The red Fry Guy is struggling to climb out of the van, but his only way out is through the driver's side window that is now above him.

The enormous paws of the beast walk past the front windshield. Beyond, there are two more wolves gathering, all of them biting and scratching at the smashed vehicle on the side of the road. The man inside is still alive, and still screaming for help.

"Why are there so many of them?" the sergeant yells at my brother. "There's not supposed to be so many of them."

My brother just wants the sergeant to get off his mustache.

I can't see it, but I can hear the wolf peering down at us from above. Its growls are so loud that it feels like the entire van is inside the beast's mouth.

The sergeant gets his door open and tries to climb out, but once he turns he sees something that makes him duck back inside.

"Look out," he says, closing his eyes and bracing himself for another impact.

The van is hit again, but it doesn't roll over. It's just pushed into a spin across the road. Pete screams in a girlish voice.

"What do we do?" I ask my brother.

He doesn't say anything.

"We can't just hide in here," I tell him. "We have to get out and run. If we scatter maybe some of us will make it."

My brother tries to adjust his position, squeezing as much of his large frame under the dashboard as he can fit.

"If we go out there we're dead," he says. "None of us would make it."

The sergeant doesn't even have the chance to scream as teeth tear through the metal, bite into him, and rip him out of the vehicle. Looking through the windshield, we see the black wolf thrash him just once to break his neck. Then it lies down, holding the corpse down with its two front paws, as it gnaws on his body like a small doggy biscuit.

The other wolves have finally torn the armed vehicle into halves, and fat brown wolf was able to beat the others to the morsel of food inside. Once they've realized they're not getting any, the other two wolves move on to our van.

We hear them barking and snapping at each other as they claw at the van, fighting over which one gets the meat. The hole created on the driver's side of the vehicle is where they begin. A brown wolf with one eye, much smaller than the black wolf, sees my brother down in the hole. It digs its snout inside, sniffing at my brother's blue suit.

Guy doesn't scream. He just tries to flatten his body out so that it can't reach him. Then the wolf begins to lick. Its massive tongue is a wet bed of pink flesh, and fills almost the entire cab. It laps at the seats like it's drinking from a water bowl. The tip of the tongue squishes into Guy's chest, but the creature cannot lick him out. His blue uniform becomes soaked with slobber.

The other wolf digs through the top of the van. I see its reddish-brown fur and monstrous face looking down at me as it opens up the vehicle. The creature's head is as big as the van itself. Its hot breath pours onto me. It salivates when it sees us inside, drooling and baring its fangs. There's nothing protecting us now. We're just a bowl of dog food to it.

Like bobbing for apples, the red-furred wolf sticks its head in and catches the man with nine arms. He punches it with all of his fists at once as it takes him out of the van.

"Run," says the man in the white suit.

We don't question him. While the wolf has the nine-armed man in its mouth, we make a break for it. I follow the man out of the van, helping Pete get his fat ass through the hole the wolf created so that he doesn't cut himself on the jagged edges.

I look up at the reddish-brown wolf as it slurps down the mutant man in one bite. He keeps thrashing with all of his limbs as he goes down its throat.

The other wolf sees us running into the woods. It gives up on trying to get to Guy and chases after us. The black wolf comes after us as well, leaping over the van.

Once we're in the forest, the wolves have difficulty running as fast as they can, because they have to weave around trees.

"Go for the dense region," says the white suited man. "Running in the direction of a cluster of trees."

Pete and the short man with three pairs of legs cannot

move very fast. All of their extra limbs make it difficult to move.

The black wolf quickly catches up to the short man and bites into him. Within seconds, he's inside of the creature's mouth and chewed to death by teeth larger than his arms.

Once we reach the dense part of the forest, the wolves aren't able to follow. They are just too big to get through the trees. Pete makes it to safety last, but he's so exhausted that he collapses the second he gets through the first row of trees. He's too close to the perimeter.

A brown wolf charges forward and rams its head through the trees to get at Pete. But the trees are too close together. It can't get its shoulders through. Pete rolls out of the way and comes over to us. Now the brown wolf's head is stuck. It whimpers and struggles to pull itself free.

The black wolf stares at us. It is not a stare of hunger, but a different kind of stare. As though it wants to play with us in a violent, cruel kind of way before killing us. It circles the perimeter of the trees, looking for a way in.

"What are they?" Pete asks us, kneeling on the ground to catch his breath.

"Our women," says the man in the white suit.

"Huh?" Pete says.

"When we banish them from our city, they continue to grow and become more wolf-like," he says. "That is what they eventually become."

The man in the white suit points at the black wolf. It's difficult to think that the enormous creature was once a woman. Its legs and arms do kind of resemble human limbs. I can see large mounds on the wolf's chest which could have once been human breasts. But I think it's the eyes that are the most familiar. Although they are yellow and look completely animal-like, there's something behind the eyes that seems human to me. I sense emotions that only a human could feel.

In the distance, a pack of giant wolves surround the van. Guy is still trapped inside. He's not screaming, but I know he's not yet dead. They bite and claw at the vehicle, flipping it over and tossing it around the street, sticking their tongues and paws into the hole to get at him.

When we were younger, Guy was the one who got all the girls. Even though he was so serious all the time, he was still a ladies man. Aside from November, I wasn't very popular with the girls because I didn't have enough meat on my bones. Guy, although not as fat as the average McDonaldlandian, was always really big and beefy. He was the captain of the foosball team, just like dad. Grandpa was a high school sports hero as well, but back then they played a game called football instead of foosball.

Football was a game where you actually used your entire body to play instead of just your hands. It was like you actually were one of the pieces on the board, and the board was the size of a city block, and you had to take the ball all the way down the block to score a goal. That is the kind of game I would have wanted to play. A game where you actually moved around. But after my grandfather's time, people were just too fat for sports that required much physical activity, so foosball took over.

If you're the captain of the foosball team you can have any girl you want. Well, unless it was somebody like Nova, who wouldn't have liked my brother at all. But being so desired was almost a curse as well as a blessing, because he couldn't have sex with any of them. That kind of attention was probably torture on his hyperactive teenage sex drive. Of course, if anybody was able to control his sex drive it was my brother.

It seems things have not changed much for him. Seeing all of the giant wolf women fighting over his body down on the street, it appears that Guy is still popular with the ladies. Hopefully none of these women are as determined as Molly was back in high school. Once she set her eyes on Guy, she didn't rest until she had gotten what she wanted.

The black wolf bites into a tree on the perimeter, trying to gnaw through it. The bark peels off of its sides, but it is not chewed through so easily.

"Let's go," says the man in the white suit. "We need to get deeper into the woods."

Pete doesn't take his eyes off of the black wolf. "Can it get through?"

"If we stay here it will keep trying until it does," he says. "But it's not getting through any time soon."

The two of them move on, but I stay standing where I am, watching the crumpled up van down in the road.

"We can't do anything for him," says the man in the white suit. "We need to move. There could be smaller ones in the area who won't have problems getting through the trees."

I give it one last look, squinting my eyes to see if he's still alive in there. I swear I can see a little blue dot in the window of the vehicle, but I can't tell if it's alive or dead.

Chapter 4

Ronald Krall

About a quarter of a mile through the forest, the trees become sparser. It feels less safe to go through this terrain, but the man in the white suit continues ahead.

We hear snarling and howling coming from the south, back in the direction of the road. It is another giant wolf, but it's alone. Instead of going in the opposite direction, the man in the white suit goes toward the snarls.

"Where are you going?" Pete cries.

The man in the white suit hushes him.

We sneak through bushes toward the noise, keeping a safe distance. The snarling becomes louder the closer we get. I can see hair and movement through the leaves. We get so close that I can almost feel the body heat of the enormous beast.

The man in the white suit motions for us to get down once we are close enough to see. We lie on our bellies and peek out of the bushes at the creature in front of us. The beast is not just snarling, it also appears to be moaning and breathing heavily. We also hear a man's muffled cries.

Lying in a meadow, we find the blonde wolf who had attacked us on the road. She is on the ground, on her side, with her paws in her crotch. She is wiggling and thrashing her hips. Then we see the man. The yellow Fry Guy who the blonde wolf had carried into the woods. We only see his yellow legs, but we can tell it is him.

The wolf is shoving the man into her furry crotch with the pads of her paws. Most of his upper body is inside of her, inside of the wolf's vagina. The creature is fucking his entire body.

The man in the white suit speaks quietly over my

shoulder, "The more they grow, the bigger their sex drive."

The blonde wolf seems to orgasm with the man inside of her. As she orgasms, her body grows. There is a stretching and popping sound coming from her muscles as her flesh expands.

"And the more they have sex, the bigger they grow."

The man shrieks inside of her, as if he can feel her growing bigger around him.

"With that kind of sex drive, she might continue raping him over and over, and she'll just get bigger and bigger."

Then the blonde wolf digs her muzzle into her crotch and sucks the yellow man out of her vagina. We listen to his muffled cries as she chews and swallows him.

"Or maybe she's more hungry than horny," adds the white suited man.

The blonde wolf curls into a ball and closes her eyes, relaxing after sex, lunch, and a growth spurt. Women are always drained after they go through a transformation like that. They almost always go into a deep sleep after sex.

We don't have any problems sneaking away, even with Pete stumbling over his third leg.

"We need to get to the facility," says the man in the white suit, leading us west through the woods.

"What's the facility?" Pete asks.

"It's where they were taking us before we were attacked," he says.

"Shouldn't we go back to the city?" Pete asks.

"We won't be able to get in there," he says. "They'll just let us rot outside the walls until we get eaten by the wolves. Our only chance is to make it to the others like us."

"What others?" Pete asks.

"The other men who are carrying the advanced parasite," he says. "All the men with extra limbs are taken out of the city and brought to the facility. In the beginning, men with deformities were just thrown out of town and left for the wolves. But the strong ones survived, banded together, and formed an army to fight the wolves. They turned an old military facility into a fortress. Now the Fry Guys always bring people like us to join them in their war against the wolf women."

"What do you mean *people like us*?" Pete says. "I don't see any extra limbs on you."

"That's because I've been good at keeping them hidden," he says. "Until yesterday, when they popped a surprise physical on me and my staff."

We stop walking. The man in the white suit takes off one of his black gloves and shows us hands. He has two hands, one on top of the other, that fit into the same glove. He pulls up his sleeves and pants. He has an extra pair of arms and an extra pair of legs, but he has them strapped so tightly together he appears to only have two legs and two arms. He has two feet in each shoe, two hands in each glove.

"It took a lot of practice to get the new limbs to move in sync with the originals," he says. "The hardest part was getting two feet to fit into each shoe, but with my small feet and these large shoes I was able to make it work."

I stare at his feet. He has them curled around each other, with one foot taking up most of the toe area of the shoe and the other near the heel of the shoe. They only overlap in the center.

"Who are you, anyway?" I ask him, staring him in the face.

He originally looked my age, somebody I might have gone to high school with, but now I can tell that he is actually much younger.

"I'm Ronald Krall," he says. "I worked in Research and Development. I was one of the people trying to find a cure for the parasites that are infecting more and more of the male McDonaldland citizens."

Then he goes on to tell me all about the parasites:

They are a hyper-evolved species of flatworm similar to the species Riberoria trematode, which most commonly infects frogs. Riberoria is a flatworm that infects frogs while they are still tadpoles. As the tadpoles become frogs, the parasite causes them to grow extra limbs, as many as forty. It does this in order to make the frogs easier to catch by predators. After the frogs are eaten by large mammals or birds, the parasite is able to grow into adulthood in the new host's stomach as the frog is being digested.

This new parasite, that we call the Oryculous trematode, does basically the same thing, but it infects humans instead of frogs.

"So that we can be easier prey?" I ask him.

"Yes," he says. "For the giant wolves."

He says that, before he was taken away, he was trying to prove a theory that this parasite also has something to do with the lycanthrope virus that turns women into wolves. Recently, they discovered that it wasn't a virus but a parasite that causes lycanthropy. It only affects women. Oryculous only affects men. Krall believes that the two parasites have a sort of symbiosis. He thinks perhaps they are male and female of the same species, and use this process for mating.

So the female parasite infects a woman, turning her into an enormous predator. The male parasite infects a man, turning him into easy prey. The woman eats the man, and as she digests him, the parasites are able grow into adulthood and mate within the woman's stomach.

61

I ask Krall, "If that were the case then how come women have been turning into wolves for a hundred years and men have been growing extra limbs only recently?"

"It's not as recent as you might think," Krall says. "The real question is why the parasite infects all women of McDonaldland but not all males are infected. The number of males infected has increased dramatically in the past couple of years but only two decades ago it was incredibly rare."

"No," I tell him. "I think the real question is how the heck are all these parasites getting into the food?"

It makes Krall laugh, as if he thought my question was meant to be a joke.

We hear engines roaring in the distance, although they don't sound anything like the electric engines of the McDonaldland vehicles.

"That's them," Krall tells us.

We run out of the woods toward the sound, hoping to get to the army before we run into more wolves. On a dirt trail, heading away from the main road, we see a caravan of cars and motorcycles. The cars are similar to the ones that escorted us into the wasteland, but these are uglier, more battle-damaged, and have old fuel-powered engines in them.

I wave all four of my arms at them to get their attention as we run out of the woods, down a hill toward them. The caravan stops. Two of the soldiers on motorcycles leave the motorcade and ride through the clearing toward us. Each motorcycle rider has two legs and two arms, and each of them holds a machinegun with their extra hands.

They stop about twenty yards away. As they get off of their bikes, I realize that they are not two people with extra limbs, they are four people with the natural number of limbs. Each motorcycle had a passenger on the back.

And when they speak, I realize they are not men, but women.

"Don't move, fat boy," says one of the women, as Pete tries to scurry back into the woods.

They keep their guns pointed at us as they approach. We hold up our hands. When they get closer, their wolf features become clear. They are female McDonaldlandians who were outcast for having illegal sex.

Two of them stay with the motorcycles. One of the women has bright red hair, yellow eyes, furry red wolf ears, whiskers and a long red wolf tail. The rest of her is pretty much human. Her legs sticking out of her plaid skirt are not furry, her arms sticking out of a ripped up tank top are normal except for patches of red fur on her shoulders. She's actually pretty cute for a wolf girl, apart from the gun she is sticking in my face.

The second one, on the other hand, is not so cute. She is wearing leather pants and a spiked leather jacket zipped all the way up to her neck. Chains and bullet belts are wrapped around her torso. The only parts of her that are not covered with leather are her hands and face, which are both covered with thick black hair. She looks even more transformed than Molly, but she has yet to develop a muzzle.

"You escaped our big sisters?" the black one asks, her voice hisses through her teeth.

"You mean those giant wolves?" Krall asks. "We hid from them in the woods."

When he turns to point at the woods, the black-haired girl pokes him in the side with the barrel of her gun. He hunches over for a second but tries not to show pain in front of them.

"You ruined their meal," says the red-haired wolf girl, pouting at him.

Although she looks like she's in her mid-twenties, her voice sounds like a six-year-old's. She also has an awkward little girl's posture.

"I'm sorry to have inconvenienced them," Krall says.

She looks at the black-haired one and gives her a sad face, "Poor Tessa is probably *so* hungry now. She didn't get to eat any of them."

Black Hair exposes her teeth in a grin at Pete and says, "Maybe we should feed her this fat one. He'd fill her up nicely."

Pete backs away.

"Yeah," says Red Hair, giggling, "I'd want to eat him too if I were Tessa."

One of the women with the motorcycles yells at them.

"Pippi, Slayer, stop teasing them," she says.

Red Hair, who I would guess is the one named Pippi, turns around and says, "Aww, but that's the funnest part."

"Let's go," the woman says.

The wolf girls put their guns to our backs and push us in the direction of the motorcycles. The woman waiting for them seems to be the oldest of the four and seems to outrank them. She's wearing spiked plates of armor made of boiled leather and old rusty pieces of metal buckled to her breasts and shoulders. She doesn't carry any guns, but has two axes strapped to her back. Her wolf features are very prominent, yet she is not very hairy. She has a fully extended muzzle, but her face is still mostly bald. Thick brown fur grows down the sides of her neck and face like fuzzy sideburns. Her human hair is braided into multiple thick long locks, giving her a medusa-like quality.

The woman says, "They call me Talon. I'm second in command of this tribe. You are now prisoners of our clan. Our law states that anything a woman captures becomes her personal property. These two captured you, so you now

64

belong to them. It is up to them whether they use you for food, labor, or entertainment purposes."

Pippi shakes my shoulders excitedly and cheers into my ear.

It seems that I have become Pippi's property. Pete and Krall have become Slayer's property. Why Slayer gets two and Pippi only gets one is probably because Slayer is the alpha of the two females.

I am put on the back of Pippi's bike and ordered to hold onto her with all four arms. Slayer gets on the bike behind me, squishing me into Pippi as hard as she can. Krall doesn't get to ride on a bike and has to run alongside Slayer with a chain around his neck.

On the other motorcycle, Talon and another wolf girl have Pete on a chain and he also must run alongside the bike. He'll never be able to keep up.

As we take the short ride back to the caravan, Slayer laughs at Krall as he tries to keep up with the motorcycle. Pippi looks back and giggles. She slows down and then speeds up really fast and slows down and speeds up, to make him stumble. Every time he stumbles, Slayer chuckles and yanks the chain to make him stumble even more. Pete seems to be doing surprisingly better than Krall. Although he is huffing and puffing, Talon does not drag him faster than he can keep up.

Being squished between the two wolf women is overwhelming my sense of smell. Slayer, encased in her leather outfit, completely reeks of skunky animal sweat. And Pippi, although much more human-smelling, has probably not worn deodorant in years. As my four arms are wrapped around her, she squeezes the upper pair with her wet armpits to keep me in place.

When we get to the caravan, we see that each car has been patchworked together from several different cars. Much of the metal used is either rusted or filled with bullet holes. There are several different layers of plating around the exterior of the vehicles, reinforcing them so that even a giant wolf would have difficulty biting through. A variety of weapons have been attached to each of the cars, many seem to have been scavenged from the black armed vehicles that the Fry Guys drive.

The wolf women in the vehicles are in all different stages of their transformations. Some look mostly human, others hardly resemble humans at all. One of them, standing at a machine gun turret in the roof of a van, looks to be eight feet and 350 pounds of pure muscle and hair.

The motorcycles pull up next to a truck with a metal cage in the back. Slayer gets off the bike and pulls the chain around Krall's neck until he follows her toward the truck. Talon brings Pete to the truck as well. When they open the cage, I see that there is already a man in there. A man in a blue suit.

Guy? I try to get off the bike to see if it is really my brother, but Pippi grabs me by the wrist.

"Where do you think you're going?" she says.

Her grip is really tight on my arm. Although she's pretty small, she seems twice as strong as I am. I knew wolf women became stronger as they transformed but I didn't know they were this strong this soon in their development. Also, I just noticed that, although her arms are completely human, she has long wolf-like claws growing from her fingers, digging into my skin.

Slayer backtracks and handcuffs me to Pippi. She handcuffs my original arms to my new arms around Pippi's waist and over her shoulders in a criss-cross fashion, so that it feels as if she's wearing me like a backpack.

I stretch my neck up as much as I can and squint my eyes at the cage. It is definitely my brother in there. However, it doesn't look like he's moving.

After they get Krall and Pete into the cage, the caravan starts to move. Slayer doesn't get back on the bike. She rides on top of the truck with her new captives, poking them in the cage with a stick.

The dirt road leads to an old highway and we take that east. The highway is littered with long abandoned cars. Most of them seem to have crashed into each other, as if there had been some kind of demolition derby here a hundred years ago. Or some kind of war.

Pippi's tail is between us. It wags against me if I hug my arms too firmly around her body, so I try to touch as little of her body as I can to prevent this.

This is the closest I've ever been to a wolf girl. I've seen them, of course, interacted with them sometimes, but I have never been wrapped around one like this. While sitting behind Pippi, I'm able to get a closer examination of her wolf parts. Her red fuzzy ears are just like that of a German Shepherd's. They flop backwards in the wind, sometimes perking upwards or twisting to the sides when she hears something.

Her red fur isn't just on her shoulders. It grows from her head down the back of her neck, her shoulders, and down the majority of her back like a cape. It probably goes all the way down her ass. Beneath the fur I can see a collage of freckles. She must have been a real red-headed freckled girl before becoming wolf-like.

Upon closer examination, I notice that some of the specks beneath Pippi's fur are not all freckles. Some of them are fleas.

Chapter 6

Puppi

Two hours down the highway, we arrive in an old city. The buildings have crumbled to all but their skeletons. Vines and trees have taken over the town, growing over and through most of the streets and structures.

The caravan finds an open lot that is surrounded by buildings. They create a circle with their vehicles, and set up camp within the middle.

It seems that these wolf girls do not have a permanent home, but live like nomads. If they're being hunted by the Fry Guy army or the mammoth wolves, it would make sense for them not to stay in one place. They also seem to live like scavengers, which makes even more sense.

When Pippi gets off her bike, she doesn't uncuff me from her back. She grabs her gear and machine gun from the side of her motorcycle and then struts around the camp as if she's showing off the guy she captured. She's either trying to humiliate me, make the other girls jealous, or both. It's incredibly childish.

"Look, I got another one," Pippi says to some of her hairy friends, pointing at me with her thumb.

"Great," they say to her.

They don't seem to care.

"It's the tenth one this year," she says, giggling as she brags.

"So what are you going to do with this one?" asks a blonde girl with a beard.

I'm beginning to get the feeling that Pippi's prisoners do not last very long.

"I don't know," she says. "I was thinking of feeding him to Tessa, because she didn't get anything to eat today."

"You have to stop feeding our big sisters," one of them says. "They're going to follow us around, expecting to be fed all the time if you keep doing that."

"But Tessa was my best friend," she says. "I just want to look out for her."

"Tessa can take care of herself," they say.

From the tone of their voices, I can tell that Pippi is a bit of an annoyance to a lot of the wolf girls around here. She continues to bother people as they are setting up camp, dragging me along with her, until Talon confronts her.

"Get that thing off of your back and put it with the others," she tells her.

Pippi's ears fold backwards.

"Okay," she whines, like a kid who doesn't want to clean his room.

As she's walking me to the cage, a little girl runs up to Pippi and tugs on her skirt. The girl is completely human and must have been born outside of the walls of McDonaldland illegally. Judging by how wolf-like the women of this camp appear, they must be having sex. Most likely, it is with their prisoners.

The little girl says, "Pippi, Pippi."

Pippi looks at her with an annoyed face. It is the same annoyed face that the other wolf girls were giving her.

"I got one too," she says, pointing at the cage.

She is pointing at my brother.

"The blue one," she says. "I found him under a truck."

"Ashley," Pippi says, "what did Grandma tell you about lying?"

"I'm not lying," she says. "Ask Grandma. I pointed him out and Grandma said I could keep him."

"You're not old enough to keep him," Pippi says.

"Grandma said so," says the girl.

Pippi storms away from the girl as if she's jealous. The expression on her face is saying, "Letting *her* have a man is such a waste."

I saw the same expression on all the other wolf girls' faces while Pippi showed me off.

When she puts me in the cage with the others, she looks at me through the bars.

"If Tessa comes by tonight, you're dinner," she says. "Otherwise, I'll have to think of something else to do with you."

In the cage, Krall is tending to Guy's wounds. Although he is beaten up, he appears to be in one piece. The wolves weren't able to get to him while he was in the Fry Guy van, but they must have crushed him inside the vehicle and tossed him all around the street before they had given up.

"How is he?" I ask Krall.

The scientist appears to know what he's doing while stitching up my brother's wounds, so he must have at least some medical knowledge.

"He'll survive," Krall says. "For now."

This cage is different than the one on the back of the pickup truck. It is more like a pet mouse cage, but large enough to accommodate half a dozen men. A tarp covers the top so that we don't bake in the sun. The floor is a bed of soft dead grass and leaves. There is a bowl of water in the corner.

71

It is exactly like we are in a pet cage.

"Who are they?" Pete says, hiding in a corner. "What are they going to do to us?"

Even though the question was directed at him, Krall ignores the fat man and focuses on my brother.

"Judging by the fact that there aren't any other male prisoners," I say, "I don't think they're going to keep us around for very long."

"Are they going to feed us to the big wolves?" Pete asks.

"I don't know," I say.

Pete moves to the other side of Guy, so that the doctor will pay attention to him. He asks Krall, "Do you know who these women are? You knew about the giant wolves."

Krall finishes stitching the large gash in my brother's chest. After getting a look at it, I realize how serious it must have been. If Krall wasn't here my brother probably wouldn't have lasted the night.

"They're obviously women who had broken the sex laws and were cast out of McDonaldland," Krall says. "They must have banded together in order to survive. I didn't know a group like this existed in the wasteland, but doesn't surprise me. People are stubborn animals who won't die very easily."

"Even women?" Pete says.

"Especially women," Krall says.

❧

I'm stunned to hear Krall, one of the McDonaldland elite, say such a thing about women. The majority of men in McDonaldland culture are incredibly sexist. Ever since the parasite began infecting women, men began viewing women as dangerous, disgusting monsters whose actions and appearances must be restricted and concealed.

Pete is one of those men who are scared and disgusted by women. He was married once. When I first met him, he had recently been married to a nice plump girl named Becky.

While most people are excited and happy after they are married, Pete seemed incredibly nervous. Whenever his coworkers asked him about his new wife, a look of panic crossed his face. It was as if he married her only because that is what a good McDonaldlandian is supposed to do. He's the type who believes you get a job at McDonald's, get married, have kids, eat at McDonald's, and that's all there is to life.

But I believe Pete has a phobia of women. It is a common fear for men to have these days. Some men are terribly afraid that women are going to turn into wolves at any moment and eat them alive. Perhaps they have heard stories of fathers having their throats ripped out by their wolf-like mothers in the middle of sex. It is something that little boys tell each other at lunchtime to scare the pants off of the more gullible children.

When Pete was trying to make a baby with Becky, he was incredibly paranoid. She really wanted children, but there was a problem. They weren't able to get pregnant. They tried several times and obtained two sex permits, but all it did was make Becky become more and more wolf-like.

It was weird for a guy I barely knew to tell me these things, but I was the only one he could really talk to about it. He told me all about how horrifying it was to have sex with her. Not only did it feel like he was having sex with an animal, but he thought he was going to be killed at any minute.

When Becky wanted to get her rich uncle to pull some strings for her to get a third permit, Pete divorced her. Divorce is looked down upon in McDonaldland, but Pete couldn't live with her anymore.

"It's like living with a monster," he always told me.

Now he's the prisoner of an entire army of monsters.

I wonder if Pete lost his mom when he was very young, because I never really thought of wolf-like women as monsters. Being around my mom all the time, it seemed perfectly natural for women to be big hairy wolves. Perhaps the wolf features were unnatural side effects of the parasites in her body, but I didn't know any better.

My mother actually died much younger than most mothers. She died while giving birth to her third child. It is not uncommon for mothers to die while giving birth a third time. After a woman has transformed so many times, it is perfectly reasonable for there to be complications during child birth. One in three mothers die during their third pregnancy. Two out of three third-born children die before birth.

When Guy wakes, he has no idea where he is or who he is with. All he knows is that he has a sticky substance in his mustache that he needs to comb out. Once he realizes that the substance is a mixture of blood and wolf slobber, his memory floods in.

"What happened?" he asks, feeling the stitches on his chest. I just realize that the stitches are baby-blue, so Krall must have taken them from Guy's suit.

"You survived the wolf attack," Krall says. "You are one lucky son of a bitch."

He gets a look at his surroundings, "Where are we?"

"We've been taken prisoner by a band of wolf girls who have been surviving out here in the wasteland," I tell him.

"The Bitches?" Guy says, going to the door of the cage to look out at the wolf women who are starting campfires in the center of the lot.

"No," Guy grunts. "I am one unlucky son of a bitch."

74

Guy tells us about the wolf women. They call themselves The Warriors of the Wild, but to their enemies they are known as The Bitches, or The Beast Bitches, or some just call them animals. Most of them were sent out into the wasteland because they were raped by men in McDonaldland, so they have a deep hatred for the men who run McDonaldland as well as males in general. For those young women who do not hate men when they are adopted into their clan, they are quickly educated to hate them. They convince the young women that it was the men who cursed them with the disease that turns them into wolves, so they must embrace this disease in order to use it against them. They capture men and have sex with them so that they will become more animal-like, so that they will become stronger soldiers in their war against McDonaldland.

In another section of the wasteland, there is an army of males who protect McDonaldland from these women and the giant wolves. It is the secret army of multi-limbed mutants that Pete, Krall, and I were supposed to join. They have been at war with the Bitches for decades, but they are a long way from winning. With the number of mutants and the number of giant wolves increasing every day, this war just keeps getting bigger and bigger.

Although they have been trying to keep it a secret, it won't be long before the people of McDonaldland get involved in this war.

Being a Fry Guy, my brother has gotten involved in the transportation of men and supplies to the mutant camp, but they have yet to take an offensive position against The Bitches. The only other thing they have done is stopped releasing women into the wasteland after they break a sex law. They can't allow their numbers to grow anymore. However, this practice has only gone into effect recently so it will be quite some time before their numbers are decreased enough to defeat them.

Guy says they have become vicious, heartless creatures who want nothing but the destruction of the peaceful McDonaldland way of life. He says that if we want to live we must try to escape as soon as we possibly can.

Krall and I tear holes in our clothes so that we can put our extra limbs through. Now that we're out of McDonaldland, there's no need to conceal them.

Krall tells Guy that there is no way for him to escape in his current condition, at least not today. Pete agrees that it is not a good time to escape, but it's only because he's too afraid to try to escape now. He surely will feel the same way tomorrow. Pete is the kind of person who feels safer in a cage.

I sleep for a couple hours, because I haven't been to bed since yesterday. But I could only manage a couple hours. It's a bit difficult sleeping on itchy weeds in a cage in the afternoon when the sun is beating down on you, and even though there is a tarp over my head it only seems to make the cage more like an oven. But worse than the light, the heat, and the discomfort, what really kept me from sleeping was the fact that Pete took a dump in the corner of the cage.

When I wake up to the smell and see the shit, I say, "What the fuck, Pete?"

But he just points at Krall and my brother, saying, "That's what they told me I was supposed to do."

"Damn it," I say, swiping at the air in front of my nose.

"And there's no need to swear," Pete says.

I spend most of the day watching the wolf girls hanging around the camp. They don't seem like vicious, heartless animals. They seem like normal girls, laughing and joking around with each other.

I watch Pippi and Slayer as they cook cans of food in a fire and then eat out of them like bowls. I can't understand every word they are saying but they seem to just be having normal conversations, teasing each other from time to time. Slayer pushes Pippi playfully with her black paws, knocking Pippi off her cinderblock. Pippi giggles and shoves her back. Then they continue their conversation. They don't seem like the types of people who would murder us just because we are men.

After watching Slayer and Pippi for a while, a wolf girl in a spiked metal bikini walks past them. She is probably the least wolf-like girl in the camp, and I wouldn't have even known she was a wolf girl if I couldn't see her glowing eyes from here.

Pippi turns around and says to the girl in the metal bikini, "Hey Nova," and then tosses a spoonful of her food at the girl.

I'm not sure if I heard it correctly, because I can hardly hear anything from this distance, but I swear she called her *Nova*, as in November, as in *my* November.

Slayer laughs as the girl in the metal bikini kicks the cinderblock out from under Pippi, causing the childish wolf girl to fall on her ass again.

Although that is exactly what Nova would do in that situation, I don't recognize her at all. It has been quite some time since I've seen her last, but there is nothing about this girl that reminds me of my old girlfriend. I wonder if I just heard her name wrong. I wonder if it's just wishful thinking that I would actually find her in the wasteland.

I yell out her name, just to see if she will look. I yell *Nova*, and then I yell *November*.

All three girls hear me, but only Pippi and Slayer look my way. They stop laughing and give me cold growling faces to keep me in line. The girl in the spiked metal bikini just walks away.

It might have been my Nova, but it probably wasn't.

I spend hours wondering... What if it really was my Nova? Could she be mine again? Would she be able to convince them to let me go? Would she save me from being killed by her friends? Or would she be a completely different person who was convinced to hate all men? Perhaps she will think I'm the enemy and let Pippi do whatever she wants with me, even if she feeds me to her giant wolf friend, Tessa.

I keep watching the camp to get a better glimpse at the woman in the spiked metal bikini, but I don't see her again. Even though it is still afternoon, most of the women are going to sleep, so maybe she is one of those who went to sleep early. I continue to keep an eye out for her, but she doesn't make another appearance.

Awhile after it gets dark, we are let out of our cage. The wolf girls seem to sleep in the afternoons and wake up around dusk. Perhaps they are becoming nocturnal.

We are the prisoners/pets of Slayer, Pippi, and the little girl, Ashley, so it is up to them to take care of us. Slayer cleans the shit out of the cage as Pippi gives us our food. We are fed cans of McDonald brand dog food.

Although McDonald's has not changed their menu in over a hundred years, they have added a pet menu. The pet menu features McDogfood, McCatfood, McBirdfood, and McMousefood. Although some poorer children will make pets of the wild lizards and snakes that they find, these four are the only types of pets that people are able to buy at the McPet Store.

We are not given utensils, so we must eat it with our fingers. McDogfood tastes surprisingly good. Kind of like a bunch of McDonald's hamburger patties mashed up with some gravy, although I think the pet food is made out of the leftover cow parts not used in the regular McDonald's food.

The little girl, Ashley, doesn't say much. She shyly gives Guy his food and says, "This is for you." Then she runs away. Her little dress is handmade, probably by herself, which I respect, but it is hideous. It was poorly sewn together from various other clothes and blankets. It also looks like it has never been washed before.

Pippi sits next to me and puts a leash around my neck.

"Give me a bite," she says, digging into my can of dog food with her long-nailed index finger.

She slurps down the dog food and smiles at the flavor. Although it originally seemed like Pippi was forcing us to eat the McDogfood as a way to humiliate us, I now realize that this is the food she must have been eating from a can earlier in the day. Out in the wasteland, they are probably used to eating whatever they can get their hands on.

Although he looks like he could eat anything, Pete is the only one who can't stomach the dog food. Guy and Krall shovel the food into their mouths as fast as they can so that they don't have to taste much of it. They only eat it because they both know that they need to keep up their strength.

"Where'd they get the McDonaldland food?" Pete asks Krall.

Slayer kicks his food out of his hands. "No talking, Meat."

The can of McDogfood splatters across the dirt. Pete seems almost happy he doesn't have to eat it until Slayer says, "Now lick it off the ground."

She points down at the food in the dirt. Pete obeys. As he eats the slimy meat on the ground like an animal, Pippi laughs at his enormous butt facing them.

"We got the food from you," Slayer tells him. "Our big sisters attack the McDonaldland vehicles. They eat the drivers and leave us the food and supplies the vehicles were transporting."

"We also capture any men that survive the attack," Pippi says. "But our big sisters usually eat them all up."

After they get bored with humiliating Pete, they stop paying attention to us. They pretend we're not sitting right next to them, even though the conversation revolves around what Pippi is going to do to me.

"I don't smell Tessa at all," Pippi says. "I don't think she's coming."

Although I listen to their conversation, I focus more on trying to spot the girl in the metal bikini. I have to know for sure whether or not it is Nova. I watch every biker wolf girl as they walk around the camp, fixing their vehicles and moving supplies.

"You should have him work for you or rent him out," Slayer says. "That's what I'm going to do with mine."

"That's boring," Pippi says.

"If you're going to kill him," Slayer says, "you should make use of him first. Play with him. Trade nights with them for some food or gas rations. You always waste them too soon."

"I hate sharing," Pippi says, rubbing her claws along the back of my neck as she examines me closely. "But I always wanted to keep one around for a while, to make the fun last longer."

I don't look at Pippi as she digs one of her claws deep into the skin between my neck and collar bone. She smiles and watches me carefully as I wince at the pain. It pleasures her into twisting her nail deeper, causing a stream of blood to trickle down my chest. When she sees the blood it makes her giggle.

She licks the blood from my neck with her long dog tongue, as I continue to scan the camp in search for Nova. I try not to respond too much to what she is doing, because I know it would only make her want to escalate the pain. I don't see the girl in the metal bikini, perhaps because it is so dark, but I keep watching.

Because I don't react, Pippi removes her nail and continues to speak to Slayer.

"How many times do you have to have sex with them before you can get a baby?" she asks.

"I don't know," Slayer says, cleaning her machine gun. "I've never had a baby. Maybe you do it once. Maybe a dozen times. Why would you want to have a baby anyway?"

"It would be fun," she says. "I always wanted to have a baby."

"You would be a terrible mom," Slayer says.

Pippi's whiskers quiver as a pissy expression crosses her face. "I would be a great mom!"

"Your kid wouldn't survive a week," Slayer says. "You'd get bored with it after a few days and then get rid of it."

"No, I wouldn't."

"Or you'd forget about it and leave it in the hot sun

81

until it baked to death."

"You're wrong," Pippi says, licking my blood from her claw. "I'd be the best mom. My kid would kick ass."

Slayer just laughs at her. "Actually, that would be a sight to see a little Pippi running around with you. She'd be a little terror."

"See!" Pippi says. "I'd even teach her to throw knives as good as me. She'd be throwing knives into everything!"

"Grandma would be so pissed." Slayer laughs. "She just got you to restrict your knife-throwing to the trees. Now that I think about it, I don't think the Warriors could handle having another Pippi around here."

"They'll just have to deal with it," Pippi says. "Baby Pippi is going to come whether they like it or not."

The two of them look at me and I accidentally look back. They both smirk at the look on my face, which I believe they are interpreting as fear.

"Oh, poor Meat," Slayer says, smacking my shoulder with her paw. "I almost feel sorry for you."

A large brown wolf girl, who looks more like she is turning into a grizzly bear than a wolf, approaches our campfire.

"I heard you got some Meat," she says to the wolf girls. "Can I use one for the night?"

"No," Pippi stands up. "You can't use mine."

The grizzly girl looks down at Pippi. "I wasn't talking to you." Then looks at Slayer. "How much?"

"Five cans of food," Slayer says.

"Five?" the grizzly girl snarls.

"*And* five gallons of gas."

The fur on the back of the enormous wolf girl stands up.

"I'll give you two gallons of gas and three cans of food," she says.

"No deal, Alyssa," Slayer says. "I'm not haggling with you."

Alyssa, the large wolf woman, bares her teeth. In an aggressive stance, she tries to intimidate Slayer into cutting down her price. Slayer, nearly half the size of this monstrous woman, casually cleans her gun and doesn't appear to be threatened in the slightest.

"So do you want it or not?" Slayer says.

Alyssa relaxes her posture. "Fine."

"Great." Slayer looks up at Alyssa and leans her gun against my back. I consider grabbing it, and turning it on them, but quickly change my mind. "Do you want the skinny one or the fat one?"

The grizzly woman looks between me and Pete. She doesn't realize that her choice is between Pete and Krall, but I am the skinniest of the four men so I can understand her confusion.

"I'll take the fat one," she says, salivating. "He'll make a good snack if I turn."

The look on Pete's face is one of shock as well as confusion. I don't think he realizes what is in store for him. He watches the back of the grizzly woman as she walks away.

"If you turn," Slayer yells, "I get to keep all of your stuff."

Alyssa yells back, "I'll pick him up when I'm ready."

Pippi and Slayer see the look of terror on Pete's face and they laugh.

"This is going to be fun," Pippi says, giggling.

On the way back to the cages, Pippi decides to take the long way around to show me off to more of the wolf girls. She takes me by the leash and jerks on it hard so that it chokes me in front of them. She aims for a particularly large group of wolf women, all of them standing around snarling and laughing as they speak. I look for the girl in the metal bikini in the group, but I can only see their backs.

There is one girl who seems like it might be her. It looks as if she is wearing a bikini because most of her back is exposed. She seems less wolf-like than the others. She has short black hair and dark skin, just as Nova did. There is a strip of fur going down her back and ending at a small tail just beginning to form. It is more of a cat tail than a wolf tail.

I keep my eyes on that girl. As we pass, the girl turns around and walks away from the crowd. She walks right in front of me. It doesn't look like the Nova I remember, but there is something incredibly familiar about her. I can't place it. When she gets closer to me, I figure out what it is. She looks like Nova's mother.

"November?" I say to her.

The girl stops and looks at me. I study her. She looks like she has changed quite a bit since I saw her last, but I swear it is her. Her face and neck seem longer, and her chin

84

more pointed. Her eyes look bigger, wider. But her cheeks and lips are Nova's. Her posture is Nova's. Aside from her wolf eyes and ears, all the scars on her arms and belly, and the long fingernails, she looks just as she would have had she aged ten years. It's her.

She looks at me with a questioning face.

"Nova?" I ask. "Is it really you?"

She cocks her head at me as a confused dog would.

"Yeah," she says. Her voice is Nova's.

Pippi gets annoyed that I'm talking and yanks on my collar. I resist her.

"It's me!" I cry. "Daniel!"

She cocks her head slightly the other way, examining me.

"You're not allowed to talk anyone else, Meat!" Pippi says, yanking the choke collar so hard that it feels like my neck is going to break.

"Don't you remember me?" I ask.

She just shakes her head.

Pippi grabs me by my second upper arm, digs her claws into my flesh, and drags me away from Nova. I try to resist, but her animal strength overpowers mine.

I watch Nova walk away, toward her tent.

"You know me, November," I yell across the camp, catching the glares of the wolf women around me. "You were my Novey."

When she hears the word *Novey*, she freezes in her tracks. As Pippi drags me away, I see Nova turn around and look at me. Her mouth dropped wide open. There is a look of recognition in her yellow eyes. She remembers me.

"Daniel?" she says.

It's too far away for me to actually hear, but I believe that is what she said. She doesn't come after me. She just watches as Pippi pulls me back to the cage.

Chapter 6

Alyssa

When Nova was a teenager, she was one of the toughest kids in school. If any of the plump foosball cheerleaders made fun of her at lunchtime she would just jump up on their table and kick them in the face with her yellow factory-worker boots.

If a guy made a vulgar comment about her sexuality she would slam his kneecap into the pavement by jumping on the back of his legs butt-first. If there were a whole group of foosball players who wanted to bully her she wouldn't back off. She would just go after their leader and pop him in the face with her tiny bony fists repeatedly until his lips were bloody. If the others tried to pull her off of him she would elbow them in the eye and squirm out of their grips. She said she wasn't afraid of them because they were way too out of shape to do anything about it. She said all she had to do was run away and they wouldn't be able to catch her.

Now that I know Nova is in the camp with me, I feel a lot safer. Although I was in pretty good shape, too, I wasn't the aggressive type. If a foosball player made fun of me I would just take it, walk away, and laugh it off. But I felt safe when I was with my Novey. She taught me how to be brave and confident. Just knowing that she is nearby, after all these years, is filling me with a bravery and confidence that I haven't felt since the day we were separated. She has always been my inner strength.

The day I lost her, much of my inner strength was cut away from me. It was a shock to hear she had been raped. It seemed impossible. If any woman could protect herself from an attacker it would have been Nova. She could take on the entire foosball team single-handed. But they said the guy

87

had a gun. I guess she couldn't outrun or outfight a guy with a gun no matter how good of shape she was in. It still pains me to this day to know this happened to her.

When I tell my brother that November is still alive and living in this camp, he just grunts and rubs his mustache. It is as if the information is not news to him.

After an hour, Slayer, Pippi, and a new wolf girl, who has short boyish hair and about a dozen piercings in her face, take us out of our cage.

They release Guy, Krall, and I, but as Pete is about to leave, Slayer says, "You stay."

She only has to hold out her black paw to get him to obey. I notice that although her hands are mostly human-shaped, her palm has black pads on them like that of a dog. The rest of her hands are coated in dark fur and her thick dog-like nails are also black.

Slayer closes Pete in the cage. A few more wolf girls come forward and pick up the cage, with Pete still inside, and carry it over their shoulders to the center of the camp.

I look at my brother and Krall. They just shrug at me. The wolf girl with the piercings pokes at us with a jagged saw-toothed sword, indicating that we have to follow after our masters carrying the cage.

When Pippi and Slayer put it down in the center of the camp, they leash us and back us away from the cage. They make us kneel at their feet. Sitting in the dirt, with Pippi hovering over me, I watch Pete curled up in the middle of the cage as a crowd gathers around him. Pippi cups her hands around the back of my neck, fidgeting with my collar, as she watches over my head.

The entire camp seems to have gathered, creating a circle around the cage. All of them are at complete attention and grow more and more silent. The only one not paying attention is the little girl, Ashley, who sits down in front of Guy and pulls out a bag of marbles. She pulls out marbles one at a time and shows them to my brother, but my brother completely ignores her, too focused on Pete to acknowledge her presence.

After a long moment of silence, three women make their way through the crowd to the cage. One is Alyssa, who is now wearing an ornate purple robe. It is the only clean article of clothing I have seen anyone wear in this camp since I arrived. The one to Alyssa's right is Talon, the second in command of the Warriors of the Wild. The one to Alyssa's left is an old woman. She must be the leader. She is older than any woman I have ever seen. She is half wolf, with long gray hair covering all of her body except her eyes and wrinkled black lips. She must be seventy years old, or maybe older.

I scan the crowd and lock eyes with Nova. She is standing in the crowd on the opposite side of the cage, staring at me. I look at her and try to communicate with my eyes, by winking at her. She winks back at me. First she winks with her right eye, then she winks with her left. Then she smiles. I think she is trying to show me that she remembers who I am. Even though she hardly looks the same, I feel like I'm looking at my old Novey. I can't help but smile back.

Pippi realizes what is going on and pulls my shoulders backwards, pressing the back of my head hard against her crotch. She stares down Nova until she breaks eye contact with me. Then she leans down and whispers in my ear.

"Don't you dare make a sound when Grandma is talking," Pippi says.

Grandma steps forward and gives a speech:

"In the walled city, women are forced to suppress their natural urges. We are told when we can have sex, how many times we can have sex, who we are allowed to have sex with, and that's if we are permitted to have sex at all. We are taught that female sexuality is something that must be controlled and feared. But here, out in the wild, we are free. We release our inner desires. The beasts within us are not to be feared, they are to be embraced. We will not allow our souls to be locked away, covered up, or forced out. This is our strength. This beast is the physical manifestation of our feral souls, the wild passion that defines our femininity, the keen sensing, and the creative playful spirit. This is our destiny. We belong to the wild."

She pulls Alyssa next to her. The large woman stands a good two or three feet higher than Grandma.

"Today, Alyssa will go one step closer to releasing her inner spirit. She will unleash her boundless passion without the need of permits or marriage. Perhaps this day will be the day her inner soul will completely break free of its bonds, and she will be able to join our big sisters in the freedom of the night."

After she is done, all of the women stomp their feet and howl. Their howls are not at all the same as wolf howls. They basically just sound the same as humans making howling sounds.

Grandma takes the robe from Alyssa, as Talon opens the door of the cage. Alyssa's hairy mass is almost too big to fit through the door of the cage. When the door closes, the wolf women howl again.

Pete is curled in a ball on the opposite side of the cage. The look on his face is the most horrified I have ever seen on a human being. His biggest phobia is about to come true. He is about to be raped by the biggest, most beast-like woman he has ever seen. And he doesn't know if he's going to get out alive. It hurts me to watch him as he snivels and shakes at the sight of her.

Pete is the biggest guy I have ever known. He is not the tallest or the most muscular, just really fat. He has more body mass than any man I've known in McDonaldland. But now, seeing him in the cage with Alyssa, he looks tiny. Nearly half her size. Since Pete is nearly twice my size, I couldn't imagine how I'd look if I were in the cage with her. I'd be only a quarter her size.

On all fours, she circles the cage toward him, teasing him, eyes locked on him, pretending she is already a complete wolf and that he is her prey. Her teeth chatter as she growls at him. He quivers at her. Then she attacks. He cries out as she lunges at him. She grabs him by the ankle and tugs him into the center of the cage, then pins him down. Once on top, he looks even smaller.

The crowd cheers. Alyssa seems to be putting on a show for everyone. She rips off Pete's clothes with her teeth, growling and snarling at him. To toy with him, she shreds each article of his clothing one at a time as soon as she removes them. Pippi laughs above me as Pete shrieks.

Once his clothes are gone, the girls laugh at the look of Pete naked. He's just a big pink ball of blubber. The women around me seem to be salivating, their wolf sides seeing him as a big piece of meat. Pete is more like a juicy cheeseburger to them.

"Get that fat boy!" Slayer yells.

Pippi giggles at that.

When his small boy-sized third leg is revealed, Alyssa grabs it with her jaws and playfully thrashes it around like a rabbit. Pete cries out in horror. He doesn't seem to realize that she's just messing with him.

Pete doesn't have an erection. He is too terrified to have an erection. I have no idea how she is actually going to have sex with him. She plays with him some more. To the delight of her audience, she pulls him across the floor of the cage by the leg in her mouth. He tries to reach out for the bars but she's already pulled him too far away from the sides. The wolf girls cheer and howl.

Then she licks his face with her big dog tongue. He cringes and swats her tongue away. Then she pins down his arms and licks his face more, covering him in slobber. Her jaws are stretched so wide that it seems like she could fit his entire head into her mouth.

He whines as she licks his neck and chest. He is bawling as she deep-throats his entire arm. The crowd is getting really into it. Not because of what she is doing to him, but because of Pete's reaction to her. They have probably not met a man who has been this terrified of them, who has been this tormented by just the foreplay. His fear seems to be turning Alyssa on, as well as turning on many of the women in the crowd.

Pippi is no exception. In fact, she seems to be the one most enraptured by Pete's suffering. She kneads my shoulders with her claws as she watches, giggling like a crazed school girl.

Alyssa licks his entire body until Pete calms down. I notice that he's getting an erection now. Although he is repulsed and terrified by the large wolf woman, his body can't help but react to the stimulation. She sucks his entire dick, including his testicles, into her maw. Her wolf eyes glare up at him as her tongue works itself around him. When she releases his penis, it is fully aroused.

The crowd stops being rowdy. They quiet down, get serious. This is the first time I've ever seen anyone have sex. I've never done it or seen anyone do it. I know how it works, but the closest I've come is just masturbating to pictures of naked non-wolf women in the pages of McPlayboy Magazine.

Everyone appears to be turned on. Even Nova on the other side of the crowd seems to have forgotten all about me and has her eyes locked on the cage. I am even beginning to get a little turned on myself, as I see their bodies press together in the cage.

Although Alyssa is huge, and more wolf than human, there is something erotic about her. Her features are not as bulky and masculine as some of the other more beastly women in the camp. She is massive, but her body is feminine. Her wide curves, exaggerations of the female form. Her thighs and hips are big and round, her waist is thin, her arms are slender.

As she puts his penis inside her, I realize that it is her chest that is turning me on. The only spot on her body that doesn't have hair is her chest and belly. Although her breasts are proportionate to her body, they seem enormous when they are pressed against Pete. They are each bigger than his head. She pumps slowly against him. Her breasts and belly are already drenched in sweat. The rest of her body is that of a monster's, but her human parts ooze with sexuality. As her plump breasts slide against her round belly, I can't stop myself from getting an erection.

Already, I can see the change happening. Brown fuzz is appearing on her breasts and stomach, filling in the bare spot. But even though hair is growing in, I'm still turned on by her body.

As she fucks Pete, Alyssa growls and moans. Pippi digs her claws in and out of my shoulders with each pumping motion that Alyssa makes. Her growls become louder as she fucks him faster and faster. As she nears the climax, the tension rising in the crowd, her body begins to rapidly transform. Her muscles bulge and pop under her fur. Her teeth grow longer. Her muzzle widens. Even her size is expanding as she gains more and more mass.

Pete squirms beneath her. As if he can feel her changes vibrating through his body. Perhaps he can even feel the muscles expanding from inside of her. As she orgasms she howls out in a more painful pathetic way, and all of the wolf women howl with her.

When she is done, she collapses on top of Pete. The crowd cheers. You can hardly see any of Pete beneath her enormous body. A big dumb smile stretches across Alyssa's lips as Pete wiggles beneath her. Pippi claps and hops up and down behind me, yanking on my choke collar with each jump.

It's over. Pete made it through alive. It didn't seem so bad from my perspective. I haven't experienced it for myself, so I don't know what it felt like. But it looked more pleasurable than anything else. If anyone, Alyssa is the one who has it bad. For one moment of fun, she had to sacrifice more of her human appearance and become even bigger and hairier. Now she doesn't resemble a human anymore at all, apart from being able to walk on two legs. But Pete, he just had to lie back and enjoy himself. I will have to ask him how he felt about it once we're back in the cage together.

The crowd begins to dissipate. After witnessing something like that, I'm surprised they aren't all so turned on now that they don't all want to take their own turn. But they seem to be satisfied with just watching. Perhaps it's rude to interfere with Alyssa's moment in the spotlight.

When I look over to my right, I notice the little girl is still sitting on the ground next to Guy. They are playing marbles in the dirt. Neither of them has been paying attention to Pete or Alyssa.

It is funny to see Guy sitting there, playing marbles with his usual serious expression on his face. He messes with his mustache as he flicks marbles at other marbles. The two of them do not say any words to each other. They just play the game. The little girl smiles a lot. She seems like she's having a lot of fun. Guy does not seem like he is having any fun.

"Wait," Alyssa says, her voice deeper, coarser.

The crowd stops and looks back at her.

She lifts herself from Pete. "I can feel it. I'm close."

The crowd returns, gathering around her.

"I'm going to keep going," Alyssa says. "I'm about to turn."

The wolf women are silent. Their faces become solemn. The only ones who make noise are Pippi, giggling with anticipation behind me, and Slayer, who yells out, "I get all of your stuff, then."

The others glare at Slayer and Pippi for their rudeness.

Pete cries, trying to wiggle out from beneath her. She holds him down and glares into his eyes. She grabs at his penis, trying to make him hard again. It is too flaccid. Her paws are much less human now. They have difficulty curling around such a small piece of meat. She barks and snarls at him. He screams. There's no way she is going to get him up.

I look over the cage at Nova. She is staring at me. Her face is generally concerned and apologetic. She seems to want me to watch her instead of the cage, as if she doesn't want me to see what is about to happen. But I already know what is about to happen. Even Pete knows.

Alyssa drools into Pete's face, growling, angry that he

can't get an erection. Her pelvis thrusts at his crotch, craving him, frustrated that he isn't already inside of her. Instead of his dick, she goes for his third leg. It is the size of a little boy's leg, several times larger than the biggest male penis, but Alyssa doesn't care. She drives the small leg into her vagina. In one shove, she gets it up to the knee. Her growls roar into Pete's face as she forces it the rest of the way in.

Pete shrieks as the creature fucks his extra limb. She stares him in the eyes, widening her jaws, as she slams against him. It isn't slow and sensuous. It is fast and violent. She fucks him like she is trying to break his leg off inside of her. She digs her claws into his chest and draws blood.

Her muscles pulse and twist as she transforms, growing even larger. Her limbs twist and mutate—the arms becoming the front legs of a wolf, the legs bending into hind legs that she will no longer be able to stand on. Her growls become more and more primal. Something behind her eyes disappears as her brain mutates within her head, then something cold and hungry clicks on. It doesn't look like Pete is being fucked by a wolf girl anymore. He is being fucked by a giant animal, who has become almost the size of a small car.

As she orgasms, she lets out a howl. There is no longer a trace of human anywhere in this howl. It is the howl of a wolf.

When Alyssa looks down at Pete, she no longer sees him as a mate. Her primal instinct only sees him as food. Pete shrieks as she bites into his neck, thrashing ferociously. She growls, ripping a slab of meat from his chest.

It happens fast. Pete is still alive, throwing his arms around and screaming as his blood sprays into the air. The meat is torn from his body and guzzled down the wolf's throat. She wraps herself around him, holding him in place as she chews the meat from his bones. All I see is his bloody ribcage, as his body twitches below the enormous mass.

Pippi has her hands around my throat, holding me

tight against her legs. I hear small growls coming from her lips as she smells the blood in the air. Then I hear many barks and growls coming from the wolf women around me, licking their lips, salivating at the meat in the cage. Even Nova is no longer paying attention to me, consumed by the sight of blood and warm raw flesh.

When Alyssa is done with him, Pete is just a mangled carcass in the cage. Much of the fat on his body has been torn away. It took a lot of his flesh to fill the new wolf. Now Alyssa wants out of the cage. She attacks the bars with her teeth and claws, bending the cage outward.

The wolf girls back away. They no longer feel completely safe. Slayer takes Krall and Ashley back toward the vehicles, but Guy is left to clean up Ashley's marbles. The only one who doesn't move is Pippi, who holds me in place.

Talon approaches the cage and removes one of the long-handled axes from her back. She swings it at the corner of the cage, facing the woods. The axe is sharp enough to tear a hole all the way down the side. Then she jumps clear.

Alyssa lunges at the hole, rips it wider with her claws and pokes her head out. The cage bends and twists around her as she pulls her mass through. By the time she gets free, the cage is a contorted jumble of wire. She charges toward the woods, but stops, turns around. She looks back at the camp, at her sisters, but I can't tell if there is any recognition in her eyes.

After letting out another long howl, the great wolf grabs a hunk of meat that was hanging out of her crotch. It is Pete's severed third leg. With the limb dangling from her jaws, she hops over one of the armored vehicles and disappears into the forest.

Chapter 7

Mars

We are not brought back to the cage with Pete's body. Instead, they take us to the cage in the back of the pickup truck. A much smaller and less comfortable place to be put.

Pippi and Slayer don't speak when they put us back. They look winded and emotionally flushed after that experience, as if they need a McCigarette. They go back to the middle of the camp and lie down, basking in the starlight.

Krall and Guy don't say anything either. I'm not sure if it is because they feel bad about Pete or if they are worried that they will share his fate. Either way, they don't feel like talking.

Later in the night, we get a visitor to the cage. It is Nova. She comes along the other side of the pickup so that Pippi can't see her from the camp.

"Nova," I say.

She tries to talk, but can't say anything at first.

Then she says, "I can't believe I forgot about you. It seems like a lifetime ago that I left McDonaldland."

"I never stopped thinking about you."

She's taken aback, as if I were trying to insult her.

Then she says, "I'm sorry. You don't know what it's been like out here. Every day is a struggle for survival. And every time we change a little piece of our minds disappears."

She is slightly more wolf-like than she was when I last saw her. I wonder if she has had sex with other men since then. I wonder if she has taken prisoners into the cage

99

WARRIOR WOLF WOMEN OF THE WASTELAND

and forced them to make love to her.

Guy interrupts. "Can you get us out of here?"

She gives him an annoyed face for asking that question.

"You remember me, don't you?" Guy asks. "Daniel's older brother, Guy."

She cocks her head at him slowly and squints her eyes, then turns away from him. She doesn't seem to remember him at all.

"You're Pippi's property?" she asks me.

I nod.

"Pippi's the worst," she says. "If you belonged to somebody else, anybody else, I would have been able to buy you. But Pippi never sells. She doesn't even rent. It's going to be impossible for me to bargain for you."

"Can't you convince her?" I ask.

"I'll try, but I doubt she will give in. I could go to Grandma and ask her to help me, but she would not be sympathetic to my reasoning. Couplings are against our ways here. She might be more angry than sympathetic if I wanted to buy you because you were my boyfriend in McDonaldland."

"Tell her I'm like your brother," I say. "We grew up together."

"Maybe," Nova says. "But Pippi is like a daughter to Grandma. Pippi was born out here in the wasteland and her mother died when she was very young, so Grandma raised her as her own pup. Grandma is more likely to side with Pippi before she sides with me."

"What about letting us go?" Guy asks.

She looks at him. Her yellow eyes reflecting in the fire light. "You'd never survive in these woods at night. You're better off in this cage for now. Because you are a Fry Guy you wouldn't have lasted long in this camp, but because you are Ashley's property you might last years here. As long as she doesn't sell you."

She looks at Krall. "You're Slayer's property. She will keep you around as long as you are useful. Your only worry is that she doesn't rent you out to one of the girls who are about to turn."

Then she looks at me. "But you are Pippi's property. She doesn't keep her meat for longer than a week, usually. It is not uncommon for them to be killed off in the first night. She likes to hurt men. She has no sense of remorse. Killing men has been a game to her ever since she was a little girl. She was raised to be a cold-hearted hunter."

"What can we do?" I ask.

"I will talk to her. I might be able to strike a deal. Perhaps I will promise to capture her five men in the next month in exchange for you now."

"But I don't want five men to die so that I can live," I say.

"I kill men on a daily basis," she says. "By capturing them I will be taking them prisoner rather than killing them on the spot."

I glare into her cold eyes. She really isn't the same girl I used to know.

"I have to go," she says. "I will do my best to convince her."

She doesn't look very confident.

"Okay," I say.

She sticks her fingers through the cage. Her fingers are oddly long and bony. She has pointy fingernails but they are still human-like. I think she wants me to touch her hand, but I hesitate.

"I'm very happy to see you again," she says, though her voice shows no emotion. "There was a large hole inside of me for years and I didn't realize why it was there until today."

I want to tell her how happy I am to see her, but I

don't, because I'm not sure it is true. Although seeing her again is what I have wanted more than anything, she is not the same person anymore. I feel uncomfortable, almost scared to be around her.

We continue to look into each other's eyes for a few moments more, but we do not speak. Then she removes her fingers from the cage and creeps away.

I drift in and out of sleep, my face pressed against the side of the cage. The wolf girls stay up all night, chatting and barking at the moon.

I dream about the time Nova and I had a picnic on the top of the hill overlooking the farming district. It was soon after we graduated from high school. I brought some sparkling wine I had made from orange drink, and I also brought along a special lunch. Besides making wine and beer, my grandpa also taught me how to transform McDonald's food into a gourmet meal.

Using Big Macs, I removed the meat and sliced it up into strips of steak. I took the lettuce and tomatoes and made a salad, using chunks of bun for croutons and special sauce for dressing. Then I smashed the french fries up with the slices of cheese and more of the bun, to make cheddar mashed potatoes. Garnishing the meal with a slice of pickle.

The meal was presented on plates I constructed from sheets of glass, painted white and decorated with flowers. We ate the steak and potatoes with knives and forks.

"This is how people used to eat," I told her. "A long time ago."

After we were done eating, we watched the sunset together. She sat next to me and nuzzled her face between my neck and shoulder. I inhaled her perfumed black hair and smiled. It was the most intimate moment we ever shared together. For that one day, it felt like we were actually a couple, lovers on a romantic picnic.

Then we looked into each other's eyes. I thought we were about to kiss. A *real* kiss. A passionate kiss, rather than her usually friendly peck on the cheek. As we went in, our lips approaching, she stopped.

"Oh, crap!" she said, jumping off of the yellow picnic blanket. "My father's going to be home any minute!"

"What?" I asked, as she packed up her things. "So?"

"It's his birthday today," she said. "I wanted to surprise him with his present as he walked through the door. If I run I might be able to get there in time."

She kissed me on the forehead and then ran off. I fell back onto the blanket and just watched her run down the hill excitedly. Even though she was running away from me, just the sight of her in the distance made me happy. That's when I knew I was completely and utterly in love with that girl.

When dawn comes, Ashley is standing at the door of the cage looking up at us.

"What do you want?" Guy says to her.

She glances at her feet, leaning against the edge of the pickup. With her eyes facing the woods, she says, "I want to make a rock maze."

"Have fun," he says.

She looks up at Guy, and says "Ummm..."

Guy grunts at her.

I look at him and he just stares forward, petting his mustache.

"I think she wants you to play with her," Krall says.

Guy grunts at him.

"Can you help me?" she asks.

Guy thinks about it.

103

"No," he says.

She is confused by his answer.

"Why don't you just play with her?" I ask.

He looks at me. "I know nothing of rock mazes."

"You stack rocks up and then let squirrels run through," she says. "Sarah used to help me make them all the time when she was alive."

My brother glares at her. "Do you have a squirrel?"

The girl shakes her head.

"Then how do you expect them to run through a maze?"

The girl looks down at her feet, rocking her weight against the side of the truck.

"Guy," I say to him. "Just play with her."

He grunts.

The girl doesn't have an argument for him. He just stares her down until she gets uncomfortable standing there and wanders away.

The women pack up the camp and get ready to move on. Slayer removes Krall and I from the back of the truck, but she leaves Guy.

"What's going on?" I ask.

"We're on the hunt," she says.

She takes us to the motorcycles, where Pippi and the other biker girls are suiting up.

"You get to ride into battle with us," Pippi says to me. "You have the honor of being my human shield."

That is all they say to us. We stand there in their group as they prep themselves. While they speak to each other, I study their personalities and listen for their names.

It seems these eight women are the biker warriors. They are the only ones with motorcycles, so they act as if they are an elite squad of their army. They are the knights of the Warriors of the Wild.

Talon is their leader. She rides on the back of a two-person bike. The driver of her bike is called Mars, a dirty brown wolf girl with gray patches, who wears goggles and a spiked helmet.

Besides Slayer and Pippi, Talon has four other soldiers under her command.

There is Casper, the wolf with many piercings that we met last night. She wears blue jeans and is topless except for a small metal plate strapped to her chest. Her long saw-toothed blade is draped over her neck.

There is Athena, who is only slightly more wolf-like than Pippi, who has blonde hair that has been dyed several different colors. Green, pink, blue, and dark purple splotches cover the hair on her head and back. Dreaded purple spikes of hair run down the spine of her back. She also has tattoos all over her body. Her clothes are made of black ripped-up fishnets that do little to hide her sun-burnt breasts.

Then there is Venus, a girl who is almost as hairy as Slayer, but she doesn't have any hair in her face. She doesn't even have a dog nose or whiskers yet. Because she is covered in so much fur, she doesn't have a need for clothes. However, she has dyed her fur a swamp green color and has a pistol holster strapped around her waist.

Then there is Hyena. She is the weirdest of the wolf girls. She isn't completely covered in hair, but where she does have fur it is frizzled and splotchy. Her tan fur is spotted with dark brown patches. She doesn't look like she is turning into a wolf at all. It looks like she is turning into a hyena. Although she is standing around in the nude when I first see her, she straps jagged rusty armor onto her breasts, crotch, and shoulders before going into battle.

Talon, Mars, Slayer, Pippi, Casper, Athena, Venus, and Hyena; these are the elite fighters in their army.

Nova is not a member of this team. She is with the armored vehicles, sitting on the roof of a car with a crossbow on her back, sharpening a sickle-shaped blade. When she

sees me standing with the biker girls, she jumps off the car and approaches us.

Pippi puts me on her motorcycle and straps me to her back. When Nova arrives, Pippi just ignores her.

"Why are you taking him with you?" Nova asks.

Pippi straps black sun-blocking goggles to her face.

Nova looks at Slayer as she straps Krall to her back. "They are going to just slow you down."

"The Fry Guys are less likely to shoot at us if we have hostages on our backs," Slayer says.

"They don't care about hostages," Nova says, loading her crossbow. "They'll just think they're putting them out of their misery."

"Well," Slayer says, "if that's the case, at least they'll shield our backs from the gunfire."

Nova rests her crossbow over her shoulder, trying to come off as concerned for the women rather than us. "They're going to restrict your movements. They could get you killed."

107

Pippi turns on her bike and revs her engine to drown out Nova's voice. Pretending she's not even there, Pippi rolls her bike back and points it in Nova's direction. As the biker girls take off, Pippi shoves Nova out of the way as she passes her, knocking the crossbow out of her hands. Slayer spits at her feet and laughs as we ride on to the head of the motorcade.

On top of a hill, overlooking a road about two miles outside of McDonaldland. My arms have been pressed against Pippi's furry flea-ridden back for over an hour, and the itchiness is driving me insane. Our sweat dripping together in the hot morning sun is only making it more irritating. I count the freckles on her upper arms to keep my mind off of the itching, but there are just too many freckles to count. The back of her head smells like french fry oil.

Slayer and Pippi have been separated. They seem to be trouble when they are together, so during battles it makes sense for them to be apart. Pippi is with Talon, probably so that she can be kept in line. Talon and Mars are on their bike next to us. And on our other side is Venus, the green-haired wolf girl.

The rest of the biker knights are on the other side of the road, hiding behind a pile of old rusted out vehicles. The rest of the motorcade is down the road, hidden in the trees.

Mars and Venus toss a rubber blue ball back and forth to each other. They try to catch it in their mouths and then throw it back. Mars, whose dog-faced mouth is more developed than Venus's, catches it every time. Venus, on the other hand, misses every time, but her reflexes are sharp enough to catch the ball with her hand after it bounces off of her face.

"I'm going to get the most kills," Pippi tells them.

Venus laughs at her. "You never get the most kills. Talon does."

"I bet Slayer I would get more than her," she says. "I bet I get more than you, too."

As the ball bounces off of Venus's lips, she asks, "How much?"

"Half of my share of the catch," she says.

"You're on," Venus says.

The more I look at Venus, the more she stops resembling a wolf girl and closer resembles a girl in a fuzzy green teddy bear suit. The kind of outfit a mother would put on her baby during McHalloween.

We hear the electric engines of McDonaldland vehicles coming up the road. The women turn on their motorcycles. All of them but Pippi, whose motorcycle can't seem to start.

"Ready girls?" Talon asks, then she goes down the hill.

Pippi slams her heel down on the kickstarter. It rumbles for a second and then dies. She kick starts it again, and it dies.

Venus sticks her tongue out at her and then laughs as she rides down the hill after Talon.

"Damn it!" Pippi cries in a pissy tone.

She kick starts it again. This time it slowly gurgles, but doesn't die. She revs it up, the high-pitched motor roaring in my ears. Then we ride down the hill, far behind the others.

This caravan of Fry Guy vehicles is a bit larger than the one I

109

was transported in. There are three armored vehicles and two McVans. They must have arrested a lot more mutant men this time.

Slayer and the other knights reach the caravan first. The two with machine guns open fire on the armored vehicle in the middle, between the two vans. When Pippi reaches the road, the caravan has already passed and Slayer has already taken out the gunner on the middle armored car.

"Shit!" Pippi says, as she sees the man's body roll off of the roof of the vehicle. "No fair!"

The wind blows hard against my face as Pippi speeds up to catch the rear of the caravan. In front of us, Mars and Venus fire at the rear armored vehicle. Behind us, a pack of Warrior cars join in the attack.

Talon stands up on the back of Mars' motorcycle. She pulls the two axes off of her back, holding one in each hand. They are like wood-chopping axes that have been sharpened to a razor's edge. Mars fires at the gunner in the red Fry Guy uniform, using her machinegun fixed to the front of her bike. The gunner is protected behind a bulletproof shield, but her bullets make it impossible for him to fire his own gun.

Once Mars gets up to the side of the vehicle, Talon leaps off of the bike and runs up the trunk of the car. The gunner fires sloppily at Talon, mostly hitting his own vehicle, as she charges him. Talon swings one axe into the gun, splitting the barrel down the middle, and slashes the other into the side of his head.

As Pippi catches up, we ride along the side of the armored car. Talon leaps onto the roof of the vehicle and chops one of her axes into the windshield. The car swerves. As the passenger of the vehicle leans out of the window and points a gun at Talon, Venus pulls out a .50 Magnum from the holster on her waist and blows his face off.

"You bitch!" Pippi cries.

Venus looks at Pippi, lifts two fingers, and sticks

out her tongue.

With only the driver left, Talon swings her axe into the driver's side window hitting him in the shoulder. She swings again and it cuts all the way through his wrist. Blood sprays from his arm out of the window, raining on Pippi and me as we close in.

As Pippi rides us past, I look at the driver. He looks back at me. His severed hand is still attached to the steering wheel, trying to drive the car. Then Talon jumps into the vehicle with him. She snaps his neck and takes over the controls.

Pippi tries to catch up to Slayer. She rides past the first van, and fires a burst of rounds right into the cab. Pippi howls as the van spins out.

"That's at least one for me," she says.

But the van straightens itself out and continues after her.

"I don't think you got him," I say.

She lets out a frustrated growl and hits the gas.

The van drives up behind us. I can feel Pippi's muscles tense, and the hair stands up on her back, as the passenger riding shotgun releases a spray of gunfire. Pippi yelps and crouches down, so that my body will shield her from the fire. The bullets miss, but scatter ahead of us. Two of them enter the back of the wolf girl riding ahead of us. It is Mars. I see the blood pop from her dirty fur and she slumps forward. Still alive, just barely hanging on. Her spiked metal helmet rolling from side to side as if she's trying her hardest to stay conscious.

Pippi rides up alongside Mars, to put her between us and the shooter. Mars just looks at us with a pissed off face as the gunner opens fire again, tearing through her back and the side of her face. Her bike topples over and her body is crushed under the wheels of the van.

Pippi doesn't show an ounce of guilt. Besides being a good shield, Mars' body also acts as a good speed bump. After running her over, the van is slowed down too much to be a threat to Pippi.

The second armed vehicle is still standing. Slayer and her crew killed the gunner and moved on to the vehicle in the front of the line. The passenger of this vehicle has taken over the gunner station on the roof and is now firing at Venus as she comes alongside.

"No you don't, bitch," Pippi says, as she speeds up to make the kill before her rival does.

Pippi fires sloppily at the back of the car, taking out the trunk and the bumper, but missing the gunman. She fires until her gun clicks. Out of bullets. She slides the gun between my arms and her waist, as if I'm some kind of human holster. Stretching her leg out to the side, she reaches for three throwing knives that are sheathed to her thigh. With four fingernails, she is able to draw all three knives.

She rides in closer and tosses a knife into the gunner's ribs. He cries out and releases the gun. As he pulls the knife from his side, a bullet blows a hole through his chest just a few inches above his knife wound. He folds over and dies.

Pippi looks at Venus and yells, "I got him first, bitch! That was my kill!"

Venus laughs and flips her off.

"He was still breathing when I finished him off," Venus says.

Before Pippi can argue back, Venus speeds up to the other girls ahead of them.

Pippi rides up to the driver of the armed car and tosses a knife at him. The knife hits the car door, piercing all the way

through the metal shielding. The driver looks at the knife with a "Holy shit" face. Pippi's wolf blood must have turned her into one strong bitch to be able to throw a knife through metal like that. No wonder she's able to toss me around like a rag doll, even though she's half my size.

Her last knife goes through the open window, misses the driver, and flies out the other side.

"Fucking asshole," Pippi says, flipping him off.

She doesn't have anything else to kill him with so she just spits at him. The driver swerves to hit her with his car, but she dodges by riding the bike into the dirt on the side of the road.

From behind, one of the Warrior's armed vehicles closes in. An arrow pierces the back tire of the Fry Guy car and he spins out of control. He crashes into a tree and goes through the windshield.

Pippi catches up to Slayer, riding up alongside her.

"Give me a clip," Pippi says.

"Screw you," Slayer says.

"I'm out of ammo," she says.

Slayer shakes her head and digs into the pack on the side of her bike. While she digs, I look at Krall sitting on the back of her bike. He's looking at me with a smile on his face. It's like he is trying to tell me something. He moves his hands a little, showing me that his wrists are no longer bound. He's managed to untie himself.

I nod my head. I'm not sure what he's planning, but he probably wants to use this attack as a chance to escape.

Slayer tosses the clip at Pippi. "That's why you should rent out your Meat. You'd get plenty of extra ammo."

"Fuck no," Pippi says.

Slayer laughs at her.

Then a bullet hits Slayer in the stomach and she falls from her bike. No longer attached to her, Krall doesn't fall with her. He catches the handles with his extra hands and balances himself. Like a spider, he inches his way up the bike with his eight limbs.

Pippi's face is in shock as she sees Krall riding next to her. She quickly tries to reload her gun, but Krall stops and turns around. He speeds off in the opposite direction.

I look back. Instead of fleeing into the woods, Krall is racing toward Slayer. She is in the middle of the road, still alive, holding her stomach and trying to stand up.

The Fry Guy van barrels toward Slayer, aiming to run her over. The car Talon is driving is on the van's side, slamming into it. Talon doesn't see Slayer in the road up ahead. If the van doesn't hit her, then Talon surely will.

As Slayer gets to her feet, Krall rides at her. He snatches her off the road with his two left arms and cuts to the right, dodging the oncoming vehicles by mere inches. He rides off with her into the woods.

Up ahead, howling fills the road. The giant wolves come out of the trees and attack the lead Fry Guy vehicle. The four biker girls up there turn around and head back in our direction. Talon and the other Warrior vehicles slow down and then stop, allowing the Fry Guy van to continue on its way. It won't make it past the wolves.

Pippi pulls off the side of the road, looking back. She turns around and rides us into the woods, to go after Slayer and Krall. I see Talon flag down Casper, the knight with the piercings. She gets on the back of her bike and points in our direction, ordering her to follow. Talon must have seen Krall escaping into the woods with one of her soldiers. She probably doesn't know that he just saved that soldier's life.

When we track them down, the bike is tossed into a thicket of weeds. Slayer is unconscious on the ground, her spiked leather jacket unzipped to reveal small black furry breasts with red nipples poking out of the fur. Krall is tending to her, pushing hard on the wound with two of his hands, as he heats a knife with a McCigarette lighter.

"Get away from her," Pippi says, pointing the gun at him, with me still strapped to her back. "Drop the knife."

Krall doesn't obey.

"If I don't stop the bleeding she is going to die," he says.

Pippi keeps quiet after he says that. She uncuffs me from her torso and goes to Slayer's side. At least there is someone in this world that Pippi cares about.

We watch as Krall cauterizes the wound. The smell of burnt hair and flesh fills the trees. By the time Talon and Casper arrive, Krall is already finishing up.

Talon immediately recognizes what is going on.

"How is she?" Talon asks.

"She'll be fine," Krall says. "The bullet missed her major organs."

"Were you able to get it out?" she asks.

"Didn't need to," Krall says. "It passed through her."

Krall lifts his shirt to show a dark red hole in his own belly. Talon glances at his wound and then moves away from him to see to her fallen soldier. Slayer is beginning to regain consciousness. Krall comes to me and squeezes on his wound like a zit.

"Are you okay?" I ask him.

He nods. "It's not very deep."

He squeezes until the bullet pops out into his hand. It barely went in an inch. A line of blood leaks down his abdomen. As he lights the knife to cauterize his own wound,

116

Slayer gets to her feet. She staggers over to him and rips the knife out of his hand and puts it back into its sheath on her leg.

"Pick up my bike, Meat," she says to him.

Krall obeys.

She gets on her bike and re-straps him to her chest, crushing his wrists with her paws as she binds him.

"If you ever free yourself from my bonds again I will kill you," she tells him.

I can't believe what I'm hearing. I say, "He just saved your life!"

She looks at me with a snarl and says, "I didn't ask him to do anything for me."

Then she starts her bike and rides it out of the woods.

Once we all get out of the forest, we see the wolves taking apart the vans to get at the mutant prisoners inside. Unlike Krall and myself, these deformed citizens aren't making it out alive. A couple of them run for the woods, but they have even more limbs than any of the mutants from yesterday. They just aren't agile enough to get very far.

In the back of the feeding frenzy, I see half a dozen smaller wolves have joined the pack. I recognize the smallest one. It is Alyssa. With the other smaller wolves, she is scavenging for severed limbs that the bigger wolves leave behind.

The other Warrior vehicles have retreated.

"Come on," Talon says. "We'll let our big sisters have their meal. Then we'll come back later to claim the leftovers."

Then we rejoin the group.

Pippi pulls up alongside Slayer to see how she's doing. Slayer smiles, pretending she's perfectly fine.

"I got two of them," she says. "How many did you get?"

"Three," Pippi says.

Slayer laughs. "No, you didn't."

"I did!" Pippi says.

Slayer looks over at me.

"How many men did she kill?" she asks me.

I think it over for a second, but decide to tell the truth.

"None," I say.

Slayer laughs loudly, closing her eyes and laying her head back in Krall's face.

Pippi grumbles.

"Oh, you're *so* dead," she tells me. "I'm not going to keep you around long enough to impregnate me anymore."

Slayer keeps laughing, kicking her leather boot into the air.

Chapter 8

Nova

The wolf girls set up a new camp in the woods. Many of the girls are huddled around Grandma, who says a prayer for their fallen sister, Mars. The wolf girl's body is in a pile of gasoline-soaked wood, about to be lit on fire. Venus cries the most. The multi-colored wolf girl, Athena, holds Venus and rubs her green fur.

Pippi doesn't seem to give a crap about paying her respects to Mars. She is still fuming at me for telling Slayer the truth. Because I'm her property, she thinks I should be on her side.

After Talon, Casper, and a caravan of Warrior vehicles return with the McDonaldland supplies left over from the wolf attack, they ration out the booty to all women, even those who did not participate in the attack.

Pippi separates her share into halves, puts the smaller half into a sack, and throws it at Slayer like a brat.

"If my bike didn't stall out at the beginning I would have beat you," Pippi says to Slayer.

Slayer smiles with her fangs and sticks her hairy face into the sack of goods.

"You should take better care of your things," Slayer says.

Pippi tugs on my choke collar and takes me toward the cage.

"Pippi," Nova calls out behind us.

Pippi stops and turns around.

"I want to cut a deal with you," she says.

"Get lost, Nova," Pippi says. "I'm not in the mood."

"I want your Meat," she says.

"I won't share," Pippi says. "Go talk to Slayer if you want to rent some Meat."

"I don't want to rent," Nova says. "I want to buy."

Pippi's face becomes even pissier.

Nova points to her vehicle. There is a yellow Fry Guy strapped to the hood. I think it was the one who crashed into a tree and thrown through the windshield.

"I'll trade you this Meat for five others," she says. "This one I have captured will be the down payment. I'll get you the other four within a month."

Pippi looks at the yellow Fry Guy and sneers. "No deal."

"Why not?" Nova asks.

"I like this one," she says. "He's mine."

"But this one is a Fry Guy," she says. "He's worth more."

Pippi looks at the other man. "He's damaged."

Nova goes over to the man on the hood. She twists the man's broken arm and he shrieks in agony. "But this one is in pain. You like them when they are in pain."

"I like causing the damage myself," she says. "I like them fresh."

"The next four will be fresh," Nova says.

"No," Pippi says.

"Then I'll give you ten more," Nova says.

"No," Pippi says.

"I'll give you all of the men I capture for the next five years."

"No," Pippi says. "I like capturing them myself. I like damaging them myself. I have no interest in anyone else's Meat."

Nova exhales furiously.

"Look, Pippi," Nova says. "I'll tell you the truth. I know him. We grew up together in the walled city. He is not like the other men. He is good. I don't want him to die."

Pippi smiles.

"I promise, I'll do anything you want. I'll give you half of my rations for a year. Anything. Just let me have him."

Pippi looks at me and licks her fangs. "You were lovers in the walled city, weren't you? You were boyfriend and girlfriend."

"He was like my brother," Nova says.

"You love him," Pippi says.

Nova puts her hands on her hips.

"Okay," Nova says. "Yeah, I loved him. If I would have stayed in the city we might have been married. Please, let me have him."

Pippi giggles. "No way!"

"Please!" Nova looks as if she is going to hit her.

"He's mine now," Pippi says. "I'll do whatever I want with him."

"I'll have Grandma convince you to sell him to me," Nova says.

Pippi leans in close to Nova's ear and whispers, "He probably won't last that long."

Then Pippi walks away, giggling, yanking on my choke collar as hard as she can so that Nova hears me whine.

Pippi takes me back to the cage with Krall and Guy. Guy is pretending to be asleep, probably so that the little girl doesn't ask him to play with her again. Krall is stitching up the hole in his stomach. Nova comes by shortly after to deliver her new Meat to the cage. The yellow Fry Guy looks to be in bad shape. He isn't bleeding very much, but he's incredibly banged up from the car accident. Nova tosses him in the cage like he's just a sack of potatoes. Krall stops working on himself and goes to the aid of the Fry Guy.

Nova looks at me with her solemn wolf eyes as she closes the cage door. "I'm sorry," she says. "There's nothing I can do."

She breaks eye contact and rubs her black wet nose.

"That's it?" I ask. "You're not going to ask Grandma?"

"It wouldn't do any good," she says.

"You're just going to let her kill me?"

She takes a deep breath and steps back.

"I'm sorry," she says. "You're her property. She can do whatever she wants with you. It's against the law for me to even be speaking to you without her permission."

Before I can say anything else to her, she turns her back and walks away. I watch her as she moves toward her tent. She really isn't my Novey anymore. From behind, she doesn't resemble her in the slightest. The stripe of fur going down her back, the black ears sticking from her head, the fuzzy tail. She is more interested in embracing her animal side than reclaiming her human past. Even the way she steps through the weeds is more animal than human.

Krall shakes his head as he examines the Fry Guy. The man is in a delirious state. He doesn't know what is going on around him.

"He's not going to make it," Krall says. "I don't think he will last the night."

"What's wrong with him?" I ask.

"For starters, his spine is broken," Krall says. "Some major organs are badly damaged. They should have just put him out of his misery back there."

Nova surely would have put him out of his misery back there, if she didn't want to use him to trade with Pippi.

Even though it seems hopeless, Krall doesn't stop helping the man. He resets some of his broken bones. He rips strips from his white suit to use as tourniquets. I watch him, surprised he would go through so much trouble to help this man who is surely going to die, even though he has a hole in his own stomach that still hasn't been completely stitched up.

"Why did you do it?" I ask Krall.

He doesn't know what I'm talking about.

"You could have escaped," I say. "Why did you rescue that wolf girl instead of saving yourself?"

"She would have died," he says.

"You could have gotten away."

"I thought it would be easier to save her life than it would be to save my own," he says.

"But she didn't even care," I say.

He shrugs.

Krall says there was a time when he never would have risked his own life to save another, especially not a woman. In McDonaldland, Krall was raised to believe that women were vile, disgusting, inferior creatures, who deserved to be treated like animals.

When he was young, Krall didn't have any exposure to women. He was raised by two fathers. One of them was on The Blessed McDonald's Corporation's board of directors. The other was the head of Research and Development. The two men were homosexuals. It wasn't uncommon for the citizens of McDonaldland to engage in homosexual activity, because sex between men was perfectly legal. However, it was not at all common for homosexual men to live together

124

as if they were married.

Krall's dads did live together and considered themselves married, even though it was not legal for two men to marry. With high positions in the McDonald's government, these men were on a mission to change the way of life in McDonaldland. The two of them hated women. They thought women were beasts and should be treated as such. Like cattle, they wanted women to be raised on farms. They wanted men to live together, marry each other, and when they were ready to have sons, the men could impregnate a woman on one of the farms and then take the male babies from her after they're born. Outside of carrying the children, the women would have no function. They would grow babies then be tossed into the wasteland once they became too wolf-like to manage.

This is what his fathers taught to Krall. For a long time, he believed that women were animals to be used and thrown out. He didn't even believe they had souls.

He was privately schooled and completely sheltered from women for most of his life. His real father, the head of Research and Development, wanted him to follow in his footsteps and become a scientist. Krall agreed.

In McMedical School, Krall was the most ambitious student they had. He was ruthless, snobbish, abrasive, and an absolute genius, just as his fathers had trained him to be. He could handle any task thrown at him, and would step on any of his peers to get ahead. By the end of his schooling, there was not a single person who didn't shrink before him in fear and respect. Even some of the teachers couldn't help but cringe with unease when he was around. He had a way of making his superiors feel stupid.

Upon graduation, he was assigned to the parasite division of Research and Development, which mostly worked on ways to cure females of their lycanthropy. This was the first time he really interacted with females. At first, he just treated them as he would a lab rat or a cadaver. He didn't bother speaking to them. If they tried to communicate he would inject them with something to make them too drowsy to talk.

About this time, his two fathers were separating. They fell out of love for each other and wanted to move on. This upset Krall. He never thought that his fathers would ever be apart. They meant everything to him. Out of spite, Krall told his fathers that he would never speak to either of them again until they got back together. They never got back together. Without the influence of his fathers, Krall's perspective on life was beginning to change.

One day, Krall decided to talk to one of the women he worked on. She was a young teenaged girl who had started practicing masturbation soon after puberty. Her parents tried to pretend she was being home-schooled and hid her in their basement, but the Fry Guys eventually found out. That's when they took her to Krall.

The girl wouldn't shut up. She was crying so loud that Krall couldn't hear himself think. He was about to inject her with a sedative, but then she said, "Please don't let them send me away. I want to go home."

Krall knew that after he was done with her, she would just be thrown out of town, most likely to her death. He had never cared before. Women were animals to him. But this time, he became intrigued and even a little saddened by her situation. He asked her about her family and about her life. He learned that, besides her wolf-like features, she was just as human as he was.

When they took her away, Krall began to feel sick. He felt as if it was his fault she was being taken away. After communicating with other females that were brought to him, he soon realized that these women were all just victims of McDonaldland society. It was the fault of The Blessed McDonald's Corporation that they had these parasites. He realized that his fathers only wanted to get rid of women because they thought it would be easier than curing their lycanthropy.

That's when he promised to dedicate himself to finding a cure for the parasite. He knew that he had the power to help women like these, and so he was going to do it. He worked day and night for several years. Although he never came any closer to finding a cure, he kept trying.

Every woman that came by him he treated with complete respect and tried to make them feel as comfortable as possible. It killed him every time he had to let them go, but he quickly developed a thick skin so that he wouldn't let his emotions get in the way of his work.

Then the male parasite was discovered and Krall was transferred to work on that project. It infuriated him to know that all of his work would just be passed on to some lesser doctor, so he decided to work on both projects at the same time. That is when he theorized that the two parasites were of the same species. But before he could come to any conclusion, he was discovered for having the deformation and was sent out of town. He says he will some day continue his research, even if he has to do so in the wasteland, even as a prisoner of the Warriors. And someday he will find a cure to bring back to McDonaldland.

He says that he recognizes a few of the Warriors from McDonaldland. They were some of the women he studied before they were sent into the wasteland. He says they haven't recognized him yet, and he'd like to keep it that way. Even though he was pleasant with some of them, he doesn't want them to think of him as that man. He'd rather just be Meat.

Pippi comes to the cage with a spear.

"What are you doing?" I ask.

127

She points the spear at me.

"This is for pissing me off," she says.

She stabs the spear through the bars of the cage at me. I jump out of the way. She stabs again. A smile appears on her face. She giggles and sticks the spear in again, piercing it into my foot just a little.

I jump around the cage as she stabs at me. Krall pulls the yellow Fry Guy into the corner with Guy, leaving me to defend myself.

"Hop!" she cries, jabbing the spear at me. "Hop like a toad!"

The spear pierces my hip. As I wince at the pain, she sticks me again in the back. Not very deep. Just enough to draw blood.

I continue trying to dodge the spear attacks as she giggles and barks, but my movements are becoming slow. At first, I think it is because of the wounds, but then I realize even my thoughts are slowing down. I feel like I've been drugged.

I stop moving, sitting upright in the center of the cage. Pippi sticks me one more time in the upper thigh.

"Nighty-night," she says.

The spear must have been tipped with poison. My eyes are heavy. The dizziness becomes too overwhelming to fight. I fall onto the floor of the cage. The last thing I see before I close my eyes is Nova, sitting casually on top of her vehicle. She was watching as it happened and didn't do a thing to stop it.

I awake upside-down. I'm in midair, looking down at the ground which is maybe fifty feet below. I look up at my feet. They are tied together at the ankles.

Pippi is up in the tree above, glaring down at me with

a big smile. She is holding the rope that is attached to my ankles, dangling me from a branch.

"You awake now?" she asks.

"What the fuck are you doing?" I cry.

"Good," she says.

She rings a bell.

"What the fuck are you doing?" I repeat.

She giggles at me and continues ringing the bell, looking off into the distance.

The trees crack and rumble in the direction Pippi is looking. I twist my neck so that I can get a better view. A giant wolf is coming through the forest, creeping toward us.

"Dinner time," Pippi says.

The wolf steps beneath the tree, its eyes locked on me. It is a bus-sized wolf with curly dirty blonde hair. Its long frizzy ears look more like that of a cocker spaniel than a wolf.

"I got a treat for you, Tessa," Pippi says.

The wolf is salivating, licking its lips. Pippi lowers the rope and I find myself moving within range of the beast. I try to lift myself to grab hold of the rope at my ankles, but gravity pulls me back.

The wolf opens its mouth. Its tongue, twice as long and twice as wide as I am, rolls out over its teeth. The back of its throat pulses in anticipation. The cavernous gullet is wide enough to swallow me whole. The uvula dangling in the back of her throat is the size of my torso. It is something that proves that she was once human, because wolves do not have uvulas. The giant animal sits obediently, waiting to be fed, as if this is a common routine.

I am lowered far enough to feel not only the heat, but also the moisture, of the creature's breath. I wiggle to reach my ankles, but my struggle only makes Pippi laugh and enjoy herself more.

129

As soon as my body goes past her teeth, into the creature's mouth, I accept my destiny. If I'm fated to be dog food, then so be it. But as the wolf's mouth closes around my body, Pippi yanks the rope and pulls me out. The beast's mouth closes, without me inside. It locks its eyes on me again, licks its lips again. Then Pippi lowers me back into its mouth. As the wolf bites down, Pippi pulls me out in the nick of time.

Pippi's laughs fill the woods. She continues to tease the wolf with my body. She lowers me, the wolf bites, and she pulls me back up. But each time, she lowers me deeper into the mouth to see how far she can get before pulling me out. It is a game to her. The wolf is getting angry, growling. It salivates so much that spit and drool splatter out across me every time it tries to take a bite.

Pippi drops the rope and I fall completely inside the wolf's mouth. My body splats against its tongue. I feel wet taste buds between my fingers as my face peers down the dark chasm of Tessa's throat. Her growling vibrates through my entire body. Right when I feel the wolf's mouth closing and her throat muscles squeezing together to gulp me down, I am sucked out into the air again.

Tessa is now leaping up into the air, snapping at me, barking loudly. Pippi is cackling, wanting it to last as long as possible. I try not to scream. I know she wants me screaming before she lets me go.

A black form leaps over Tessa's head, diving from an adjacent tree toward Pippi. It is November. She punches Pippi so hard that the girl falls from the tree. I drop only a few feet before Nova seizes the rope.

Pippi catches herself on a branch just above me. As Nova pulls me up, the wolf gets even more ferocious, leaping up and biting at the air mere inches away from me. Pippi pulls a throwing knife from her ankle and tosses it at the rope. The knife pierces the center of the cable, lodging itself up to the handle, but the rope does not snap. Yet. By the time Pippi pulls another knife, Nova already has me by the ankle. Pippi aims her second knife for my head.

As the knife darts at my face, Nova yanks my body into the air and I find myself standing safely on the branch next to her. Nova seems to be just as strong as Pippi. She doesn't even look at me as I wrap my arms around the trunk of the tree, focusing instead on her opponent. She jumps down to the branch below and punches Pippi before she can draw another knife. She punches her in the throat and then punches her in the stomach.

Pippi begins crying and gagging, trying to breathe through her damaged windpipe. Nova kicks her in the kneecap, causing her leg to twist sideways, knocking her off balance. Pippi falls from the branch, but Nova catches her by the ankle.

Now it is Pippi dangling over the giant wolf's maw. The bratty wolf girl shrieks as the beast leaps for her, snapping and growling at her.

"Tessa, no!" Pippi cries at the wolf. "It's me! It's Pippi!"

Nova holds her there for a moment.

"Do you want me to drop you?" she asks.

Pippi cries in response. Then she says, "Tessa, it's me..."

"It's not nice to tease our big sisters with food," Nova says. "Do you want me to give her what she wants?"

"No," Pippi cries.

"Are you sure?" Nova says, lowering her a foot.

Pippi shrieks. "No!"

"I want you to give me Daniel," Nova says.

"He's my Meat," Pippi says.

"I could just feed you to Tessa," Nova says, leaning her in even closer to the wolf's reach. "After you are dead, I can claim him as my own."

"Fine," Pippi says.

"You'll give him to me?" Nova asks.

"He's yours," she says. "Have him. I don't want him anymore."

"Promise?" Nova asks. "On your word as a Warrior, promise you will leave him alone and never speak of this to anyone."

"I promise," Pippi says.

132

When Nova lifts Pippi back onto the branch, Pippi's eyes are drowning in tears, her voice is croaking, she can hardly catch her breath.

"If you fuck with me again I will kill you," Nova says, glaring deep into the girl's eyes.

Pippi doesn't respond. She leaps out of the tree into the next one, climbs down and runs out of the woods. The giant wolf stays below us, instead of following after the girl. Its eyes still locked on me.

Nova climbs up the tree to my branch and sits me down.

"I thought there was nothing you could do?" I ask her.

She looks at me with her cold eyes and gives me a look as if she regrets having saved me.

"I didn't think I could live with myself if I just let it happen," Nova says.

"Thank you," I tell her.

I look down at the beast growling below.

"Now what?" I say.

"She won't leave until she is fed," Nova says. "Pippi got her too hungry to just walk away now. We'll have to wait and hope she gives up soon."

"You should have just fed Pippi to her," I say. "That would have been easier."

Nova snaps at me. "Pippi is a rotten little brat, but she is still my Warrior sister. She just needed to be taught a lesson."

"Pippi doesn't see you or any of the other Warriors as her sisters," I say. "She was pretty much responsible for getting your sister, Mars, killed today. You would have been doing your group a huge favor by killing her."

Nova doesn't respond to that, so I don't push the topic.

"We should be silent," Nova says. "And keep as still as possible. Tessa will get bored sooner if there isn't any sound or movement coming from us."

I stay quiet for a moment, then I say. "I missed you, November."

She takes my hand in her elongated fingers, but she doesn't say another word.

I used to sit with Nova in trees a lot when we were kids. She was usually always happy when she was up in the trees. It was her escape from the world.

Sometimes, though, she was quiet and reflective. When she was in a bad mood, she would go up in a tree to work out her problems. During these times, she would either ask me to leave her alone or we would sit together in silence.

Usually, when this happened, it was something her father did to piss her off. He was a domineering son of a bitch who always wanted her to be a normal girl, follow the rules, stay away from troublemakers like me. But she never listened to him. Nova was wild. She would break rules just out of spite. But, still, sometimes he would get to her. Sometimes he would make her feel so miserable that all she could do was hide in a tree. I don't know why November loved her father so much.

Sitting in the tree, I wish I could think of more pleasant times with Nova. There were so many moments where we would talk for hours up in the trees. But, sitting here in silence, all I can think about is how her father used to make her so sad. Then he had her kicked out of town after being raped at gunpoint.

Chapter 9

Athena

Tessa does not leave. She sits at the bottom of the tree, waiting.

An hour passes. We hear motorcycles coming near. The leading motorcycle is Hyena, who cackles through the woods as she rides. She is dragging the yellow Fry Guy through the dirt, tied to a long rope. When the large wolf sees the bloody mess of the man, she goes for it. Hyena speeds through the trees, the wolf chasing after, leading it out of our vicinity.

Nova helps me climb down the tree. Once we get to the ground, we see a crew of pissed off wolf girls standing by their bikes, staring us down. Pippi, with a swollen neck and a black eye, stands in the back. Slayer stands in the front. Athena and Casper are on her sides.

Slayer is too pissed off to speak, she just stares us down. She also is still in a lot of pain, too much pain to be as aggressive as she wants to be. Pippi seems too scared to approach Nova. She hides behind Slayer. So it is Athena and Casper who come forward to confront us.

Casper draws her saw-toothed sword and holds it out in front of her. Athena pulls out a long club with rusty spikes sticking out of it. They circle us, as if we are prey.

"You try to kill your own sister for this Meat?" Casper says, snarling at Nova.

Casper's voice is low and raspy.

Athena, frizzing her motley colors of hair, smacks her spiked club into the dirt as she circles us. She says, "You betray us, after all we have done for you?"

Athena's voice is high-pitched and squeaky.

"I didn't try to kill her," Nova says. "If I wanted her dead she would be dead."

Casper scratches her sword against a tree as she passes it. "You attacked her and forced her to give you her property. That's stealing."

"Stealing property from a sister is a terrible sin," Athena says.

"This man was my property before he was Pippi's," Nova says. "I was just stealing back what was rightfully mine."

"You sicken me," Casper says, spitting at her feet. "Meat is only Meat."

Casper cuts my arm with her saw-like sword, just enough to break the skin. Then Athena swings her club at my legs.

As she's leaning down to swing, Nova leaps into the air and kicks Athena in the face. The multi-colored wolf girl falls back, unable to finish her swing.

"That's it," Casper says, swinging her sword at Nova's face.

Nova ducks and jams her two long fingers up the girl's nose. She sticks them so far up there that Casper begins twitching, almost paralyzed, unable to fight back. Nova sneers at her, gripping her face like a McBowling ball, digging her fingers in even deeper.

"Don't you fucking touch my man," she says, snarling in Casper's face, "ever again."

Slayer just watches. She doesn't speak or join in. Pippi continues to hide in the back.

Athena gets onto her feet and slams the blunt end of her club into Nova's kidney. Nova topples over, releasing Casper from the nose-grip. Once the fingers are free, Casper pukes into the grass. Blood leaks from her nostrils and she coughs and sneezes at the pain.

While Nova is stunned, Athena comes down on her. I

137

try running between them, but Athena just punches me in the eye. With one punch, I crumble to the ground.

Athena wraps her club around Nova's neck and pulls her back. The spikes dig into her throat, but Athena does not apply enough pressure to pierce the skin. When Casper finishes coughing and wheezing, she punches Nova in the stomach. Nova doesn't cry out.

"Get her!" Pippi cries.

Casper punches her again.

"Kill her!" Pippi says.

Casper punches her in the face, then holds her jagged sword at Nova's mouth, as if wondering whether or not she should ram the sword up November's nostrils as payback.

"Cut her fucking face off!" Pippi yells.

"Enough!" shouts a voice from behind.

It is Talon.

The wolf girls recoil. Casper lowers her weapon and Athena releases her grip around Nova's neck. Talon steps forward. The green-haired wolf girl is with her.

"Venus told me what happened," Talon says. Then she looks at Pippi. "You should have come to me with this."

Then she glares at Athena and Casper, who shrink in the presence of their Alpha leader.

"I will not stand for Warriors taking justice into their own hands. Nova will be punished in the Warrior way, not your own."

She turns to November.

"You have committed crimes against your own sister," Talon says. "You attacked her and stole her property. You are under arrest."

Nova tries to defend herself. "What about my property? They just stole my Meat that I captured today and fed it to Tessa. They must give me this Meat," she points at me, "to replace it."

Talon doesn't even look at her anymore. "You have broken the law. You no longer have the right to own property."

"Casper," she says to the pierced wolf girl. "Tie them up and bring them back to camp."

Casper gets to work.

Then Talon looks at the wolf girl with the crazy colored hair. "Athena, track down Hyena and tell her to come back to camp."

Athena goes to her bike and gets on her way.

"Pippi, Slayer, let's go," Talon says.

Then we set off for the camp.

When we get back to the camp, I am separated from November and put back in the cage. Nova is taken into Grandma's tent with Talon. Pippi, Slayer, and Casper are left behind. While Nova is answering for her crime, Casper and Slayer seem to be confronting the green-haired girl, Venus, for squealing on them. With Talon and Nova preoccupied, Pippi takes the opportunity to deal with me.

The red-headed girl comes to my cage and kneels down to talk to me. She isn't her usual smiling and giggling self. The look on her face is one of pure wrath.

"Next time, that bitch won't be there to stop me," she tells me.

That's all she says. She stands up and goes back to her friends, rubbing her bruises with her paw.

While waiting to see what is going to happen to November, I watch the women who confronted us in the woods: Athena and Casper.

Athena, the motley-haired wolf girl, is sitting by a fire with containers of ink. She has a gun-shaped needle and is tattooing herself with it, drawing what looks to be a red dragon. I'm not sure why, but something about her looks familiar.

As I look more closely, I suddenly recognize this woman from when she lived in McDonaldland. Her real name isn't Athena. I think it was Samantha. Athena was just her stage name. When Casper and Venus sit beside her, I realize that I recognize the two of them as well. They all used to be famous in McDonaldland, about seven years ago.

They were in a band called The Griddler Girls, which was McDonaldland's official musical act for a little less than

140

a year. In McDonaldland, creating your own music is pretty much illegal. There is only one official band allowed in McDonaldland at a time. Before The Griddler Girls it was The Happy Meal Gang, a rock group featuring 10-year-olds, and before that it was Mac Tonight, a lounge singer with a moon-shaped face. The point of these bands was to entertain the young people in McDonaldland, while also promoting McDonald's food and values.

The Griddler Girls were supposed to be a hip all-girl rock group. There were five of them: A singer, a drummer, a bass guitar player, and two guitarists. They were the most successful McDonaldland band in decades, because they really connected with the teens. They sang happy songs about Chicken McNuggets and holding hands.

But the Griddler Girls started to change their image without the permission of The Blessed McDonald's Corporation. While researching ancient rock bands, the Griddler Girls came across a long dead style of music called Punk Rock. They read about their sounds, styles, and attitude. That's the type of music they wanted to play.

Then they started dying their hair multiple colors, piercing themselves, getting tattoos, dying their clothes black and ripping them up into new original styles. They only played one show as punks, and it was a show that McDonaldland would never forget.

There was Athena, the singer, with her crazy dyed hair and tattoos screaming about rebelling against the government. Then there was Casper, the lead guitar player, who had a dozen metal rings pierced into her face, with a tall black mohawk. There was Venus, the drummer, who had a short green pixie haircut and wore a green Fry Guy uniform to be ironic. There were two other girls, one with long purple hair and another with dark red hair and a lot of black makeup. I wonder if one of them was the dead wolf girl, Mars.

I went to the first half of that show. I was on a date

with some annoying, ugly girl my brother forced me to go out with. She was fat and conservative. She was always quoting passages from the McDonald's Bible.

Her favorite band was The Griddler Girls, which was a band I didn't care for. I liked to make up my own songs and whistle them in my head, just as grandpa used to do. When I saw The Griddler Girls perform their new punk songs, this conservative girl was pissed off. I, on the other hand, was highly entertained. It made me happy to see these girls playing their own music, dressing in their own style, and flipping off the authorities.

They were definitely trying to inspire change and ignite rebellion in the hearts of their teenaged audience. Unfortunately, I seemed to be the only person who appreciated their performance. Everyone else in the crowd was upset and angry. They didn't like these songs. They didn't like what they were saying about the McDonald's government and religion.

Some people stayed behind to boo the girls and throw milk shakes at them, while the majority of people just left the stadium to go home. The girl I was with forced me to get her out of there. I wanted to keep watching, but she was insistent. I told her I would take her home only if she promised never to talk to me again. She agreed.

I wasn't there to witness it, but I heard that The Griddler Girls were escorted out of McDonaldland after that performance. They were the only girls I knew who had been kicked out of McDonaldland for doing something besides having sex. Within a week, McDonaldland had a new act: Skaberry Milkshake. This band renewed the ancient music called *ska* while promoting McDonald's milkshakes.

It's weird to see The Griddler Girls again. They don't look the same as they used to. Since entering the wasteland, they have started to have sex or at least masturbate, causing their wolf features to manifest. They have also expanded on

142

their punk styles, with more tattoos, piercings, and accessories than they had in the city. They have also become angry and violent.

These days, instead of playing instruments and reviving punk music, they are riding motorcycles and killing Fry Guys. They are also bullies who wanted to kill my Novey. It is depressing to think of what becomes of the people once they enter the wasteland. I used to think of them as heroes, now I just think of them as petty thugs.

Nova doesn't leave Grandma's tent until dusk. I watch from my cage as she is taken out to the center of the camp. She has been stripped of all her clothes and her hands are tied behind her back.

The wolf girls gather around Nova, Talon, and Grandma.

Grandma says, "Nova has committed a terrible crime against her sister, Pippi. She has been found guilty of assault, thievery, and the endangerment of a sister's life. Nova will be stripped of her rank and all of her possessions. Her punishment will be Trial by Claw, which will be carried out immediately."

The wolf girls stomp their feet and howl. They create a circle, stomping their feet in rhythm as if they are banging on drums. Talon brings Nova, naked and bound, into the center of the circle. Once she is in place, the women end their stomps.

"Nova," Grandma says. "As you know, committing a crime against a sister is the same as committing a crime against all your sisters. So retribution will be carried out by each and every one of your sisters. The severity of your punishment from each sister will be left to their individual judgments. Do you understand?"

November nods her head at Grandma.

"Then let us begin."

The wolf girls howl and begin stomping their feet again. Venus is the first to enter the circle with Nova. She swipes at Nova's back with her green paw and then steps out of the ring. Judging by the crowd's booing, it was a weak cut.

Athena comes up next and slashes her on the back with her claws, in the exact same spot as Venus, but this cut is so deep that blood splashes from Nova's skin. Casper takes Athena's place and attacks Nova's face with her claws, right across her cheek and nose. Hyena yips and cackles when she enters the ring, leaping into the air and stabbing her claws right into Nova's side.

One at a time, the wolf girls approach Nova, cut her with their claws, and then step out. Some of them cut her deeply, others just barely scratch her. The only one who doesn't cause any damage at all is the little girl, Ashley, who just runs up to Nova, presses her hand against her thigh for a second, and then runs back to her place. But no matter how big a cut she is given, Nova does not cry out for any of them.

The final three are Talon, Slayer, and Pippi. When Talon enters the ring, she claws Nova across the palms. The crowd gasps when she does this. They stop howling and stomping. It doesn't look very painful, so cutting across the palms must mean something dishonorable among the wolf girls. The crowd is still silent when Slayer enters the circle. Slayer, with her incredibly wolf-like claws, cuts her on the ass. The cut causes a lot of bleeding, but I'm surprised she didn't slash her in a more tender area. It's almost as if she pitied her, or was too weak from her own wound to do more damage than that.

When Pippi enters, the eyes of every woman in the crowd widen. Pippi looks sternly at Nova. She touches the bruised and swollen spots on her face. Pippi approaches Nova. She holds her hands out, extending her claws. Then she digs her nails beneath Nova's shoulders as deep as she can go. For the first time, Nova cries out. She cries at the top of her lungs. And her cries only turn into shrieks as Pippi drags her nails down her chest, ripping deep trenches into her flesh. Pippi cuts as slowly as she possibly can, tearing eight enormous gashes down her body. She slices down her breasts, over her belly, and down her thighs. Nova doesn't stop screaming until Pippi is finished.

When the trial is complete, Nova is standing there, quivering, covered in blood. Judging by the number of scars covering Nova's body, I realize that she has been through this ceremony a number of times before. This one, however, was probably the worst of them. Even among the Warriors, Nova has been an outsider.

Pippi doesn't leave the circle after her turn is done. She just stands there, smiling, admiring the damage she has caused. Then Pippi sticks out her tongue and laps at Nova's wounds. She licks the claw mark from Nova's thigh, up her belly, over her breast, to her neck. I can't tell if she did it as a way of forgiving Nova or a way of humiliating her further. Pippi whispers something into her ear. Then Nova falls to her knees and collapses in the mud.

Grandma tends to Nova's wounds personally. She cleans out the gashes with water, applies ointment from a clay pot, and wraps her in clean bandages. When she is finished, Grandma hugs her, as if she genuinely cares about her. The old gray wolf woman is quick to punish her children and quick to forgive. They don't speak a word to each other throughout this.

"We have to get you out of here," Guy tells me from

the back of the cage.

Both Krall and Guy are looking at me, concerned about what Pippi is going to do to me now.

"I don't want to leave without Nova," I say.

"You don't belong together anymore," he tells me. "Your presence here is only causing her trouble. She would be better off if you left."

"Even if I could escape, where would I go?"

"The other camp," Guy says. "Your place is with the men's army. Her place is with this army."

"I don't want to join that army," I say.

"If you stay here you will be killed," he says. "You are not allowed back in McDonaldland. You would not survive out in the wild alone. There is only one option for you."

"But if I joined that army," I say. "Nova would be my enemy, wouldn't she?"

Guy exhales through his mustache.

"In the wasteland," Guy says. "Men and women just can't be together. It will never work between you two. You are destined to be enemies."

I shake my head.

"It would have been better if you had never reunited in the wasteland."

Talon comes to our cage with Ashley hugging her leg.

"She says you have not been playing with her when she asks you to," Talon says to Guy.

Guy grunts.

"You must do as she tells you to do," Talon says. "If she wants you to play then you play."

"I am a man," Guy says. "I do not play with children."

Talon opens the cage for Guy to exit.

146

Guy does not move.

"Are you really going to protest to playing with a little girl?" Krall asks him. "Pete's owner rented him to a woman who raped him and then ate him alive. Your brother's owner wants to kill him for fun. All your owner wants is for you to play with her. But you complain?"

Guy looks at Krall, then leaves the cage.

I know my brother. He is a proud man. It hurts his pride to be ordered around by a child. His pride is more important to him than living or dying, so he doesn't consider himself as lucky as Krall does.

Ashley hugs herself to Guy's leg as he walks away from the cage with her. He steps slowly, looking down at the weird girl like some kind of pesky canine humping his leg. If we weren't in such a dreadful situation I would have found my brother's awkwardness hilarious.

My brother was always awkward around children, especially his own. He was proud of them. He liked to show them off like trophies. But he never seemed very comfortable around them.

His first child was the worst for him. Molly would hand him the child and he would just look at it, like he wasn't sure what to do with the thing. It would make me laugh when the look of panic would cross his face as the baby would crawl across the floor toward him.

Even though it was just a baby, he would not stand for it breaking the rules. His biggest rule was that the baby didn't spit up on his Fry Guy uniform. Of course, the baby didn't know any better. Whenever it spit up on his uniform, he would punish the baby by having it sit in the corner by itself to reflect on what it had done.

He expected his children to be responsible, mature

147

adults instantaneously upon birth. He did not have the patience to deal with their infantile behavior. He did not approve of crying, bed-wetting, runny noses, or monsters under the bed.

It's good that he had Molly. If she wasn't around, Guy would have probably gone completely insane trying to control his kids' childish conduct.

Talon doesn't leave with Guy and Ashley. She stays by the cage, staring at me.

"Is it true?" Talon says. "Were you and Nova in love when you lived in the walled city?"

I nod my head. "I loved her more than anyone."

She looks down for a moment. When she looks back there are tears in her eyes. They drip down her hairless snout. Her sudden emotion causes me to inch back a little.

"I'm so sorry," she says.

For some reason her tears are beginning to make me cry. The only thought that goes through my mind is that Nova has just died from her wounds and this is her way of telling me, but that couldn't be it. Nova looked like she would easily recover.

"I wish it would have worked out for you," she says. "I wish Nova would have captured you rather than Pippi. I wish *anybody* would have captured you rather than Pippi."

She puts her paw on the cage.

"I'm sorry," she says.

This is the toughest warrior of the wolf women. I doubt many people have ever seen her cry like this. At first, her tears made me feel confused and worried. But now, still confused, I also feel somewhat honored.

Chapter 10

Casper

Engine sounds fill the woods.

Talon stands up. There are dozens of vehicles and motorcycles coming toward us through the forest. Headlights brighten the trees. The voices of men yell and holler all around us. Talon pulls the axes off of her back and runs away from the cage.

The wolf girls in the camp all get to their feet and rush to their tents or their vehicles to arm themselves. But the attackers arrive too soon, before any of them are ready.

Mutant men in armored trucks crash through the perimeter, emptying their machine guns into the women. Two wolf girls are shredded by bullets and tossed over a campfire. Another huge muscled beast of woman roars in the center of the camp, firing a shotgun at the invaders, only to be quickly run over by a massive six-wheeled vehicle.

I look across the camp for any sign of Nova, but she must still be in Grandma's tent. As the trucks blaze through the camp, unloading on every armed and unarmed wolf woman, I see Guy carrying the little girl away from the center of the conflict, using his own body to shield her from the gunfire.

I notice the door of the cage has been left unlocked. I'm not sure whether Talon left it that way on purpose or not. I look at Krall and he nods his head.

The first thing we see when we get out of the cage is a man with four arms and four legs riding his motorcycle past us. He is able to ride his motorcycle and fire machine guns at the same time. Unfortunately, he only has two pairs of eyes, so when he passes by he only sees us with his peripheral vision and doesn't realize that we are male prisoners. His bullets fire over our heads as we duck. Even though he is able to shoot and ride at the same time, it appears as though he is not able to aim proficiently while riding.

We crawl behind an overturned Warrior vehicle, trying to get across the camp to Guy and hopefully Nova. A truck slams into one of the parked Warrior vehicles ahead of us, tossing it into the car we're hiding behind. In the back of the truck, a fat, bearded man with eight arms holds eight semi-automatic pistols, firing them at the wolf girls who try to get to their cars.

Venus is one of the girls he shoots at. She leaps into a car before the bullets can hit her, but one of her friends isn't as lucky. She falls dead against the car door, her blood splattering against Venus' green fur. The green-haired girl fires her .50 Magnum at the eight-armed man, but misses. He's able to get off too many shots for her to aim properly. The bearded man jumps from the back of the truck before it drives too far out

151

of range for his guns. He steps slowly, firing eight guns at a time as fast as a machine gun, and with the advantage of being able to fire in eight different directions at once. As he closes in, Venus is not even able to fire a single round. She just ducks behind the seat, covering her head.

The man gets within five feet of the car when three of his limbs fall from his body. He cries out, turning around to see an axe landing in his face. Talon hacks him two more times just to make sure he is dead. Then she pulls Venus from the vehicle and pushes her in the direction of Grandma's tent.

Talon seems to be fine with taking the men on single-handedly. She runs at one of the six-wheeled armored vehicles, which look more like tanks than trucks. The four men on the top of the vehicle firing at her are just not quick enough. Once she leaps fifteen feet off of the ground and lands on the roof of the vehicle, her two axes chop into two of their backs before they can even turn around. One of them points his gun at her

and is sliced down the middle. The last just trips over his seven legs as she decapitates him from behind, his head bouncing off the roof of the vehicle onto the driver's side windshield.

Although Talon is able to take down the men quickly, her sisters are being cut down just as easily. All around her, she sees them fall. Many of them are able to kill a man or two before they die, but others fall before they can fire even a single round.

I notice that there are many different kinds of mutants. Although most of them are of the multi-limbed variety, there are also other mutations. Some of them have blistered lizardy skin. Others have eyes that bulge out of the sockets. Some of them have large swollen heads twice the size of their bodies. One of these swollen-headed mutants standing on the roof of a vehicle has a very strange deformity. It appears as though his head is in the shape of a giant hamburger.

Guy is nowhere to be seen. He must have escaped into the woods. I'm surprised he hasn't joined the mutants in the fight against the Warriors. I'm sure that's what he would have wanted me to do, but all I care about right now is making sure Nova is safe.

Krall and I pick up some machine guns from dead mutants and run across the camp into Grandma's tent. If any wolf women were to see us with these guns they would shoot us on the spot, but we take the risk. This is my chance to escape, but I don't want to do it without Nova.

Grandma's tent is filled with blood and bullet holes. There is one woman's body in here, but it is neither Grandma's nor Nova's. We go through the back door of the tent. Out here, the woods are filled with crashed vehicles, mostly mutant trucks. A small group of wolf women defend the rear of their camp here. They are spread out through the trees, shooting at the trucks and motorcycles coming their way.

153

I see Grandma fighting with them. She does not appear to be a defenseless old lady, even though she is much older than any human being I have ever met before. With an ornate golden shotgun, Grandma blows holes into every vehicle that gets in her range. She aims for the tires first, then the passengers.

Krall and I decide to stay far away from this fight. Nova doesn't appear to be among these girls, so we head into the woods away from the battle.

We circle the camp for what seems like hours, though it has probably only been minutes, keeping our distance from the perimeter and away from the fight. The sounds of gunfire and roaring engines echo through the forest in all directions around us.

Heading toward a large bonfire far away from camp, we crouch behind bushes to see what is going on. There is an overturned Warrior vehicle. It was a large van that had been used to transport pregnant wolf women or the younger, weaker women who did not yet have the skills for battle. The van had crashed into a mutant truck. While the truck had exploded into a mountain of flames, the van is only just now beginning to catch fire.

There are still many women alive, hiding in the van. Outside the vehicle, there are a handful of wolf women, protecting their weaker sisters, as dozens of mutants close in on them. Some of the mutants circle the van on motorcycles, firing handguns. Other mutants are on foot, carrying multiple swords and axes in their many hands.

There are already four dead Warriors lying in the dirt. Pippi is among them, although she appears to only be unconscious. I can see her bloodied face in the firelight. Her eyes are closed and her breathing fast. Still standing, I see Slayer, Casper, Athena, and Hyena, as well as two others:

154

one with Asian eyes and one in a horned helmet.

The one in the horned helmet dies before I get a better look at her, shot from behind by one of the mutants on motorcycles.

Casper hacks into a mutant with her saw-toothed sword as he approaches the van. Her blade doesn't just slice through him, it shreds his flesh like a chainsaw. Athena clubs another mutant with such power that his head explodes into nothing, his brains spraying against the side of the van in tiny wet pieces. Slayer and Hyena are the only two with guns. They fire conservatively, as if they are both running low on ammo. Slayer is at the front of the van, while Hyena takes the middle. The two wolf girls who were guarding the rear have already fallen and I doubt the others have even realized it yet.

The fire is spreading across the van. The women inside begin banging on the back door, trying to get out. The door is jammed. They scream, trying to get the attention of Slayer and the others, but their protectors are too busy fighting off the mutants to notice them.

When Krall sees this, he doesn't hesitate.

"Stay here," he tells me, as he runs out of the bushes toward the van.

I decide to follow him.

When we get to the van, the women are crying and panicked. Some of them are not conscious. Krall picks up a rock and slams it against the glass, but it doesn't break. Bullet proof. Krall drops his gun and picks up an axe from a fallen Warrior and jams the blade into the crack of the door, then tries to pry it open. I take a knife from a dead mutant and try to do the same. It bends open an inch, but that's all.

We ignore the guns fired around us as we work on the door. A mutant circles around the back of the van on his motorcycle, firing a handgun at us as he rides. He only shoots twice, missing both times. Krall removes his hand from the axe and grabs his gun. Before the mutant on the bike rides away, Krall fires his machine gun into the man's back. Then he goes back to work on the door.

As I try to push the door open, I see the Warriors are getting beat down and the number of mutants is increasing. Slayer looks exhausted. Although she appears to still have some ammunition left, she is now fighting off the mutants with a spear. She fires the gun with one hand and jabs with the spear in the other.

A mutant with six arms begins firing arrows at the women. With so many arms, he is able to load and fire two bows rapidly at the same time. Casper, with lightning animal reflexes, catches an arrow in midair as it flies toward Athena's chest. The mutant archer fires more arrows at the two of them. Casper swings her bulky sword, cutting an arrow in half in midair before it reaches her face. She catches another before it hits her chest. But one arrow pierces through her arm, and another hits her in the neck. She catches the one in her neck

a split second after it hits her, preventing it from going all the way through, but it's still buried several inches.

Casper continues shredding up mutants with the arrow in her neck. She holds the wound with her free hand, trying to stop it from bleeding too much. Another arrow hits her in the hip and she falls to her knees.

When her friend, Athena, sees this she shrieks with her squeaky voice and clubs through the mutants that try to get between them. She swings her bat so hard that it splits limbs into pieces and grates large chunks of meat from mutant torsos. She hits one man so hard that he breaks in half at the waist.

As the archer closes in on them, rapid-firing his arrows, Athena uses a dead mutant to shield Casper from his attacks. After a minute, the corpse becomes a porcupine of arrows. Athena drops the body, rolls beneath his projectiles, then tosses her club at him. The spiked weapon spins through the air and hits him square in the face, the nails penetrating his brain, killing him before he hits the ground.

As Casper gurgles blood at her motley-colored friend, a bullet hits Athena in the back. She crumbles to the ground and dies at Casper's feet. The pierced wolf girl looks down at her fallen sister. No fight left in her, she wraps her body around her friend's corpse and caresses the pink hair on her forehead.

Hyena sees Krall and I struggling to get the door of the van open. She points her gun at us, cackling. But then she realizes that her sisters are trapped in the vehicle as it is consumed by flames. She lowers her weapon and comes to our aid.

With the help of Hyena's beastly strength, we are able to pry open the door and get the women out. She and Krall help them down one at a time, many of them too stunned from smoke inhalation to move very fast.

When we look out at the fight, we see the Asian-eyed wolf girl's legs shot out from under her. Only Slayer remains to fight off the horde. She empties the last of her rounds into two mutants with oversized heads. Then she takes on three men at the same time with her spear. Although they have several weapons in their multiple arms, Slayer is able to strike and defend with only her spear. She stabs one through the eye, slices another's guts out, and trips the third with the pole of the spear.

As she drives the spear into the tripped mutant's chest, a man on a motorcycle comes up behind her and clubs her in the back with a mallet. She goes down.

When Krall sees her fall, he holds up his gun and charges to Slayer's aid. As I help the last coughing wolf girl down out of the van, I watch Krall as he stands between Slayer and the mutants and guns them down. Like an expert marksman, he takes out each of the motorcycle riders no matter what their distance. Slayer looks up at him, her face in a state of complete shock, as he takes out a dozen of his own kind to save her.

Hyena and I join him. The three of us form a triangle around the wounded women. Hyena fires at the mutants coming from the back and I take them coming in from the middle. Although I have never fired a weapon before, I do my best to take the mutants down, and need to use all four arms to keep the weapon steady.

Without any ammo left, the mutants retreat. Hyena and I fire at their backs as they flee into the woods, but Krall drops his weapon into the dirt. He's not interested in killing vulnerable men.

After we're finished, I notice the silence. The gunfire throughout the woods has ceased. There are no more sounds of battle, only the sound of vehicles moving quickly away from the camp. It's over.

Hyena looks at me with a smirk. I smile back. Then I realize her gun is pointed at me. I lower my weapon and she takes it, but otherwise she leaves me be. She helps a pregnant woman up from the ground.

Krall and Slayer are locked in a stare. Slayer is back on her feet, in an aggressive stance. She has the gun Krall dropped and is now pointing it at his belly, snarling.

"Why did you do it?" she asks him. Her tone is angry. I don't think she liked the idea of being saved by a man.

"Because you would have died if I didn't," he says.

The black fur covering her entire body stands up in frustration. Krall's answer was not satisfactory.

"You killed maybe twenty men," she says. "Just so I would not die?"

Then she bares her teeth at him. I realize that she's not mad because she was saved by a man. She is mad because Krall's actions do not make sense to her.

"I had to kill them," Krall says, "or they would have

159

WARRIOR WOLF WOMEN OF THE WASTELAND

killed all of you."

Slayer relaxes her stance. She closes in toward him, almost as if she is preparing to passionately kiss him, or bite his face off.

"I cannot have my Meat fighting like a Warrior," she says.

She turns her back and looks at her wounded sisters around them. The pierced wolf woman by her feet is still breathing, still wrapped around Athena's corpse. When Slayer sees them, she looks back at Krall.

"If you can repair Casper the way you did me," she says to him, "then I will forgive you."

Krall doesn't even nod his head in response. He just goes to Casper's side and gets to work.

I am looking down at Pippi asleep in the dirt when Slayer comes to my side. She kneels down and brushes the crusty blood from her sister's freckled face.

Without looking at me, she says, "If you knew what she plans to do with you once she wakes up, you never would have helped save her life."

Then she stands back up and says, "She'll only repay you with an agonizing death."

As Slayer steps away from me, I see a group of wolf women staring down on us from the hill. I recognize two of them as Talon and Nova. When I see Nova, a wave of relief washes over me. I should have known that she could take care of herself.

It looks as though they have been there for quite some time. By the expressions on their faces, I believe they witnessed the end of the battle we just fought. They must have seen Krall and I giving up our freedom in order to save their sisters.

Talon gives me a nod of respect, but Nova shakes her head at me as if I just made the stupidest decision of my life.

160

The giant wolves smell the blood in the air and can be heard howling. Grandma orders the Warriors to pack up the camp and leave the dead where they lie. I am reunited with Guy in the cage on the back of the pickup truck. Apparently, he did not take his chance to escape. He protected Ashley through the entire fight, guarding her in a nearby barn. He doesn't say whether or not he had to kill any men in order to protect her. All he says is how disappointed in me he is for not getting away.

Krall stays with the wounded, patching up several wounded wolf girls, including Pippi. Casper seemed to be in pretty bad shape when I left them, but he said she would make a full recovery. He said the wolf women are strong and can heal quickly.

I do not regret anything I did back there. Perhaps I would have been better off if Pippi and Slayer died.

When we leave the camp, half of the Warrior women are lying dead across the field. Many destroyed vehicles are also left behind. I see the large yellow eyes of giant wolves coming out of the woods as we evacuate. Tonight they will fill their bellies with their fallen little sisters.

On the road, Pippi rides her motorcycle up to me at the back of the pickup. Her head is bandaged where a mallet had hit the back of her skull. She seems fine, although she is riding her bike a little crooked.

She throws a dead rabbit at the cage and its head gets caught between the bars. Her eyes meet mine. An almost friendly smile crosses her face.

"This is for you," she says, yelling over the engines.

I pull the bloody rabbit carcass into the cage with me to examine it. I have never seen a real rabbit before.

"They said you helped save my life," she yells. "Take this as a reward."

"A dead animal?" I say, not sure if she can hear me.

"You're welcome," she says.

Then she speeds away.

When I look down at the rabbit carcass, I notice that its blood is still warm. She must have just caught and killed it moments before we left camp. And by the look of the teeth marks, it appears that she caught the thing in her own jaws.

They set up a new camp, by a quiet river in a rocky valley. At the top of the mountain above, there appears to be an ancient shopping center that has been slowly crumbling down the mountain. Half of it is lying in pieces along the bank of the river, the other half is still dangling on the cliff, ready to give way at any moment.

After the Warriors are settled in, they have a prayer for their departed sisters. Then Guy, Krall, and I are brought into the center of the crowd to have an audience with their leader.

Grandma sits on a log with her golden shotgun lying across her lap. She looks us up and down. Ashley, Nova, Talon, Casper, Hyena, Slayer, and a handful of other wolf girls step out of the circle and gather behind us.

"They say you fought like Warriors," Grandma tells us, nodding at the women over our shoulders. "You protected them, you killed men for them, you healed them, all at the expensive of your own freedom. Deeds like this must not go ignored. All of these women have borne witness to your actions and feel that you could be of benefit to our community if you were to become more than just Meat.

"Men have joined the Warriors of the Wild in the past. It is rare, but some men have given their allegiance to us and fought alongside us as one of our own. If you wish it and if your owners permit it, you may become members of our tribe. Your rank will be lower than that of the lowest female Warrior, without any chance of advancement. You will be expected to obey all of our laws. Your punishment for breaking our laws will be more severe than it will be for your female counterparts. If you ever show any sign of betrayal or lack of loyalty, you will be demoted back into property."

Guy and I look at each other. He seems angry with this outcome rather than pleased. Krall, on the other hand, doesn't seem very surprised.

"We will take this on a case by case basis," Grandma says. "Please state your names."

"Ronald Krall."

"Guy Togg."

"Daniel Togg."

When Grandma hears our names, her eyes light up, she says to us, "You wouldn't happen to have been related to a man named Steven Togg, would you?"

"Yes," Guy says. "He was our grandfather."

Grandma smiles. "Fate is an interesting thing. The first male to ever join the Warriors was your Grandfather. There is much that we owe that man."

"Is he still alive?" I ask.

She shakes her head. "He died many years ago, but much of his wisdom lives on in us."

Grandma motions to the little girl. "Ashley, bring your Meat forward."

The little girl holds my brother's hand and they step forward.

"Ashley," Grandma says. "This man protected you and saved your life. Do you wish to free him?"

Ashley nods her head.

Grandma looks at my brother.

"Guy Togg," Grandma says. "Your grandfather used to speak about you. He used to tell me how frightened you were of wolves. I'd like to know, how do you feel to now be surrounded by wolves?"

She smiles, showing her fangs through her wrinkled black lips.

"There is not a Fry Guy working the wasteland who does not fear the giant wolves," he says.

Then Grandma asks him, "You were a Fry Guy in the walled city?"

"Yes," Daniel says.

"A high ranking officer?"

"First Lieutenant," Daniel says. "The highest rank of uniformed Fry Guys."

He says this with pride.

"You are the one I worry about most," Grandma says. "I believe you will always be loyal to the walled city. Because of this, I cannot give you full rights as a Warrior. Your movements must be restricted to the camp. You are not permitted to carry weapons. You are not to go anywhere unescorted. You will have to gain our trust in order to have more freedoms.

"Your function in this camp will be to act as Ashley's guardian. You will look out for her as if she were your own child. In the future, we might have you look after more children. You will become the nanny of our community."

When she says Guy will be a nanny, his face contorts into one of extreme concern. A nanny is probably the most embarrassing position you can give to a man like him. Some of the Warriors giggle when they see his reaction.

"Do you agree?" Grandma asks.

Guy hesitates only for a moment. "Yes."

"Then welcome to the Warriors of the Wild, Guy Togg."

The Warriors howl.

164

"Slayer, bring your meat forward," Grandma says.

Slayer and Krall step forward.

"This man saved your life. Twice. He helped save many lives and he healed many of our wounded. Several of our sisters would not be alive now if it weren't for him."

"Slayer," Grandma says. "Will you free this man and allow him to join our community?"

Slayer looks Krall deep in the eyes. Without breaking her gaze, she says, "This is not Meat. This one acts more like a sister than Meat. I have no use for Meat that does not know its place. He is free."

She doesn't stop staring in Krall's eyes, even when he turns away.

"Ronald Krall," Grandma says, "you have more medical knowledge than any of the Warriors. Your abilities are far greater than even my own. You will become the doctor of the Warriors of the Wild. Although you have proven yourself a skillful fighter, you will not be allowed to use weapons except in the event of an emergency. Because your skills are unique, you are too valuable to risk losing in battle. Do you agree?"

"Yes," Krall says.

He doesn't hesitate for a second.

"Pippi, bring your meat forward," Grandma says.

Pippi, who was not among the women standing in the circle beside us, comes in from the back of the crowd. She grips my shoulder tightly and brings me forward.

"This man helped save—"

"No," Pippi interrupts. "I'm not going to let him free."

"But, Pippi," Grandma says. "This man helped save

165

the lives of many of your sisters, including your own. Will you reconsider?"

"I already gave him a reward for saving my life," Pippi says. "I think that is enough. He does not deserve freedom."

I turn to see Nova stepping forward, as if ready to clobber Pippi. Grandma holds out her hand and Nova ceases her advance.

"Pippi," Grandma says, "you have always been the most stubborn of us. I cannot force you to give up your property, but I ask you to reconsider. If Daniel is anything like his grandfather, I guarantee you he will be an asset to our community. Please, for me, let him free."

Pippi looks at me with trembling lips.

"No, he's my Meat," Pippi says. "I captured him. He belongs to me."

"Pippi ..." Grandma pleads.

"No!" Pippi cries.

Grandma sighs and shakes her head.

"Very well," she says. "I cannot force you to give up your property. However, I still believe the Warriors owe a large debt to this man. Because of this, I am giving you an order to treat your Meat with respect. You are not permitted to physically abuse him. You are not allowed to murder him. You are not allowed to rent him out to anyone who might possibly turn."

"But he's mine!" she says. "I have the right to do whatever I want with him!"

"You do not have the right to disobey my commands," Grandma says. "If you disobey my commands you will be stripped of rank and lose all of your property, including your bike, including this man. And if you decide to go against my orders and murder this man, or even attempt to murder this man, you will lose the right to own Meat or advance in rank for as long as you live."

Pippi does not say another word. She just grinds her teeth and clenches a fist around my shoulder.

As the meeting breaks up, the women who came to our defense congratulate Krall. They only give a slight nod to Guy (except for Ashley, who gives him a hug around his legs) and they don't even look in my direction.

Hyena and the Asian-eyed wolf girl shake Krall's hand and pat him on the back with their paws. They say, "Welcome, Sister," and he laughs with them. Slayer stares him down, still bewildered by his actions. She doesn't shake his hand or say a word. Casper stays by Slayer's side. Although she came to our defense, Casper also does not say a word. Perhaps she can't speak with the wound in her throat or perhaps she is still traumatized by the loss of her sister, Athena.

As Pippi takes me back to the cage, alone, we run into Nova. Pippi and Nova glare at each other, growling under their breaths.

"I'll be watching your every movement," Nova says. "If you mistreat him in any way Grandma *will* find out."

Pippi flares her nostrils.

"This is all your fault, isn't it?" Pippi says. "You're the reason why I can't use my Meat the way I want to."

"You're going to regret not letting him free," Nova says. "I promise you."

"He's my Meat," Pippi says. "I might not be able to kill him, but I still have control of him. And I say that the two of you are not allowed to speak to each other anymore. If he so much as looks at you again I'll whip him until he bleeds."

"You're not allowed to physically abuse him anymore," Nova says. "There's nothing you can do to him that will stop us from speaking to each other."

"There's other ways to punish him besides *physically*

WARRIOR WOLF WOMEN OF THE WASTELAND

abusing him," Pippi says. "Maybe I'll rub my shit in his face and make him eat it."

Pippi giggles. Nova mock-giggles for a second and then grabs the red-haired wolf girl by the ear and pulls her into her face.

"If you don't make him as comfortable and happy as possible you *will* regret it," Nova says.

"Oh yeah?" Pippi says, ripping her ear out of Nova's hand.

"He's only your property for as long as you live," Nova says.

"Do you think you can threaten me?" Pippi says.

"Yeah, I think I can."

They glare at each other for a moment, inches away from each other's eyes. Then Pippi smiles.

"Hey, Talon," Pippi yells, still looking in Nova's eyes.

Talon breaks from a group of her friends and looks at us.

"Prepare the ceremonial robe," she says. "I'm going to wear it tonight."

Talon nods her head.

Nova's mouth drops open. "You fucking bitch!"

Pippi smiles.

"He's my Meat," Pippi says, "and there's nothing you can do about it."

Then Pippi pushes me away from Nova and walks me across the camp. I try to turn my head to look at her, but Pippi holds the back of my skull firmly so that I have nowhere else to look but straight at my cage.

Chapter 11

Slayer

After sitting in my cage for a while, I see Krall heading in my direction. He has a smile on his face. If I knew any better I would think he was coming to tease me for still being a prisoner, or perhaps he wants to congratulate me on being able to survive. Although I am still Pippi's property, it is nice to know that I will be able to live. I'm not sure what life will be like for me, but at least I don't have to worry too much about being killed any time soon.

Before Krall makes it to my cage, Slayer steps into his path. Her full-body spiked leather outfit is clean and shiny now. She must have just washed the dirt and blood from it. Although now it looks almost greasy, as if she waxed it up to look nicer.

"I would like you to walk with me," she says to him. "I want to take you into the woods and show you what it means to be a Warrior."

Krall nods his head awkwardly.

"Since you were originally my property, I feel it is my responsibility to get you accustomed to your new life. You will be my little sister."

"Okay," he says, chuckling a bit at being called her little sister.

She leads him away from the camp, into the forest. Krall turns around and looks back at me, noticing I had been eavesdropping on their conversation. He shrugs his shoulders at me and then turns back, trailing closely behind his new sister.

An hour of sitting in my cage alone on the back of the pickup.

I hoped Guy would come talk to me, but he seems busy playing marbles with Ashley. He doesn't look like he is having much fun. He curls his mustache with such force that I can tell he is mad. I bet he would have preferred to be in this cage with me than be that little girl's permanent nanny. Of course, I'm sure he doesn't plan on staying. Next chance he gets, he will attempt to escape. He has his own family he needs to return to.

I scan the camp for Nova. She is sitting by herself, her eyes toward the woods. I wish she would come over and talk to me, but she probably knows it wouldn't be a good idea. Maybe she's plotting ways to kill Pippi. Maybe she's regretting not tossing the little bitch into the giant wolf's mouth when she had the chance.

A group of wolf girls come to me. They gather around the pickup and then lift up the cage with me still inside. They carry me into the center of camp where many of the wolf girls have gathered. I don't see Krall and Slayer, nor Guy and Ashley. Though I do see Nova, sitting on a log near the back of the crowd.

It isn't until I see Pippi emerge from Grandma's tent wearing the ornate purple robe, that I realize what is happening.

Grandma and Talon stand on Pippi's sides. Both of them seem annoyed, perhaps angered, by the girl between them. They surely know that Pippi is only doing this out of spite, to hurt her sister, Nova, and prove that she has complete dominion over her Meat. Pippi doesn't recognize their disappointment in her. She is too wrapped up in her own satisfaction to pay them any mind. A smug smile spreads across her face, pointed in the direction of November, as Grandma gives her speech.

Grandma's speech is similar to the one she gave when Pete was in the cage, but this one has been edited down. She doesn't say it with much emotion. She just wants to get it over with.

She ends it with, "Today, Pippi will go one step closer

171

to releasing her inner spirit."

Then Grandma leaves. She goes back into her tent, not interested in viewing the ceremony.

Talon is left behind to supervise. She removes Pippi's robe, exposing her naked body in the moonlight. Her freckles extend all the way down the front of her body, with only a small space of white freckleless skin on her belly and chest. Her breasts are small and pointy, almost sharp, and curved slightly upwards. She doesn't have any wolf fur on the front of her body, but her back is covered in it. Her back is a coat of red fur, like that of a fox. Her entire ass is covered in a thin layer of fur, which stretches down the backs of her thighs. When she turns around, it looks as though she is wearing a skin-tight pair of red fuzzy pants with a fluffy tail attached to it.

Although Grandma was not interested in the ceremony, the other wolf girls quickly embrace the spirit of the occasion. They stomp their feet and howl excitedly. I see Nova does not join in with the howls. A couple of the others also seem to remain quiet, including Pippi's friend, Hyena.

When she enters the cage, Pippi gives me a big ravenous smile. Her wicked yellow eyes shimmer in the firelight. She crawls on all fours toward me as the cage door closes behind her.

"Do exactly what I tell you to do," she says. "I can be sweet or I can be rough."

She pulls off my pants.

"You won't like it if I'm rough."

Unlike Alyssa, who ripped the clothes off of Pete with her teeth, Pippi removes my clothes gently, seductively. It is not the treatment I would have expected. When we are naked together, she rubs her hand down my chest and watches Nova's reaction. Nova's cold stare makes Pippi smile.

Pippi crawls around in a circle around me, imitating an actual wolf. As she passes behind me, she whips her tail in my face. Her tail releases a strange smell that is both sweet and musky. It is so strong that it makes my nose water.

172

She turns around and slaps me with her tail again, filling my nostrils with the scent. It makes me dizzy this time, as if the smell is some kind of chemical.

After she is finished circling me, she spreads her knees, squats down low, and urinates in the corner of the cage.

"Sniff it," she says, pointing at the puddle of urine on the ground.

"What?" I say, almost yelling at her.

"Smell my pee," she says.

I go to the puddle and smell it. The urine is also thick with the strange odor. I now realize that she didn't have me smell her urine to humiliate me, she is doing it out of instinct. I remember reading about the mating rituals of wolves, and how the females release sex hormones in their urine as a way to show the male she is ready to mate. I've never heard of wolf-like women doing this before, though. I'm just happy she is satisfied with only one sniff.

Pippi puts her foot in my face. Now that she isn't wearing boots, I see that her feet are much more wolf-like than her hands. The feet are long and deeply arched, with thick hooked toenails, and patches of red fur on the top. They are absolutely hideous-looking.

"Lick them," Pippi says.

She can tell that I find them repulsive.

"Now," she says.

I stick out my tongue and slide it against the side of her foot, where it most resembles a human's. Pippi looks over at Nova and giggles.

"Suck on the toes," she says.

Reluctantly, I do as she asks. I put two of her smaller toes into my mouth and suck on them. They do not have the pungent taste I was expecting, from walking around in leather boots all day. They are clean. Looking at her body, all of her skin seems clean. She must have bathed in the river prior to this ceremony.

She curls her toes as I suck on them, digging the toenails into my tongue. It is a little abuse she can give me that nobody else can see.

Then she pulls herself closer. She sits down between my legs, facing me, and squeezes her knees around my waist. I feel the heels of her feet against my butt. Her tail wags, tickling me as it brushes against my inner thighs. She wraps her arms around my shoulders, and presses her breasts against my body, looking down at me.

"Hold me," she says.

She places my arms around her back, all four of my arms. She has me caress the fur on her back with my multiple hands as we embrace. She gives Nova a glance, teasing her as she rubs her hands up my body.

Now I know why Pippi is being so gentle. She is trying to make it look as passionate and tender as possible, because she knows it will piss Nova off even more than if she were rough. Pippi rubs her cheek lightly against mine, I feel her wet nose on my temple and her hot breath on my ear.

She looks me in the eyes. When they are only inches away, her eyes seem even less human than before. Soulless.

"Kiss me," she says.

I look at Nova, as if she might be able to do something to stop this, but she's not looking at me. Her cold gaze is locked on Pippi, as if she's imagining all the horrible things she wants to do to her. Pippi pulls my face to her and kisses me. She wraps her lips around mine and I kiss back, but only slightly.

"Kiss me better," she says.

I kiss her for real, but her fangs make it impossible, they poke and cut at my lips and tongue. Pippi pushes my face away.

"Kiss me deeply," she says in an annoyed tone. "With passion."

I don't know how to kiss somebody I hate with passion, but she does all the work for me. She closes her eyes, holds the back of my head, and presses my face hard against hers. She sucks my tongue into her mouth and swallows my lips. Her whiskers tickle my nose as we make out. When her tongue enters my mouth it feels strange. It's much thinner and wider than a normal human tongue.

Although I put no feeling into my kiss, it almost feels as if she really is kissing me with passion. She rubs my back as she kisses, pressing her breasts against my chest. She pushes one set of my arms down her back past her tail and I find myself squeezing her soft furry ass as I kiss her.

The wolf girls surrounding the cage begin panting and breathing heavily. They do not howl or stomp their feet. It is as if they are witnessing something they have never seen before in this ceremony. They are probably used to fierce violent sex, not this gentle affection. Whatever the case, they appear to be mesmerized by the presentation.

Pippi doesn't stop kissing me as she lies me down on the floor of the cage. She only releases my lips for a second, to look down at my crotch. Her hand curls around my penis. The long wolf-like nails scratch against my inner thigh as she strokes it into an erection. Part of my brain tells me that I should resist her and make this as unpleasurable an experience as possible for her. But there is another part of my brain that can't resist. I have never made love to a woman before, so my hormones are going wild. Of course, my hormones might just be reacting to the pheromones Pippi released from her tail and urine.

She puts her legs around me and then guides my dick

toward her crotch. The fur around her vagina is soft and delicate. It is not stiff and curly like my pubic hair. She wraps her mouth around my neck and sucks on my throat as she slides me into her. While pushing me in as far as it can go, she licks my face. As if she's doing it to be playful, she slips her tongue down my forehead and coils it into my eye. Her fangs poke into my cheek and then she wraps her lips around my eye socket, as if trying to suck my eyeball out of my head.

As she fucks me, her tail points up into the air. She turns and looks at Nova, who is staring back with more rage than ever. While looking her in the eye, Pippi begins to moan. She opens her mouth wide and groans at Nova with each push of her body. Her eyelids loosen and she stretches her head back, making love to me with as much passion as she can feign.

"Make noises," Pippi whispers in my ear.

I realize she wants me to moan with her, to make Nova angry.

"Show everyone how much you love sex with me," she says.

177

I make slight panting noises.

"Louder," she says. "You have to moan as much and as loudly as I do, no matter how loud I get."

I moan louder. I do it in such a mockful way that Nova would know I am only doing it because I was told to. Pippi moans louder and so I moan louder. Strangely, many of the women in the audience begin to imitate our noises, moaning with us. Then my moans turn from pretend to genuine. Pippi smiles and laughs at Nova as our wails of ecstasy become thunderous. She savors the moment, riding me slowly, sensuously.

When she comes close to climax, she begins growling and barking between moans. She howls and her sisters howl back. I grip her coat of fur with all four of my hands and we come together. As she orgasms, I feel her changing. Her moans of pleasure mix with screams of agony, as her body mutates. The muscles in her arms flex and grow, popping out like metal balls under her skin. Her teeth grow longer, sharper. I feel her limbs extending and building mass. Her face lengthens, the jaw stretching forward an inch, the beginning formation of a muzzle. A thin strip of hair rises up the bridge of her nose.

After the transformation is complete, she feels heavier on top of me. Her breaths are hard and fast. She keeps her eyes closed tight and holds my arms in place around her back. The women around us howl and cheer. Talon opens the door of the cage, but Pippi doesn't get out. The crowd begins to disperse.

"I'm not done," Pippi says, exhausted. "Close the door."

"That one was a big change," Talon says, "You won't have the energy for another round."

"I know," Pippi says. "But I want to stay."

She wraps her arms around my body and lies all of her weight down on top of me. Her breaths become slow as she cuddles me, forcing me to cuddle her back. Many of the wolf women look at her confusedly as she snuggles with her Meat in the cage. Nova is not confused about it, just angry. She knows the red-headed bitch is only doing it to piss her off.

When the wolf women carry the cage back to the pickup, Pippi is still inside. She has fallen fast asleep around me, snoring coarsely into my ear. Just before dawn, Pippi wakes up and has sex with me again. This time, she does it without an audience. She doesn't do it to spite Nova or to punish me, she does it for herself. When she's done, fur sprouts from her arms, going from her shoulders down to the back of her hands. She also appears to have grown several inches taller.

When she leaves the cage, she kisses me on the neck and says, "You're mine. Don't you forget that."

Then, so that I would remember, she cuts a claw mark across my back. Not deep enough to be counted as physical abuse, just deep enough so that the pain will linger until I see her next.

I wake to the morning sun glaring in my eyes. Many of the wolf women are just now waking up, heating McDonald's brand coffee in the fire pits.

Krall steps out of a tent with his white coat thrown over his shoulder. One of the wolf girls at a fire offers him some coffee and he takes it in a small paper cup. He talks with her as he drinks it. The girl is that Asian-eyed wolf girl. She has a friendly smile and wears a frilly corset over a mesh tank top.

Asians were a race of people from a long time ago. They were very common in the old world, but only a tiny portion of them became a part of the McDonaldland civilization. After a hundred years, most Asian blood has mixed into the population. There aren't any full Asians anymore. However, many people are still born with Asian traits. You will find people with Asian eyes every now and then. My grandpa was the one who told me that Asians were once a race. Most people in McDonaldland just think it is a certain shape of eye.

There used to be a large variety of races when the world was bigger. In McDonaldland, they are all pretty much mixed together. My grandpa said that culture was a big part of defining a race, but once The Blessed McDonald's Corporation required its citizens to embrace only one unifying culture, races seemed to disappear. There are still a variety of hair colors and flesh tones, but there's really only one McDonald's race.

The Asian-eyed wolf girl looks more Asian than any woman I have seen before. Her skin and facial structure are definitely Asian. She might only be a third or a quarter Caucasian. Of course, her wolf-like features are going to take over eventually.

She catches my gaze. Although her eyes are Asian-shaped, they are still the yellow eyes of a wolf. If she ever becomes one of the giant wolves I wonder if any of her Asian traits will carry over with the change.

Krall comes over to my cage carrying a second cup of coffee. He hands it to me. The paper cup seems like it has been reused at least a dozen times. They don't let anything go to waste around here.

"It's from Apple," Krall says, pointing over to the Asian-eyed wolf girl.

Apple waves at me and smiles. I wave back.

"She rides with your friend, Nova," Krall says.

"She's Nova's friend?"

"I don't know if they're friends," he says. "Apple just said that Nova's on her team. Apple is the driver, Nova rides on the roof with her crossbow."

180

I nod my head.

"Where were you?" I ask.

"I slept in Slayer's tent," he says, stretching.

"You slept with her?"

"We didn't have sex or anything," he says. "But we did share a sleeping bag. She said that new Warriors, which they call *little sisters*, always share a sleeping bag with one of the higher ranking women for the first few nights of joining their tribe."

"That's strange," I say.

"It's so they can keep safe and warm," he says. "You wouldn't believe how warm their fur can be when you're sleeping with one."

"But it's not all that cold out," I say.

"Yeah, I guess not," he says.

"So what did you do last night?" I ask, hoping that he doesn't ask me about my night.

"I just went on a stroll through the woods with Slayer," he says. "We had an interesting conversation. If I didn't know any better I would say that she was hitting on me, but I think she is just trying to be nice to thank me for saving her life."

I nod my head. It seems Slayer isn't as big of a bitch as I had thought.

Krall tells me more about Slayer. He says that she, for some reason, told him a lot of weird things about herself, things she wouldn't have told many of her sisters. Maybe because he's a doctor, maybe because it's easier to talk to a stranger, or maybe she really does like him and blurted out random weird facts about herself out of nervousness. In any case, Krall isn't keeping this information private.

He tells me Slayer is actually still a virgin. She has never had sex or even masturbated. When she was kicked out of McDonaldland at the age of thirteen, she was accused of masturbating illegally, even though she has never masturbated before.

Slayer has clitoromegaly (an enlarged clitoris), due to excess testosterone. It is nearly two inches long. Because of this, it is very easy for her to become sexually stimulated. As a kid going through puberty, her clit was a major annoyance. It was so sensitive that just the act of walking around in tight pants would irritate it and cause burn-like pains. But after puberty, she found walking around in tight pants kind of arousing. She knew that touching herself there was bad and against the law, but she didn't know that wearing tight pants without underwear was a problem, so she did that sometimes because she liked how it felt.

When she started riding her bicycle to school, she realized that the act of riding intensified this sensation. Sometimes she would go out for a ride just to feel it. When thick black hair started growing on her thighs and belly, she thought it was just because of puberty. Her mother told her that she would grow hair on her legs, in her crotch, and in her armpits, but nobody told her how much hair she would grow.

It wasn't until she had her first complete orgasm that she knew that riding her bike was turning her into a wolf. On the way to school one day, she decided to get up extra early to ride through the farming district of McDonaldland. As her enlarged clitoris became stimulated against the bicycle seat, moisture building between her legs, she pedaled faster and faster down the long windy road.

When she had the orgasm, she squeezed her thighs together, unsure of what was happening to her. She just knew that it felt good. Then her muscles went limp and she crashed into a fence. Quivering in agony on the ground, she assumed the pain was caused by hitting the fence. It was actually caused by her body transformation.

She didn't know she had gone through the change

until she arrived at school and everyone was looking at her funny. Although nothing she could feel on the outside of her body had transformed, her eyes had become yellow and wolf-like. During her first period of class, her teacher nearly fell over when she saw Slayer's eyes glowing in the back of the classroom. The teacher took her by the ear out into the hall and straight to the principal's office. Then the Fry Guys came and took her away.

In the wasteland, Slayer learned how to survive on her own. She lived like a wild animal, teaching herself how to hunt and hide from the giant wolves. Her home was a little foxhole dug into the earth, surrounded by bushes.

She continued to have orgasms, in her sleep. She would have dreams about riding her bicycle and would rub her thighs together in a circular motion until she came.

A year had passed before the Warriors found her and brought her into their tribe. By then, Slayer was already covered in a thick layer of black fur. From all the transformations, she had lost much of her memory, including her own name. They called her *Bear Slayer*, because, when they found her, she had just finished killing a black bear with only a sharpened stick. Talon was the one who found her, and she said that she had never seen a more wild and vicious killer in all her life. Her name was eventually shortened to *Slayer*, once they realized that bears were not the only creatures that she was proficient at killing.

These days, Slayer has to wear a cup on her crotch when she rides her motorcycle, to prevent undesired orgasms. Although she has owned many male prisoners during her eight years as a Warrior, she has not had sex with any of them. She has already transformed so much at such a young age. If she starts having sex it won't be long before she completely turns.

Talon, Hyena, and a handful of Warrior vehicles come back into camp. They have concerned looks on their faces. When Grandma comes out to greet them, she is smoking a long wooden pipe.

"There was nothing left," Talon says. "The Meat had beaten us to the camp and stripped the vehicles clean. There wasn't anything left."

"Hmmm." Grandma releases puffs of smoke from her gray fuzzy beard. "We did inventory here. It seems that the majority of our supplies were left behind during the attack."

"What should we do?" Talon asks.

"We'll have to go on another raid today," Grandma says.

"I don't think the girls are ready for another one so soon," Talon says. "Not after what happened last night."

"We have no choice," Grandma says.

They order the rest of the women to take down the camp and get ready to move out. So many of them are wounded, I don't know how they'll be able to attack another McDonaldland supply run.

Apple, with one leg bandaged around a splint and another taped at the knee, limps over to Nova using a stick as a crutch and tells her that she doesn't feel confident driving their vehicle in her condition. Nova says that she has to do her best. There just aren't enough drivers left to pull off a successful raid without her.

Casper is also convinced to ride, despite all of the arrow wounds in her body. Krall reinforces her bandages so that she will be able to fight without ripping her stitches open, but he says she really shouldn't take any unnecessary risks or she might seriously damage herself. After having lost her close friend, Athena, Casper just looks like she's ready to kill people and doesn't care what happens to her.

While the camp is taken down, Grandma paces along the river, smoking her pipe and mumbling to no one in particular.

Chapter 12

Venus

The Warriors attack a small McDonaldland motorcade at high noon. There are only two armed vehicles and one van this trip. It shouldn't be too difficult for them, even with the lack of soldiers.

The wounded knights stay back as reinforcements, while Talon, Venus, and Hyena lead the strike. I am on Pippi's motorcycle, strapped to her back again. Perhaps this time she will purposely let Fry Guys fire at her rear, to get me shot, so that she can still kill me without seeming at fault.

While wrapped around Pippi, it feels like I am holding a completely different person. She has changed, not only physically but also mentally. She seems more serious than before, more mature. It's like the new wolf in her has eaten away her childish sense of humor.

"This is going to be over too quickly," Pippi says. "I better catch up if I want to get any kills."

We speed up to get to the others. Bullets fly past our heads as the armed vehicle in the back of the motorcade fires on us. As long as Pippi doesn't get ahead of this vehicle, I should be safe.

Talon rides on the back of Venus' motorcycle. She stands up on the back, balancing herself, her axes out to her sides. Venus howls as they get to the back of the armed vehicle. As Venus pulls along the side of the car, she draws and points her .50 Magnum at the gunner. She fires and blows off his shoulder.

As soon as Talon jumps from Venus's motorcycle, the Fry Guy vehicle hits the brakes. Talon wasn't ready for that. She hits the back windshield with her knees, flies over

186

the gunner, and hits the street in front of the car.

Then the other two vehicles in the motorcade hit their brakes. The van ahead pulls over and opens its back doors, releasing a dozen armed Fry Guys. They weren't transporting mutants. They came here to fight.

"It's an ambush!" Hyena cackles, hitting her brakes and skidding her tires sideways down the road.

Venus doesn't have time to hit the breaks. She drives straight into the crowd of armed soldiers, without so much as raising her gun in defense. Their bullets tear through her green fur and she flies backwards off of her bike.

Then, ahead, I see an army of vehicles heading our way. Trucks filled with mutant men, coming to assist their Fry Guy colleagues. The two armies must have planned this attack together. They are trying to finish off the Warriors once and for all.

Pippi turns around before they start firing at us. She follows Hyena back toward the other Warrior vehicles.

"Retreat!" Hyena yells at her sisters who don't yet realize what is happening.

The warrior motorcycles and vehicles turn around, some of them veer off the road, others drive in reverse. I see Apple turning her vehicle around, off into the dirt. Nova has her crossbow aimed to take on the first truck of mutants that reach us.

As Apple turns her car around and speeds up to make their escape, Pippi rides up alongside. Nova doesn't see it coming as Pippi reaches out her hand and grabs her by the ankle. I squeeze Pippi's arm, trying to stop her, but Nova is already tumbling off of the back of Apple's car into the dirt.

I look back and see Nova hit her head on the road. She doesn't move. Beyond her, the mutant trucks race toward us, firing machine guns and hollering with multi-fists waving in the air.

"That's what the bitch gets for fucking with me," Pippi says.

"What the hell!" I scream.

I look around at the other warriors. None of them saw what happened, not even Apple. They are just going to leave Nova for the mutants.

I don't know what to do about it myself. I just look back at her body in the road. My mouth droops open. A pain wells up in the back of my throat. My eyes water. I don't know what to do but cry into Pippi's furry back.

As the mutant trucks get closer, Pippi breaks off from the group. She turns into the woods, riding up a hill, away from the conflict.

Looking at the back of Pippi's head, I can just imagine the smug little smile she has on her face right now. I can't believe what has just happened.

Nova...

"You'll never see her again," Pippi says, as if she can read my mind.

"You evil little bitch..." I say, my voice cracking.

"She had it coming," she says. "Now you can pay all of your attention to me and forget about her."

As we ride up the hill, I realize that I can't just do nothing. I can't let Pippi get away with this. The next thing I know, I'm biting Pippi's furry ear. She shrieks.

I drop my legs down until they hit the ground and then I go flying off of the back of the bike. Because my arms are still tied around Pippi's chest, she falls off with me. We tumble down the hill together, rolling over one another. She hits her head on a tree and yelps at the pain, growling and hissing as we fall.

When we stop, I pull myself up so that her arms will slip out of my tied limbs. She struggles to keep me attached to her, but I wiggle her arms out. Then I turn and run out of the forest toward the road, my four arms still bound together.

Pippi shouts at me, chases after me, but she doesn't follow me out into the road. I turn and see her get back on her bike and retreat into the woods.

Nova is surrounded by mutants on the side of the road. Although most of the mutants went after the retreating Warriors, some of them stayed behind to deal with their new prisoners. Next to Nova, Talon is in hand and ankle cuffs. Venus is there as well, but she is convulsing on the ground, coughing up blood. Her green fur has been stained red.

When I approach the men, they raise their weapons to me. I freeze and show them my bound hands.

"Don't shoot," I say. I feign relief for having found these men. "I escaped from the wolf women. I was their prisoner."

They take me closer.

A bald mutant with a claw-shaped scar across his face takes me into the group at gunpoint. He brings me to a young teenaged mutant with three legs, "Is this one of the men who shot at you?"

The boy looks at me. "I don't know."

"Last night," the bald mutant says to me, "a bunch of our brothers were killed by men in the Bitch camp. The assholes were fighting on the side of the fucking bitches. Are you one of them?"

"No," I say. "I was their prisoner."

One of the mutants steps out of the crowd.

"Dan?" he says.

I recognize that voice. As the man comes forward, I realize that it is my old friend, Robby. My old poker buddy who disappeared a few months back. Judging by the feet growing out of his crotch and the hands growing out of his chest, he must not have moved to the other side of town as I expected. He must have been discovered by the Fry Guys and banished from the city.

"Robby?" I say.

He shakes my hand within the bondage.

"You know him?" asks the bald mutant.

Robby says, "Yeah, I've known him for years. He's a good guy."

"He might have joined forces with the enemy."

Robby waves his hand in the air. "Are you kidding? His brother is one of the highest ranking Fry Guys in McDonaldland. He's loyal. There's no way he'd team up with the Bitches."

"If you vouch for him," the bald mutant says, as he cuts my bonds with a mud-caked machete, "then he's your responsibility."

Robby is a short, chunky man with naturally dark skin and a scraggly beard. He used to work at the fish hatchery, where they would raise the meat required for the Filet-O-Fish. We met because we lived in the same crappy side of town and were both pretty happy people despite having such crappy jobs.

"How are you doing, man?" he asks, a machine gun dangling over his shoulder.

"Things could be better," I say, looking over at Nova, who has been staring at me. She seems to be in okay shape after having fallen from a moving vehicle, but I have no idea how long they're going to keep her alive. I'm prepared to kill each and every one of these mutants, including Robby, to prevent her from being killed.

"So you were a prisoner of those Bitches?" he asks me. "Did they force you to have sex with them?" Then he points at the bald mutant. "Captain Kongun over there says that the Bitches force their male prisoners to have sex with them so that they can grow into those big wolves."

I look away from Nova to shake my head at him. "Nope. Nothing like that."

He pats me on the shoulder.

"Well, you're safe now, bud. The Bitches aren't going to last much longer. Captain Kongun says we'll defeat them by month's end."

I nod my head and pretend to be excited about that.

A group of Fry Guys come toward us from the van down the road. They are led by a fat, dark-skinned, white-haired man wearing a blue uniform with red arm bands. I recognize him. He is Duncan Charles, the Chief of the Fry Guys. November's father.

He recognizes his daughter instantly. When Nova sees him, her yellow eyes widen and her lips tremble. It has been almost ten years since the last time they saw each other. Her father acts as if it is not a strange reunion.

"November," he says, nodding his head at her.

Then he turns to Captain Kongun. "Will your men be able to finish them off?"

"We didn't expect them to retreat," the bald mutant says.

Captain Kongun has six chainsaws strapped to his back. He has two extra limbs growing out of his chest and two more growing out of his back. Unlike most mutants, his uniform has been custom tailored with sleeves for each of his six limbs.

When Kongun speaks, he talks with all six limbs. "You should have waited until we were closer."

"Your soldiers failed last night," the Chief says. "I

don't see how they will succeed today."

"I've never known them to retreat from a fight," the Captain says. "At least we know they are weaker than ever before."

Chief spits at the mutant's shoes. "Let's just get off the road before we attract some Giant Bitches."

The bald mutant orders his men to pull out. As the soldiers lift the wolf women to take them back to their trucks, the Chief points at Nova.

"Be as humane as you can with that one," he says.

"Why?" asks the Captain.

The Chief rolls his tongue in his mouth at him.

"She's my daughter," he says.

Apart from what little Nova told me about her father, I didn't know very much about him. Most of the time I would just see he and Nova get into arguments. He would be yelling at her as she left the house, or he'd run into her in public and tell her to stop messing around and go home to do her homework.

There was only one confrontation I had with him that has stuck in my memory. It was during November's sixteenth birthday. She was born in the month of November, which is how she got her name. Every birthday, the Chief always stated that it was not his idea to give her that stupid name.

We gave her presents and she blew out the candle on her hot apple pie. We clapped. Most of the people there were not friends of Nova's or mine. They were friends of her father's and the children of the friends of her father's. These were the people he wanted Nova to be associating with, rather than me.

That day, after the Chief introduced Nova to a nice young man who was the son of a Fry Guy Lieutenant and backed them into the kitchen together, he took me by the arm and led me outside. At first, I figured he was only doing this so that he could give his daughter some privacy, but then I realized he also had something to say to me.

"I don't want you hanging around my daughter anymore," he told me.

I didn't know how to respond to that.

"We've been best friends for years," I told him. "How can I just not be friends with her anymore?"

"She has become a woman," he says. "She has to start looking for a husband soon. I don't want you to get in the way."

"But we're just friends," I said.

"Men and women can't be *just friends*," he said. "I know that you're only her friend because you're in love with her."

"That's not true at all!" I said.

"You're the kind of kid who would try to sleep with her illegally," he said. "I used to be a young man your age, so I know how it is. You have to be responsible and disciplined in order to control hormones at your age, but responsibility and discipline are two things you know nothing about."

"I would never try to persuade Nova to sleep with me," I say.

"Maybe so," he says. "But I don't want you hanging around her anymore. Just in case."

"You can't stop me," I told him. "And I doubt you'd be able to stop her, either."

"Maybe you're right," he said. "But I can persuade you."

He went into his wallet and pulled out twenty McDonald's bucks. Each one was worth a hundred credits.

"I'll give all of this to you if you never speak to her again," he tells me.

Then he put the money in my pocket. I tried to take it

193

out, but he just pushed it back in.

"This is the easy way," he told me. "You don't want to do this the hard way."

He wouldn't let me back into the party, so I walked home with the money. The next day I told Nova all about what happened. She decided that we should spend the money and then hang out even more than before.

"But what if he tries to separate us *the hard way*?" I asked her, as we sat up in a tree.

"That's what he always says," she said. "Don't worry about it. I know how to threaten him a lot more than he knows how to threaten me."

"Oh yeah?" I ask.

"Yeah. I'll just tell him that if he tries to separate us again then I'll have sex with you out of spite."

When she looked at me, she noticed my face was blushing. It made her smile.

Before we get into our vehicle, the Chief looks at me. He squints his eyes and then nods his head.

"You're the Togg boy," he says.

"That's right," I say.

"Funny meeting you here," he says, digging his finger into his ear and then examining the wax he collected. "Back when you were kids, it seemed every time I saw my November outside of the home you were always there by her side. Even in the wasteland, you two won't stay apart."

"She saved my life from the Bitches," I say, hoping that Nova doesn't hear me using the term *bitches*.

"It's like old times," he says, sniffing at his finger. "Old times."

194

They load us into the trucks and head off down the road. I ride with Robby and the Captain, wishing I would have been in the same vehicle as Nova and her sisters.

When we get to the facility, it is a much larger place than I had expected. The building is ten times the size of the McDonaldland mall. It is like a small city inside of a fortress. The only thing I like about it is the drab gray color of the buildings, which is much more pleasant to look at than the yellow and red of McDonaldland.

Past the main gate, we pull into a parking lot filled with trucks and armored vehicles. We drive up to a building and are greeted by a swarm of mutants with machine guns. When I exit the vehicle, I see Nova being escorted by gunpoint away from the direction I am supposed to go. She looks back at me, her eyes begging for me to do something. I only look back at her with an apologetic expression. The same one she gave me when I was prisoner of the wolf women.

Inside the facility, it looks much like an abandoned mall. Long empty hallways, brown and yellow stained concrete floors, faded white brick walls, paint peeling off of the ceiling. It is unpleasantly warm and emotionally sterile.

Captain Kongun takes me into an office the size of a bathroom. He has me tell him everything I know about the wolf girls. I tell him how many they are, how badly they were crippled after the last attack, and how they are short on supplies. Basically, I told him everything he already knew. If I had any useful information I probably wouldn't have given it to him, even though I owe the Warriors no favors.

By the end of the conversation, he believes I'm someone who can be trusted and says I will be a good addition to their army. He calls Robby into the office. Robby walks into the room with the hands on his chest curled into fists, like they are fist-shaped breasts.

"I'm going to make him a probationary recruit," he says to Robby. "I want him by your side every second of every day for the next three months. He's your responsibility. If he fucks up, you share the consequences."

Robby nods.

"Now, show him to the barracks," says the Captain. "There's an orientation later today. Make sure he attends."

Robby salutes and then escorts me from the room.

"So how the hamburglar have you been doing?" Robby asks me with a big smile on his face, as we walk through the dreary corridors toward the barracks.

"Okay," I say, not in the mood for small talk.

As we walk, we pass mutants of all varieties. They are not in as high spirits as Robby. Most of them look exhausted and depressed. They wear brown jumpsuits that don't look like they've been washed in months.

"It's great to see you," he says. "I was hoping some more of my friends would join the Outlanders."

"Outlanders?" I ask.

"That's what we call ourselves."

"The Warriors call you Meat," I say.

"Warriors?"

"The wolf women. They call themselves the Warriors of the Wild."

"Oh." He laughs. "We call them the Bitches."

I nod my head, but don't laugh with him.

"You remember Frank, right?" Robby asks.

"Of course," I say.

"He was here, too," he says. "We even played poker

again a few times. Good old Frank."

"Where is he now?" I ask.

"Dead," he says. "Killed by one of those giant wolves."

I nod my head solemnly. "I'm sorry. I had no idea what happened to the two of you. We both thought it was weird when Frank stopped hanging out, then you disappeared. I don't know why I didn't think something was up."

"Well, you know," Robby says. "The people in charge of The Blessed McDonald's Corporation are a bunch of assholes. Their food causes deformities and instead of solving the problem they just get rid of those people infected."

"I met a guy who works for Research and Development," I say. "He said that he was trying to find a cure for our deformity."

Robby chuckles. "Find a cure? Are you kidding?"

As we pass a group of old gray-haired mutants with swollen heads, Robby points at them.

He says, "You see them?"

"Yeah."

"A few decades ago, the chemicals in the McDonald's new sugar substitute caused several people to grow tumors which swelled so large that their heads quadrupled in size. Those that survived were just thrown out of the city. The doctors found a cure and the problem was solved."

He points at another guy, who is covered in rough lizard-like skin. "Then another problem came along. When they tried to make synthetic pork for the McRib, they discovered that many people were allergic to it. The reaction caused permanent skin damage to those who were sensitive. So they kicked those infected out of town and put the McRib project on hold."

Robby stops and explains the history of the Outlanders.

For generations, the quality of McDonald's food has been degrading. The food has become more and more processed, infused with more and more chemicals to synthesize flavors that they are not able to produce naturally due to limited resources. Over the decades, the food has caused a number of new diseases and mutations in the McDonaldland citizenry. Every ten years or so, a new mutation will pop up. Anyone infected is kicked out of McDonaldland and forced to survive in the wasteland.

He says the Outlanders have been around for several generations. They have banded together to help each other survive. They have created lives for themselves. They have children. They live the best they can.

Each outbreak is worse and more widespread than the last. But with each outbreak, their community grows in number. The multi-limb parasite is only the newest outbreak of mutants. However, it is by far the largest outbreak in the history of McDonaldland. Because of this, the Outlander army has become enormous.

Robby doesn't know the parasite mutating the men has anything to do with the parasite that has been infecting the women for the past hundred years, and it doesn't seem like any of the other mutants are aware of this either. They just think it is the newest mutation caused by McDonald's food. Since it is the same parasite, I doubt it is going to be cured easily. They've never been able to cure the lycanthropy in women, so I doubt they'll be finding a cure any time soon for the same parasite in men.

The barracks are absurd. The room is the size of a gymnasium and the bunks go four beds high. Most of them, however, seem empty.

"They had to build this in order to accommodate all of the newcomers that have been joining as of late," he says.

He brings me to an open bunk.

"Take this one," he says. "It's better to get a bottom bunk. Just mess up the covers and people will know that it's taken."

I mess up the covers.

"Oh!" he says. "I forgot to tell you something. Your grandpa!"

"Yeah?" I ask.

"Steven Togg! That guy is a legend around here, at least among the old-timers. He really helped get this place into shape. He started their brewery. The beer is about two thousand times better than the crap you used to brew up."

"Really?" I'm suddenly interested.

"Yeah," he says. "We all get a beer ration. You'll have to try it out. Perhaps they'll even put you to work at the brewery. Besides fighting, we all have to work a maintenance job. The brewery is a good job. There's also a winery, but the vineyard is so small that we don't get much of a wine ration. It's for special occasions."

He laughs and slaps me on the shoulder. "Yeah, your grandpa did a lot for this community. He got the plumbing going. He helped build vehicles from the old wrecks around the wasteland. He's like a hero. Too bad he was captured by the Bitches. Nobody heard from him after that."

Perhaps that's when grandpa joined the Warriors.

"So what's this orientation about?" I ask him.

"You'll get to meet the Mayor," Robby says. "He's the leader of the Outlanders." Then he leans in and whispers in my ear. "He's an enormous asshole, so don't do anything to piss him off. I'm serious."

"You have a Mayor?"

"Yeah," he says. "Mayor McCheese."

199

I've heard of Mayor McCheese before. My grandfather told me about him. Back when he was a kid, he used to see the Mayor up on his balcony dictating to his people.

The Mayor was the official leader of McDonaldland. He was the spokesperson for The Blessed McDonald's Corporation. Originally, he was just a normal executive, but they wanted him to be more than just a regular politician. They wanted him to resemble the God from the McDonald's Bible. They wanted him to be Mayor McCheese.

So this executive was given reconstructive surgery to look like the fictional character, Mayor McCheese. They made him look like a living cartoon. It must have been a comical sight to see this man walking down the streets of McDonaldland in his purple suit and top hat.

Grandpa said that the Mayor and his friends were kicked out of McDonaldland because of acts of high treason. It was believed that the Mayor wanted to dismantle The Blessed McDonald's Corporation board of directors, and make himself the supreme leader of the country. My grandpa never knew what had become of him.

It appears that he has joined the Outlanders. However, that would make him almost one hundred years old now. I ask Robby about this and he says that all he knows is there is a rumor that Mayor McCheese was created with so many preservatives during his reconstructive surgery that he can live for a very long time.

Chapter 18

Mayor McCheese

When I see Mayor McCheese, he is not as comical-looking as I imagined. His enormous hamburger-shaped head is not like that of a cartoon character. It looks realistic. His head has been cosmetically modified to look like a giant hamburger. The burger, the bun, the condiments, they are all human flesh that has been stretched, twisted, and dyed to look like an authentic McDonald's cheeseburger.

Mayor McCheese doesn't dress as the mayor we know from the McDonald's bible. He doesn't wear a purple suit with a top hat. He wears a black military uniform with the sleeves removed, bullet belts strapped across his chest, and two shotguns over his shoulders. His body is bulky with enormous gnarled muscles large enough to carry his giant head with ease. His hamburger face is not friendly, it is warped into an angry (almost psychotic) expression. He is the scariest fucking thing I have ever seen.

I am in a room with seven other new recruits. All of them must have just gotten in from McDonaldland this week. They look even more freaked out by Mayor McCheese than I am, perhaps because they didn't have anyone like Robby to warn them about him first.

With Captain Kongun following close behind, Mayor McCheese paces in front of us, examining his new men.

"I am Mayor McCheese," he says. When his mouth moves, his entire hamburger head moves with it. "Your new boss. Here in the wasteland life is rough. We have wolves as big as houses who want to feed on weak men such as yourselves. We have pirate Bitches raiding our supply runs and taking our men prisoner to use in sadistic games of mutilation. If you want to survive you have to do exactly what I say when I say it. This is an army and you must respect the chain of command."

He paces the men and stops in front of me, staring me down. His eyes are bigger than my fists and glossy. They bug out of the bun of his head like that of a toad.

"Your main job will be soldier," he says. "You will learn to fight. You will learn to work in a team. You will learn to hunt wolves. But first and foremost, you will learn to obey orders. Many of you will not survive the year. Those who do will most likely do so because they followed orders without hesitation.

"You will each be given a job, assigned to you by Captain Kongun," he points to the bald mutant at his side. "In addition to fighting, you must contribute to our society in one way or another. Perhaps you will work in the mess hall, perhaps in the vineyard, or perhaps in the garage. It all depends on what skills you possess."

He steps back.

"I will let the Captain take over from here," he says. "But, before I depart, just remember one thing: if you do not obey, you will be wolf food."

He glares at me in the eyes again before he departs.

Captain Kongun removes his belt full of chainsaws and then gives us more details about what life will be like for us as Outlanders. He mostly just gets into the etiquette involved and how we are to treat our superiors. He assures us that we will be eaten by wolves if we don't do exactly as he says.

When it comes time to assign jobs, he asks me for my experience. I tell him I am a brewer like my grandfather, Steven Togg. When I say the name Togg, he doesn't seem to have ever heard of him before.

"You have experience as a brewer?" he asks with his eyebrows lowered in an aggravated manor. "There are no brewers in McDonaldland. You couldn't possibly know anything about it."

"I brewed illegally," I say. "My grandfather was Steven Togg. He created the brewery here. He taught me everything he knew."

The Captain eyes me suspiciously. "We don't need any brewers at the moment. What we need is someone to work in meat processing. Do you know anything about meat processing?"

"I don't think so," I say. "I used to work in the fry-chopping plant in McDonaldland."

"That's close enough," he says. He waves Robby over to me. "You'll be working with your friend here."

"I work in meat processing as well," Robby says. "You're going to love it there."

When Robby takes me from the Captain, he whispers into my ear, "You're going to hate it there."

Robby takes me to the meat processing plant at the edge of the facility. He says that I'll be expected to get to work immediately tomorrow, so today he'll show me what I'm supposed to do.

"I'm sure you could use a rest after being a prisoner of the Bitches," he says, "but that's the way it is around here. Nobody gets a break unless it's to eat, sleep, or shit. The place is worse than McDonaldland."

He goes on to explain about how the Outlanders create products to trade with McDonaldland. He also mentions that McDonaldland isn't the only civilization they trade with. There are other small communities that have developed after the apocalypse. The one they trade with most is a town in southern Texas. That's where they get their oil, gasoline, and other food products that they can't grow in this area of the country. They act as a median between McDonaldland and this other community.

"Did you think McDonaldland was the only civilization in the world?" Robby asks. "How do you think they get their oranges to make their orange juice? You ever see any orange trees there. McDonaldland isn't as self-sufficient as they pretend to be. A lot of their food and supplies come from us or other outside communities."

In exchange, the Outlanders give the people in Texas beer, wine, and fruits they can't grow out in the desert. If it wasn't for the Outlanders both McDonaldland and the other culture wouldn't be as happy as they currently are.

"Then there's the meat," Robby says. "McDonaldland makes it seem as if all of their meat comes from the nu-cow farms, but it doesn't. Do you think that small herd of cattle could feed all of McDonaldland? The majority of their meat comes from us."

"This place raises cattle?" I ask.

"Not exactly," Robby says.

When I enter the plant, I see a group of mutants wheeling a giant wolf into a cage. It is the curly haired wolf, Tessa, that almost ate me the other day. They are pulling her by large chains attached to a forklift. Her mouth is bound with a metal harness. She growls deeply as they drag her into the cage.

"What is the wolf doing here?" I ask Robby.

"That's our cattle."

He takes me through the plant and shows me cages and

cages of giant wolves. Only, the majority of them don't have heads.

"We call them nu-wolves," he says.

He explains to me how McDonaldland asked the Outlanders to raise cattle to supply them with meat, as well as hunt and kill the giant wolves that plague the wasteland. But after a couple years of killing wolves, Mayor McCheese decided that he didn't want all that wolf meat going to waste. He began selling the McDonaldlandians the meat of the wolves they had killed, without telling them where the meat had come from. The Outlanders did raise cattle as well for a while, but then Mayor McCheese realized it was easier to sell them wolf meat.

The Mayor had an idea. He would not just kill the wolves in the wild. He would capture them, cut their heads off and implant chips in their bodies similar to those of nu-cows, then he could grow them even larger so that they would produce more meat.

"That's like cannibalism," I tell him. "They used to be women."

"Used to, yeah," he says. "But then they became animals and animals are used for meat."

I wonder if that's how the parasites are getting back into the McDonald's meat. The female parasites infect the women and turn them into enormous predators. The male parasites infect the males, turning them into easy prey. When the men are eaten by the women, the parasites are able to develop into maturity. They mate and lay their eggs. Then the giant wolves are turned into meat and eaten by the McDonaldlandians, who ingest the parasite eggs. I'm not sure if this works out for sure, but it sounds a bit plausible. I wish Krall were here.

Robby takes me into another warehouse twice the size as the previous one. The cages in here are much larger than the others. Inside, there are giant wolves without heads lying on the cement floor, hooked up to feeding tubes. These are much larger than any of the wolves in the wild. While the wild wolves get to be as big as buses, these wolves are as big as houses. They are just enormous blobs of furry meat.

"It's horrific," I tell him.

"You'll have nightmares about it for weeks," he says. "I promise you."

"How do they even get that big?"

"Well, sex, of course," Robby says. "The more they have sex, the bigger they get. They are having orgasms all day long. They are hooked up to machines that masturbate them nonstop. It actually doesn't take them that long to get this big. That wolf we just brought in today will probably grow to be big enough to be chopped up into burgers within just a few weeks."

My jaw goes slack.

"So *everyone* in McDonaldland is eating this stuff?"

"Everyone."

"So *I've* been eating the flesh of women all this time, perhaps even people I used to know?"

"Basically, yeah," he says. "You've probably been eating them your entire life. But don't feel so bad about it. These wolves eat men every day. All we're doing is eating them back."

"I want to show you Kroger the Mighty," Robby says, as he brings me into another large warehouse. This one has only a single cage.

"Masturbation isn't as effective at growing the wolves as actual intercourse with males," he tells me. "We don't know why, but real sex just creates a bigger transformation. That's why we have Kroger."

Inside of the one large cage, there is an enormous

207

wolf. It is bigger than any of the wolves in the previous room. While the others are as big as houses, this one is as big as an apartment building. It is fucking one of the headless wolves with a penis the size of twenty men.

"It's a male wolf?" I ask. "I thought only women could turn into wolves."

"Kroger the Mighty isn't exactly a man," he says. "It's a hermaphrodite."

The giant wolf has eight extra pairs of limbs. The hermaphrodite isn't just infected with the female parasite that turns it into a wolf, it also has the male parasite that causes it to grow multiple limbs. Even though it is covered in hair, the eight extra limbs growing down its torso makes it look like some kind of insect.

We stand there, listening to the thunderous moans as the beast fucks the blob of hairy meat. When it orgasms the creature roars and grows even larger. The headless beast beneath it also grows significantly larger.

"Feeding time," says a voice behind us.

A group of mutant soldiers are hauling a group of prisoners to the cage. The mutant prisoners are screaming and begging to be freed. Among the prisoners, there is a green wolf girl. It is Venus. She is being carried on a stretcher by two soldiers. She is mumbling deliriously and barely able to move. All of her fur is now so coated in blood that there is more red than green on her body.

"What are they doing?" I ask.

They open the cage and force the prisoners inside.

"Remember when the Mayor said *if you do not obey, you will be wolf food?*"

I nod.

"What he meant was, if you don't do what he tells

you he's going to feed you to Kroger."

When the giant hermaphrodite wolf sees the people inside of the cage, it casually snatches them up and swallows them whole. The people are so small compared to Kroger that they are but small bites of food. I watch Venus lying half dead on the floor of the cage. She doesn't resist in the slightest as the wolf licks her up into its mouth like a little green jelly bean. Her face is one of somber defeat as she slides down its tongue into its throat.

"Is that what will happen to all the women prisoners?" I ask Robby.

"No, just the wounded ones are fed to Kroger," he says. "The Outlanders have uses for the others."

Then Robby tells me about what fate has in store for Nova. He says that while many of their wolves are caught in the wild, they find it safer and easier to raise meat if they capture them while they're still in human form.

Whenever the Outlanders capture wolf women, they are restrained and put in cages. Then, one at a time, the mutant men rape them. They rape them until they completely turn. Then their heads are cut off and they become nu-wolves, where they will be grown as big as possible until they are chopped up into meat.

He also said that women who break sex laws in McDonaldland are no longer released into the wild. The Fry Guys don't want them joining the Warriors, because that would only create more enemies for them. So, just this past year, the Fry Guys started releasing women to the Outlanders. The Fry Guys don't know the fate of the women. They assume they will be used as slave labor or perhaps for sex. But the women now released from McDonaldland are only destined to become food.

209

I panic. The thought of Nova being raped by mutants, turned into a giant wolf and processed as food for McDonaldland is the most unsettling thing I've ever imagined. I pull Robby's ear to my mouth and whisper, "I need to talk to you. In private."

Robby nods his head and takes me out of the warehouse. As we pass Kroger's cage, the sound of gurgling mixed with muffled cries issues from the creature's belly as the prisoners are being digested alive. He takes me into a walk-in refrigerator filled with boxes, probably containing packaged meat.

I say to him, "One of the women captured with me is Nova. She was my girlfriend years ago, before we met. I can't let her be raped and turned into one of those head-less mountains of meat out there. I've got to get her out of here."

Robby's face becomes cold. He just stares at me for a few minutes.

"Tell me the truth," he says. "Were you one of the men who fired on Outlanders last night to save a bunch of Bitches?"

I take a couple minutes before considering my answer, but decide to go with the truth. "Yes, I did."

He deeply exhales at me. I don't care if he was my friend in McDonaldland. If he plans on turning me in I won't hesitate to kill him with my bare hands before he even leaves this room, and then feed his body to that giant hermaphrodite wolf.

Then he says, "I was hoping you would say that."

As he goes back toward the door, he says, "Come with me. I have some friends I'd like you to meet."

Robby takes me across the complex and gathers some mutants to follow us. They bring me into a small room outside the barracks. One of them stands guard outside. Most of them look just as confused as I do.

"Why'd you gather us together, Robby?" asks a five-armed mutant with a black Mohawk. "It's not even fucking dusk yet."

Most of the others seem equally annoyed.

"We've been given an opportunity that must be acted upon now," Robby says, pointing at me.

The other mutants in the room look in my direction.

"What's this all about?" I ask him.

Robby stretches the fingers of the hands on his breasts, then says, "The Mayor plans to attack McDonaldland at the end of the month. With all of the new recruits he's been getting, he's built up a big enough army to take on the Fry Guys. He wants to reclaim his throne as ruler of McDonaldland. The Blessed McDonald's Corporation might be a corrupt and oppressive government, but they are nothing compared to the cruelty of the Mayor's reign. None of us in this room want this to happen. Even though we were thrown out of McDonaldland, it is still home to our friends and family. We don't want to see it destroyed or perverted by the Mayor."

"So what do we need him for?" a fat mutant with glasses asks.

"He's friends with the Bitches," he says. Then he looks at me. "We can help you rescue your girlfriend and get you out of here, but we want something in return."

"Name it," I say.

"I want you to convince the Bitches to help us. The Fry Guys don't stand a chance against the Outlander army, but if the bitches were to help it would be a different story. As the Mayor attacks the Fry Guys, the Bitches can attack from the rear. The Outlanders would be surrounded."

"What about you?" I ask. "You're Outlanders yourself."

"Most of us haven't been here for long," he says.

"We don't have ties with any of these assholes," says the mohawked mutant. "They could all die for all we care."

"We plan to do as much damage as we can from the inside," Robby says. "We don't care if we have to die to save our families. We just can't let the Mayor take over our home."

"I can't convince them to fight to save McDonaldland," I say. "They all despise everything McDonaldland stands for."

The mutants frown at me.

"But there is one chance," I say. "Talon was one of the women who was brought in with Nova. She's the second in command of the Warriors. If you rescue her she might be willing to get the others to help your cause."

"It's worth a try," Robby says. Then he looks at the others. "There's only one problem."

"What's that?" I ask.

"I'm responsible for you," he says. "If you escape with the Bitches then I'll be the one left to answer for it. I can't let that happen."

"You could come with us," I say.

"No, I'm needed here," he says. "You'll have to stay behind. We'll get the women free and send them back to their people. You will stay here. Then, hopefully, they will convince the other Bitches to help defeat the Mayor."

I think about it for a moment. There's no way I want to stay with the Outlanders, but saving Nova is more important to me. I'd rather be apart from her and know that she's safe. Besides, the only place I have among the Warriors is as Pippi's doormat.

"Okay," I tell him. "I'll stay behind. But I get to help in the rescue."

"Of course," he says. "You're the one who will have to convince them to support our cause during the escape."

"So how do we get them out of here?"
"Leave that to us."

We go immediately to the prison block. The mohawked mutant comes with us, along with a mutant who has a long red beard and only one extra limb the size of a baby arm. The four of us walk casually through the complex until we get to the cells. Then we creep into the prison when nobody is looking.

Inside is a long hallway that ends in a lounge. It is filled with couches made of blonde wolf fur. On the other side of the room, a man is pouring himself a cup of coffee. He is wearing a black and white striped jumpsuit with a black cape. He has an enormous oversized head with red hair and a black hat. When he turns to the side, I see a black bandit mask covering his eyes and a red tie down his chest.

Robby pulls us back into the hallway.

"Fuck," Robby whispers. "It's Hamburglar."

My grandfather also told me about the Hamburglar. He was kicked out of McDonaldland with his friend Mayor McCheese. Just like the Mayor, he had undergone reconstructive surgery to look like the cartoon-like Hamburger character from the McDonald's Bible. Whereas Mayor McCheese was supposed to represent the God of McDonaldland, the Hamburglar was supposed to represent the devil.

He was the Chief of the Fry Guys. His job was to punish the criminals of McDonaldland. Back when my grandfather was a kid, if somebody was arrested for breaking an unforgivable crime, it was the Hamburglar who escorted that criminal out of town.

My grandfather also said how ironic it was to see the Hamburglar escorted out of McDonaldland himself, after teaming up with the Mayor in an attempt to overthrow the corporate government.

We have no choice but to push forward. Robby watches for the way to clear and then one at a time we sneak past the lounge through the door that leads to the cellblock.

As I sneak past, I see the Hamburglar stirring sugar into his coffee. He dips a chocolate cookie into the coffee and takes a bite. His oversized head wobbles as he chews. He doesn't turn around until the last of us gets past him.

Inside the cellblock, there is a bin filled with weapons near the door. Swords, rifles, spears, and other assorted weapons piled up in a heap. When I see Talon's two long-handled axes on top of the stack, I realize that this is where they discard weapons that have been taken from the prisoners.

Like a McDonaldland prison, the walls are lined with cells. They are filled with naked wolf women in many stages of transformation. Some look barely changed at all, as if they were just exiled from McDonaldland this week. Others have already turned into massive beasts. The largest of them is the size of a Fry Guy van, and fills the majority of her cell.

Near the end of the row, there are two guys looking into a cell, laughing and cheering. The four of us hide behind the crate of weapons. I hear Nova's voice. It is coming from the cell the mutants are looking into.

Peeking out from behind the crate, I see there is a third man inside the cell. He is taking off her clothes and smacking her as she resists. Nova's hands and legs are bound.

"I'm going to give it to you good, Bitch!" says the man in the cage.

He fondles Nova's breasts with two of his hands as

214

four more curl around her hips and thighs. Nova spits in his face and he punches her in the stomach. Then he pulls down his pants and lies on top of her.

I stand up to go to her aid, but Robby pulls me back down.

"I'm going to fuck you like the animal you are," he says.

As he tries to put his penis inside of her, Nova thrusts her pelvis at him with such force that he is tossed forward, over her. His head slams between the bars of the cage so hard it rips both of his ears off. He shrieks as his ears dangle by bloody threads. Before his friends can come to his assistance, she rolls over him and slams her weight on his back, snapping his neck between the bars.

One of the other mutants pulls a knife and enters the cage. He says, "I'm going to fucking kill you, Bitch!"

Before Robby can stop me, I grab one of Talon's axes out of the top of the weapon pile and charge the mutants. The one still outside the cell turns around as the axe comes down into his forehead. Then he drops.

The other mutant points the knife at me.

"Who the fuck are you?" he says.

Nova rolls over on the guy's legs and he trips forward. When he hits the ground, I chop the axe down into his lower back. He cries out, but he doesn't die. I try to pull the axe out, but it's stuck. The man won't stop screaming.

"Shut him up!" Robby says, as he gets out from behind the crate and barricades the door just in case the Hamburglar hears the screaming.

With my foot on the guard's back for leverage, I try pulling out the axe. But it has gone in all the way to the floor and is now caught on his spine.

The mohawked mutant grabs Talon's other axe and runs toward us. I give up on the axe and grab the knife from the screaming guard. Instead of finishing off the mutant, I bring the knife to Nova's bonds and cut her free. She doesn't say anything as she leaves the cell. She stomps on the back of the guard's head and a loud cracking noise echoes through the cellblock. He stops screaming.

Before Nova puts her clothes on, she releases Talon from her cell. Then she goes to the other cells and releases the other wolf girls one at a time.

"This isn't part of the plan," Robby says, getting between me and Nova. "We can only get two of them out."

Nova pushes him out of the way to release more of the imprisoned girls. As the girls are released, they immediately go to the bin of weapons to arm themselves.

A knocking sound comes from the door. Somebody is trying to get in.

"Shit," the mohawked mutant says. "We're fucked."

Talon comes up behind the mohawked man and takes her axe out of his hand. Then she rips the axe out of the dead man's back, taking half of his spine out with it. Although she is naked, she has patches of fur covering her breasts and ass like a bikini of hair. It is like she doesn't even need to wear clothes.

Robby runs to the other side of the room and opens a garage-sized door that leads into a large corridor designed to transfer wolves once they have become too big for the cells.

"This way," Robby says.

Nova and Talon release all of the wolf women, even the ones who have already turned. When Robby sees the van-sized wolf stepping into the room with them, he dives through the exit. The mohawked mutant and I get the hell out of there as well.

Chapter 14

Talon

Once outside the cellblock, the wolves run past us and spread out into the facility. The screams of mutant men soon echo through the corridors.

"You have to convince them now," Robby says to me, as he closes the garage door behind us. "We don't have much time."

I turn to Nova and Talon who are dressing themselves while holding their weapons between their knees.

"These guys are helping you escape for a reason," I tell them. "They need your help defending McDonaldland from the mutants."

"No way," Talon says.

"But they're saving your lives," I say. "Do you know what they would have done to you if you stayed their prisoner?"

"It's not up to me," she says. "It's up to Grandma, but I can guarantee you she will not sacrifice a single sister's life to save McDonaldland. I have no intention of convincing her otherwise."

Then I look at Nova. She shakes her head at me.

"If we could destroy McDonaldland ourselves, we would," Nova says.

Then the group of women take off without us.

"You have to go after them and convince them to fight the mutants," Robby says. "I don't care how you do it. Just make it happen. We can't let the Mayor take over McDonaldland."

"What about you?" I ask. "You said you'd be to blame if I go missing."

"Don't worry about it," he says. "I have a plan. Come on."

We run in the direction of the wolf girls. Before we get to the end of the corridor, Robby says, "I'm going to go to the meat processing plant and release more wolves. The bigger ones that have yet to be turned into nu-wolves. If I release them the entire facility will be in chaos. You'll be able to escape. And if Captain Kongun wonders what happened to you I'll tell him you were eaten by one of the large wolves."

"Think he'll buy it?" I ask.

"It's worth a try," he says.

When the giant wolves are freed, the facility becomes a war zone. Machinegun fire and the howling of wolves can be heard throughout the complex. I catch up to Talon and the other wolf girls outside the facility in a back parking lot. They have encountered a small group of mutant guards and are battling between the automobiles in the lot.

Three of the mutants are already dead on the ground. They were the ones with the guns. The four remaining Outlanders fight the wolf women with swords and axes.

Talon tosses one of her axes through the air like a boomerang and it decapitates one of the mutants. Then she goes after a mutant with four arms, two of them holding hammers. As she swings her axe at him, the mutant tries to block with one of his hammers. The axe chops off the head of the hammer, but he was able to stop it from colliding with his face. Before Talon can strike again, the mutant grabs her axe with his free hands, just below the blade, and swings his other hammer at her face. It hits her square in the forehead.

Nova takes on the other two mutants with her sickle-

219

shaped sword. Both of them have swords twice the size of hers. She blocks one of them and then strikes at the other, but can't get past their fencing skills. With the hook of her sword, she catches one of their blades as they block and lowers it down to his legs, piercing his thigh with his own sword. Then she grabs him by the neck and rips out his throat.

Talon wasn't fazed by the hammer hit to her forehead. She just shakes it off. He hits her in the face again and she just shakes it off again. Then growls at him. She tries pulling on her axe, but the mutant curls all four of his arms around it. She rips on the axe, gutting most of it away from him, but he still has a firm grip on the bottom of the handle. After failing to pull it away from him, she decides to push on it. With all of her strength, she shoves it back toward him, smashing the handle of the axe all the way through his chest. When he's dead, she pulls her axes out of the corpses and kills two more unarmed mutants who she finds hiding behind a truck.

As the final mutant comes at Nova, she kicks him in the stomach and as he's tumbling back she jumps at him like a cat. She severs his sword arm and then catches him by the collar before he hits the ground. As he screams, blood draining out of his severed limb, she just stares at him with cold animal eyes. Then she slams his face into her tits, right into the spikes on her metal bikini. The nails go through his skull and kill him instantly.

Nova and Talon go to the other wolf girls. They have picked out a couple of trucks and are loading up the younger girls and the wounded. I go after them.

"I'm coming," I tell Nova.

She doesn't look at me, loading injured women into the truck, as she says, "Are you sure you want to go back to be Pippi's Meat?"

I wasn't about to debate it. I jump into the back of the truck and we head out. We drive through a crowd of soldiers firing at a giant wolf and crash through an armored Fry Guy car. The front gate is open as panicked mutants attempt to escape their own fortress, so we drive our trucks straight through the gate and straight through the fleeing mutants.

When I look back, I see Chief Duncan Charles staring at us as we drive away, just standing there in his fuzzy blue suit as if there wasn't anything unusual going on behind him. Then I notice Nova is staring back at her father as well. She is grinding her teeth and clenching her fists. If they were standing face to face right now I bet she would rip his head off without second thought.

The new wolf girls are cold and scared. Many of them have been getting raped and abused for days. Nova and Talon don't know any of them. None of them were members of the Warriors before they were captured. Most likely, they were delivered to the Outlanders by the Chief of the Fry Guys. There are only six of them. Perhaps a dozen more never got out of the facility, because they were too wild or confused.

Talon tries to calm them down. She tells them about her sisters, the Warriors of the Wild, and how they will be welcomed with open arms. None of them seem very enthusiastic about it. They all seem to want to go back home to McDonaldland to see their families.

It's past dusk and we've decided to set up camp in the woods. It's going to take time to track down the rest of the Warriors. They are constantly on the move to make it difficult for their enemies to find them, but it also makes it difficult for their friends to find them. Talon believes she'll be able to track them down in a day or two. Until then, we're on our own.

Nova hasn't so much as looked at me since we left the facility. She's distant, troubled. I would have thought she would want to speak with me. We haven't really been able to spend much time with each other, since I was Pippi's property. Perhaps she doesn't really want anything to do with me anymore. Perhaps I remind her too much of the person she used to be, the person she thought she'd forgotten.

Talon sees me sitting alone in the dirt away from the fire, so she comes over and sits down next to me.

"I want to thank you for helping us back there," she says.

I turn to see Talon's hairless dog-shaped face pointed at me. The braids of her hair stuck within her furry cleavage look like a package of french fries.

"I had to," I say. "You don't even know what they would have done to you had I left you there."

"Rape us? Use us for meat?" She speaks as if these things are no big deal.

"Yeah," I say. "You knew?"

"No, but I'm not surprised."

"The idea doesn't bother you that you'd have been raped and then used for meat?"

She shrugs. "We do the same thing with the men we capture, but when we use men for food we eat them alive."

I don't know. The women may be crueler in this regard, but for some reason the Outlanders' way seems more disturbing to me than the Warriors' way. I think it might have to do with the thought of Nova becoming McDonaldland food.

"Why are the Warriors and the Outlanders like this?" I ask. "Both groups are outcasts of McDonaldland. I don't see why you're not united in one community."

"We used to be," she tells me. "Years ago, before even

Grandma was with the Warriors, there was only one group of outcasts. They were mostly made up of women who had been cast out of the walled city. Mutant men were a minority, but they lived together, married, raised families. They lived free and peacefully. But, eventually, the men wanted to limit the amount of sex the women were allowed to have. The men didn't want their wives turning into wolves and leaving them, but the women didn't want to be bound by laws. They wanted to have the freedom to make love at their own discretion. Many of them women embraced the idea of transforming into wild creatures without boundaries. It wasn't long before they separated into two camps. Some women stayed with the men, and some men stayed with the women. But, over time, the two camps evolved into the tribes they are today."

"So they separated because the men were too controlling?"

"It is the nature of the male species to be controlling. The only way the women could be truly free was to start their own clan with their own rules."

"They couldn't compromise?" I ask.

"There's no compromise," she says.

I stare across the fire at Nova. All I want is to be with her. I don't care if it seems impossible. I have to figure out a way to make it work.

"You don't think it could've worked out?" I say.

"I wish more than anything that it could."

Talon tells me about when she used to live in McDonaldland.

"I had two gorgeous sons, a beautiful plump husband, and a nice home on the north side, overlooking the lake," she says.

She talks about how they used to have sex illegally, after they had their kids. They would kiss and touch each

223

other for hours, teasing each other, just foreplay. When they had sex, they would only do it in quick bursts. Sometimes Talon would have an orgasm, but usually only he would. When they did it this way, she wouldn't transform so much.

Most of the time she stayed at home. She didn't socialize with any friends and when she went out she was always covered. Nobody could tell that she was changing, because nobody ever saw her.

"It's actually quite common," Talon says. "People break the sex laws and get away with it all the time, as long as they have already had kids legally."

They got away with illegal sex for years. The more she changed the more she wanted to have sex. Sometimes she was embarrassed that her husband wouldn't find her attractive the more wolf-like she became, but he assured her that she was beautiful no matter what she looked like.

But then she became pregnant with a third child. This was not something that she could hide. They thought about trying to find a way to abort the baby, but Talon couldn't get herself to do it. They made love almost every day until her stomach was large enough to show in public. By that time, her wolf features were so prominent that they could hardly be hidden by her clothing.

After saying a long goodbye to her husband and sons, she turned herself in and accepted her punishment. They said they would see each other again one day, but neither of them meant it.

She thought raising his child in the wasteland would be the next best thing to being with him, but the child was stillborn. She was denied even that.

"At the time," she says, "I wished I could have taken my family with me into the wasteland. It rarely ever happens, because most people in the walled city believe that being outcast is a death sentence. Who wouldn't rather be separated from their family than put their family in danger?

I know now that it never would have worked, but I wish things would have been different. I wish everything would have been different."

I realize that this is why she cried the other day, when she asked me if Nova was my girlfriend when we lived in the walled city. She knew what it was like to be separated from her love. She must have imagined what it would have been like to meet her husband again in the wasteland. Even if he had become the property of another wolf woman, she surely would have liked to see him again.

Nova is on the other side of the camp, gazing into the woods. I can't take my eyes off her, nor can I find the courage to go talk to her.

"Give her time," Talon says.

Talon watches me as I stare at November. Her glare is one of a concerned friend, yet also one of a ravenous animal.

"She seems so distant," I say.

"Nova's always been like that," Talon says. "Ever since we found her. She's quiet and keeps to herself."

"She never used to be like that," I say.

"I think she became that way because of *him*."

"Who?"

"Her father."

"The Chief?"

"Yes," Talon says. "He's the reason she was sent into the wasteland."

"I know. I can't believe that asshole outcast his own daughter. He had the power to make an exception with his daughter, but instead he decided to make an example."

"That's not what I mean," she says.

I look at her, not sure what she's getting at.

225

"He molested her," she says. "Nova was sent into the wasteland because she was raped by her own dad."

I'm too shocked to say anything.

Talon says, "He claimed it was an unknown assailant, and had her removed from the city before she could say otherwise."

I look at Nova. She sits there, yellow eyes in another world, tracing the scabbed over claw wounds on her belly with her index finger. It wasn't the wolf in her that made her colder. It was her past.

Talon looks at her as well. "It was probably pretty upsetting to see him again. She hasn't seen him since it happened, nearly ten years ago."

"It doesn't make sense," I say, my voice croaks a little. Tears well up in my eyes when I think of what Nova must have gone through, and how I wasn't able to be there for her. "How could he do that to his own daughter?"

I want to go over to Nova to say how sorry I am, but I realize that she probably doesn't want to talk to me about it. My head spins with frustration. I sit next to Talon for a while and just poke the dirt with my fingers as hard as I can.

Nova gets up and walks into the woods.

"You should go after her," Talon says.

"I wouldn't know what to say to her."

"Then don't say anything."

I follow Nova into the woods. She hears my footsteps behind her, but doesn't turn around. When she stops, I put my arms around her and place my chin on her furry neck.

She doesn't speak, but she puts her long fingers around

226

one of my arms. I want to talk to her about her father, figure out some way to make her feel better about it, but I dare not open my mouth.

We take deep breaths together, feeling each others' lungs expand in rhythm. She turns and looks at me with her big wolf eyes. Then she kisses me. I recoil as her spiked metal bra stabs into my chest. She takes it off, exposing her tan sliced-up breasts, and wraps her arms around me.

Communicating with our breaths as we feel each other, I tell her how much I've missed her and she tells me how she's longed for me ever since we were young. She pulls off my shirt and we kiss each other's bodies. When I lick her wounds, she sighs as if she finds it pleasurable, so I lick all of them one at a time. I press my tongue on her thigh, then slide it up across her belly and breasts in the way that Pippi did after the Trial by Claw.

Concerned that it is the wrong time and place, I resist her when she tries to make love with me. She scowls as if angry for being denied, but I give her a face that expresses my concern that it isn't really what she wants. Frustrated with me, she pulls off my pants and puts me inside of her mouth. She sucks me all the way to the back of her throat, as if she's doing it out of spite.

As she sucks on me in the forest, I look around at the shadows beyond the trees. There seems to be movement coming from the darkness. I think I see giant black legs stalking toward us. It's probably just my imagination, but I still decide to keep my eyes focused on the woods.

Nova's teeth are too long and sharp for this to be enjoyable. They scrape across the shaft of my penis, causing me to cringe at the pain every time she goes down.

When I'm about to come, she stops and lays me on the ground. Rocks and twigs dig into my back as she straddles me. She lifts her tail and then jostles my dick into her. Then she spins me around, squashing my face into the dirt, so that we are end to end. She bounces our asses together, my penis twisted awkwardly inside of her, fucking in the way wolves do. It only takes a minute before I release inside of her.

When I go limp, she pulls me out and lies on top of me. She hugs me with all of her strength and kisses my chest so hard it feels like she's punched me. Then she lays her head on my shoulder, staring forward with a blank expression. I wrap an arm around her. She closes her eyes and grinds her teeth. Her body doesn't transform, not even a little bit.

After lying in the dirt becomes itchy and too uncomfortable to bear, we put our clothes back on and walk back to the camp.

Before we arrive, we see something large and black drooping over the fire. It is an enormous wolf, the one that attacked me on the road as I left McDonaldland. Standing in the middle of the camp, it yawns widely and licks its lips. My first thought is that it is attacking the camp, but then I notice that it is just standing there, relaxed.

Talon approaches the wolf. She lifts her hand and the beast presses the side of its muzzle against her palm. Petting its whiskers, Talon hums to the creature, staring into its immense eyes.

The other girls come to the wolf as Talon waves them over. They pet its legs and neck, whatever they can reach. The wolf just closes its eyes and enjoys the rub down.

"Talon has a way with the big sisters," Nova says. "It's like she can communicate with them. Tame them."

There are more of them beyond the camp, peeking in from the woods. I see rows of giant eyes, peering in from the shadows. Talon calls the other wolves forward to meet their new sisters.

I stay back, far away from the wolves. Nova leaves my side and enters the camp to pet the black wolf next to Talon. I watch her as she rubs the beast's lower lip and fingers one of its teeth. The black wolf catches me watching Nova. It growls at me under its breath, as if telling me that I don't belong.

Chapter 16

Grandma

We catch up to the Warriors several days later. Talon found an abandoned camp and we followed their tracks day and night until we finally caught up to them.

When we arrive, the women all come out to great us. They are introduced to their new sisters and praise Nova and Talon on such a daring escape. Neither Nova nor Talon tells them it was I who was responsible for getting them out. I am pretty much ignored by the group.

Only Krall comes to greet me. He shakes two of my hands, crosswise, and asks me to tell him all about my experience. When he hears about how the Outlanders are using wolves to give meat to McDonaldland, he becomes troubled.

"It's just as I suspected," he says, his hand pressed against his forehead. He leaves it at that.

When I see Guy, all he does is nod at me. He is busy watching Ashley do handstands for him. He congratulates her for such an acrobatic feat as he combs his large mustache with a fork.

Casper comes up to Nova and I.

She asks, "Venus is really dead? She didn't make it?"

I nod at her and then she looks at Nova.

"She's gone," Nova says.

Casper's eyes dart away from us. She slinks off to her tent. With Venus dead, she's now the last of The Griddler Girls.

When Pippi sees Nova and I, her mouth drops open. Pippi approaches us and gives November a long stare down. Nova looks ready to stick a spear in her belly like a pig.

Pippi looks at me and says, "Come."

She points at the ground in front of her.

I look at Nova for help, but Nova is too busy glaring at Pippi to acknowledge me. Not sure what else to do, I go to the red-haired wolf girl.

"You're still my property," Pippi says as I approach her.

She kneels me to the ground, then says, "Wait in this spot until I return with your leash. If you move an inch you will be punished."

After Pippi goes into her tent, I turn and meet eyes with Nova. She doesn't say anything. She just turns and walks away.

Talon sees me standing obediently in the spot Pippi left me. She approaches and says, "Don't worry. You won't belong to her for much longer. I promise."

I nod at her, trying not to move an inch.

Pippi returns and looks me in the eyes. I notice that she has decorated her newly formed muzzle with two hoop-shaped lip piercings similar to Casper's.

As she leashes me, she says, "I'm mad at you for running away like that. You hurt my feelings."

She looks at me like she wants me to apologize, but I don't say anything.

"I'll forgive you this one time," she says, "but don't you dare ever do it again. You'll have to make it up to me tonight."

She brings me to a new cage near the middle of the camp. It looks like it had just been built a few days ago, to replace the one destroyed by Alyssa. As Pippi puts me inside, I see Talon, Casper, and Hyena coming toward us.

Pippi turns to Talon and says, "I want to wear the ceremonial robe tonight."

Hyena raises a gun to her.

"You won't be wearing the ceremonial robe," Talon says. "You're under arrest for assaulting one of your sisters, resulting in her capture and nearly her death."

"What?" Pippi cries.

"Nova said you pushed her from Apple's vehicle during her last raid so that she would be taken by the Meat. This is a crime that will not be taken lightly."

The red-haired girl stomps her feet. "That bitch is lying!"

Pippi looks at me as if I will come to her defense. By the look on her face, it seems as if she really believes that she's innocent.

Grandma finds Pippi guilty. Just as Nova was punished, Pippi gets stripped of rank and all possessions.

At dusk, she is put through the Trial by Claw. The wolf girls cut into her one at a time. Unlike Nova, Pippi cries like an infant as she is being cut. There are not many who go easy on her. It is as if they all had built up so much rage against Pippi over the years that they are thrilled to finally be able to take out their frustration on her, physically. Even her best friend, Slayer, gives her a good slash across her belly. The fact that she is crying only seems to make the women attack her more brutally.

By the time Nova's turn comes around, Pippi is already bloody from head to toe. Nova steps up to her and looks her in the eyes. She just glares at her, then turns away. It takes a strong individual to just walk away from this. I bet this is the way someone like Nova proves to her sisters that she is the better person of the two.

As Pippi relaxes, wiping the blood and tears out of her eyes, Nova swings around and sucker-punches her in the stomach. She punches open-handed, with her claws out. Nova's fingernails stab deep into Pippi's stomach, all the way to the knuckles. Before she lets go, Nova twists them, cutting a circle on her belly, as if she's trying to rip out her liver. Pippi screams, louder than the time Nova was cut during her ceremony.

When Nova's claws are released, Pippi falls to the ground. She curls into a ball, weeping, quivering in the mud. Nova spits on her and leaves the circle, she marches out of the camp and disappears into the woods. The other sisters disperse, leaving her in the dirt.

This time, Grandma does not help the victim of the Trial by Claw. She does not pick her up and heal her wounds. She just leaves Pippi in the mud to rot, too disappointed in the girl she raised as her own daughter to even look at her.

Talon comes to the cage and releases me.

"You're no longer Pippi's property," she says. "I claimed you and I am letting you free."

"Thanks," I say.

She gives me a nod and returns to her tent.

I cross the camp and approach Pippi. She's still crying, face down in the mud. When she looks up at me, I offer her my hand. She takes it cautiously, her furry fingers curl into my palm, and I lift her to her feet.

Her watery yellow eyes gaze into mine as blood flows down her face.

"I'm sorry," I say. "But you deserved it."

Then I walk away.

234

I'm called into Grandma's tent. She sits me down on a dusty feather cushion. Then she lights up her pipe. Four wolf girls are standing behind me. The only one I recognize is Talon. Pippi is also in the room, lying on a cot with her back turned to the group. Her wounds are bandaged. It appears Grandma finally helped her after leaving her in the mud for a couple hours.

"So you are no longer property, Daniel Togg," she says. "I assume you will be wanting to stay here with Nova?"

"Yes."

"Her sisters have sensed something is troubling her," she says. "She's going to need you."

I nod my head.

"Now, we need to assign you a place among the Warriors." She smiles and leans her head back. "Your brother tells me that you take after your grandpa."

I smile.

"Your grandpa used to make this amazing wine out of wild berries. We called it Wolf Juice. You wouldn't by any chance know how to make it would you?"

"He taught me everything he knew about brewing and winemaking," I say. "I've never made wine out of berries but I'm confident I could do it. I can make alcohol out of pretty much anything."

Grandma widens her teeth in a smile.

"Our sisters could really use something to lift their spirits about now. Wolf Juice would be perfect for that. When your grandpa was around, every night was like a celebration."

"You were friends with my grandpa?"

"We were more than just friends," she says.

Grandma tells me about the day she met my grandfather. It was over fifteen years ago. He was captured in a raid on the mutant camp, back when the Warriors were far more powerful than the Outlanders. One of the men captured was my grandpa. He was an old man. Much older than any mutant they had ever captured before. They didn't know what to do with him. None of the wolf women wanted to have sex with him. He wasn't able to do much physical labor. Even trying to feed him to their big sisters didn't work, because the giant wolves didn't find him very appetizing and wouldn't go near him. So he was just a burden to the Warriors.

His owner was tired of wasting food on my grandfather and was about to just kill him, when Grandma decided to purchase him for one can of food. Grandma says she used him for company. Being the leader of the Warriors, Grandma had to always be strong and flawless. She didn't have anyone she could share her own problems with. So my grandpa became her confidant.

He was a wealth of information and could tell her all about the old world, before McDonaldland. He told her about his family and taught her how to make use of all the seemingly useless supplies they obtained from raids on Fry Guy vehicles. He taught her how to make little sculptures out of McDonald's straws. He taught her how to make ropes out of McDonald's napkins.

Eventually, Grandma and my grandfather became lovers. Because Grandma had gone through menopause, she could have as much sex as she wanted without transforming into a bigger wolf.

My grandfather was then freed and became a member of the Warriors. He was Grandma's advisor and was a major help to the Warriors. He taught them how to build cars by combining the solar-powered McDonaldland cars with the scrapped vehicles that litter the ruins of the old world. Originally they were only getting their vehicles by hijacking Fry Guy supply trucks. My grandpa showed them that gas-powered cars could go faster than the Fry Guy vehicles, which only reach up to sixty miles per hour. They only needed to raid the gasoline supply run going between the Outlander camp and that far away community down in Texas.

But his most important contribution was making Wolf Juice, because it made life in the wasteland so much more enjoyable. It was a golden age for the Warriors.

"That's why it will be so wonderful if you can bring us Wolf Juice again," Grandma says.

"So what happened to my grandfather?" I ask. "How did he die?"

"Natural causes," Grandma says. "He was an old man, even older than myself. He died in his sleep after a Full Moon celebration. He died happy and content, without a regret in the world."

That makes me happy. Grandpa lived his life the way he wanted to, without compromise. And, in the end, he came out on top. That's exactly why I followed in his footsteps.

"So we'd like you to become our official winemaker," she says. "Are you up to the task?"

"Definitely," I say. "It will take some time to grow a yeast culture, find the berries, and ferment the wine, but I can do it."

"Excellent," Grandma says, slapping her knees, ready to say her farewell and send me away.

"There's just one more thing," I say.

Grandma nods.

"I met a group of rebels within the Outlander facility," I say. "They need your help."

I tell Grandma all about the attack on McDonaldland. I also tell her all about what goes on within the Outlander Facility, what they do to their captives, and how they are capturing their big sisters to use as meat to serve to McDonaldland. Grandma listens to everything I have to say before speaking a word.

"Because these men helped save Talon and several other sisters," Grandma says, "I am open to the possibility of helping them. However, I will not make this decision on my own. I will call a meeting and allow you to attempt to convince our sisters. If the majority is in favor we will fight."

The Warriors gather in the center of the camp. Grandma lets me explain the situation. As soon as I finish speaking, it seems as if there is not a single woman who is in favor of the idea.

"There are many innocent people who will die if you do not help," I say.

"Many Warriors will die if we do help," Slayer says. "We've already lost so many."

The wolf women stomp their feet in agreement.

"We wouldn't stand a chance," Apple says.

"I know McDonaldland is your enemy," I say, "but it is the lesser of two evils. If you help save McDonaldland then maybe they will return the favor. Perhaps they will give you food and supplies rather than the Outlanders."

Hyena steps forward and says in her cackling voice: "We are against everything the walled city stands for. They are an even bigger enemy than the Meat. I would love to see the city fall."

Several Warriors cheer her words.

"Just let the two armies destroy each other," Casper says in a croaking voice. "Then we can kill the leftover Meat while they're weak."

The wolf women clap their paws and stomp their feet. Grandma steps forward.

"Let's hear from the women who are indebted to these men," she says. Then she waves Talon forward. "What do you think we should do, Talon?"

Talon gives pause. "I am grateful that these men rescued us from imprisonment, but I would rather have died there than risk the lives of my sisters. We are just not ready to do battle with such a large force. We just barely survived the last attack."

Grandma rubs the hair on her chin.

"Nova," Grandma says. "What do you think?"

Nova creeps into the crowd from the background. She looks at me with cold eyes. Then she says, "We didn't ask to be rescued. We owe the men nothing."

Then she steps away.

Grandma looks at me, then looks at the crowd. "Is there anyone who thinks we should join this fight?"

Grandma scans the crowd. The wolf women look around to see if anyone thinks it would be a good idea. Only one woman steps forward. It is Pippi.

"I think we should go," Pippi says.

They all gawk at her, confused. Grandma asks her to explain.

Pippi says, "We're the Warriors of the Wild. We don't back down from fights."

Grandma says, "There's a fine line between bravery and foolishness."

"I'll kill Meat any chance I can get," Pippi says.

The other women don't seem swayed by Pippi's argument. Of all the women to come to my aid, it had to be Pippi. She's so unpopular with the other Warriors, especially now, that most of them would side against her just out of spite. I quickly realize there is no way I am going to be able convince them to fight for McDonaldland.

After the meeting concludes, I go to Nova and Talon.

"Why didn't you want to help?" I ask them. "McDonaldland might be a corrupt place, but it was your home."

"It doesn't concern us," Nova says.

I go to Talon. "Your husband and children live there. How could you do nothing to protect them?"

Talon turns and walks away. I follow.

"I know they are more important to you than anything," I tell her. "Are you really going to just sit back and let the Outlanders attack their home?"

She doesn't turn around.

Nova grabs me by the shoulder and says, "Daniel, stop."

"They could die," I say.

Talon keeps walking.

Nova pulls me away and looks at me.

"Don't!" she says.

"Why won't she listen to me?" I ask.

"Daniel," she says. "Her family is already dead."

Nova tells me what happened to Talon's family.

Two years ago, during a raid on the supply run between the Outlander facility and the southern community in Texas, the Warriors attacked a group of mutants. They were going after a tanker of gasoline. Talon, being the fierce and brutal warrior that she is, jumped into the back of an Outlander truck, swinging both axes at the men who were firing at her.

She didn't know that her husband and sons had been cast out of McDonaldland after contracting the parasite that caused them to grow multiple limbs. She didn't know that they had become soldiers in the Outlander army. She didn't even recognize her own sons, who had grown up to be young men, sitting in the back of the truck she was attacking.

Talon dropped into the backseat of the truck, hacked one mutant's head off, sliced another one in half, split one of their skulls open, and then drove her axe down into the driver's stomach. She didn't realize her sons were in the truck until the driver looked back at her.

Quivering and coughing up blood, the boy realized who his attacker was.

"Mom?" he said with a wheezing voice.

It was her youngest son. Only eight years old when she left the city, now he was a teenager. Before the boy lost control of the vehicle, Talon jumped into the driver seat next to him and pulled the truck over, leaving the battle.

Once on the side of the road, Talon noticed her oldest son's decapitated head in the seat next to her. She jerked her vision away from it to prevent herself from screaming. Her dying son wept as she held him in her arms tight to her chest, her axe still inside of his belly, her tears dripping onto his face. They didn't say anything to each other. He just glared up into her wolf-like eyes, two mutant arms holding her by the sleeves. As he died, Talon pressed her wet snout against his forehead and dug a fingernail under her own kneecap.

After the raid was over, Talon realized that her husband was also a part of the mutant group. He survived an arrow to the shoulder, and was taken prisoner by the Warriors. He became the property of a wolf woman named Baal, who had a severe grudge against Talon ever since she became leader of the Warrior Knights and Grandma's right hand soldier.

After being denied her promotion, Baal didn't feel she had a place among the Warriors anymore. She was interested in having sex until she turned, so that she could join her big sisters in the wild. When she captured her Meat during the raid, Baal only thought it was too perfect that the mutant had been her rival's husband.

Talon pleaded with her to let her husband go, she went to Grandma, she did all she could, but Baal would not let him go. One night, Talon went to her husband in the cage. He wanted to hold her, but she wouldn't let him. She told him what had happened to their sons. She said she killed them without even realizing it. When Talon tried to free her husband so that they could run away together, her husband wouldn't leave. He said he would rather die than go with her. Even if it was an accident, he could never forgive her.

Talon's husband didn't even look in his wife's direction as he was raped by Baal. He lay there until the Bitch turned and ripped him to shreds.

When Nova finishes telling me the story, she looks at me like I'm the biggest asshole in the world for bringing up her family to Talon. I just nod my head at her and wander away.

I go over to Guy, who is sitting by the fire with Ashley. His face displays complete annoyance as the little girl sleeps with her head in his lap.

"Is it true?" Guy asks. "Are the Outlanders really planning to attack McDonaldland?"

"At the end of the month," I say.

"After all we've done for them?" Guy says.

"The Mayor wants to be the ruler of McDonaldland, as he once was," I say.

Then Guy lowers his voice. "We have to go there and warn them about the attack."

"How?"

"We have to escape," he says. "There's no other way."

"When?"

"If they aren't attacking until the end of the month, then we have time," he says. "We'll have to wait until the moment is perfect. We have to make sure we will be able to escape no matter what."

Casper and Hyena come to our fire to warm themselves. Guy just nods at me to conclude our conversation. I don't think I want to leave the Warriors in order to warn McDonaldland of the attack. Because of my mutation, the Fry Guys probably won't even let me into the walled city. No, Guy is going to have to go by himself. I'm going to stay behind and see if I can't convince the Warriors to join the fight.

I search the camp for Nova, but she doesn't seem to be around. I don't have a place to sleep for the night and am wondering if she can put me up in her tent. Maybe she has extra blankets or a sleeping bag I can use. Maybe she will let me sleep with her.

After scouring every inch of the campsite, I figure she must be out in the woods somewhere. I decide to go out

and look for her. I'm probably not allowed to leave the camp unescorted, but nobody stops me when I go.

There's a lake a quarter mile outside of camp. When I come upon it, I see ripples on the moonlit water. A black form is swimming like a frog from bank to bank and back. I sit down and watch, focusing my eyes to see if it is Nova.

When the woman steps out of the lake, I realize it is Slayer. She is naked. Her wet fur is pressed flatly to her body so it doesn't appear that she is coated in fluffy fur at all. She has night-black skin with yellow eyes. The smell of wet dog fills the air as she crosses the beach. A bald naked man comes toward her. He wraps his four arms around her body and slicks his fingers through her wet fur. It is Ronald Krall.

They just hold each other in the light of the moon, rocking gently back and forth as if they are in a slow dance. Krall does not kiss her or try to seduce her into making love with him. He just gives her closeness and warmth. By the look in Slayer's eyes, this is something she has needed for a very long time.

When I go back to the camp, I decide to give up on finding Nova and sleep in the cage. I've grown used to sleeping on itchy dried weeds.

After falling into deep dreams with my face pressed against the bars, I awake to find a blanket wrapped around me. Somebody covered me with it while I was unconscious. It smells like an animal and is covered in red hairs, but it also has a nice perfumed scent that puts me quickly back into a comfortable sleep.

Chapter 16

Hyena

Days pass. Nova isn't speaking with me. She isn't speaking to anyone. I try to talk to her but she always just stares into the distance in the middle of our conversation and then shuts me out. Talon tells me that I just need to give her time.

I've been growing a yeast culture so that I can start making Wolf Juice as soon as possible. I'm hoping I'll become more accepted by the women once they try their first batch of the wine. The Warriors move camps every day. They have gone on one successful raid, but I didn't see any of the action. I ride with Guy and Ashley, in a truck near the back of the caravan, where none of the fighting ever takes place.

I haven't spoken with Krall in a while. He is usually with Slayer or with one of his patients, so I mostly just hang out with Guy and Ashley. Guy is usually in a bad mood.

Ashley is drawing a wolf in the dirt with a stick, as Guy and I sit by a campfire eating hamburger buns.

Guy looks at the drawing in the dirt.

"What is that supposed to be?" he says in a bothered tone.

Ashley looks up at him with her dirty face. "It's a wolf."

"Hmmm ..." Guy takes a closer look. "No, that doesn't look anything like a wolf."

Ashley scratches her neck awkwardly.

Guy sits down next to her. "If this is a wolf, then where are its ears?"

Ashley points to an "M" shaped scribble at the top

of the drawing.

"I thought that was a bow in its hair," Guy says. Then he points at the center of the drawing. "You have the nose all wrong, it's too thin. The eyes are also too high on its face. And why is its head so big compared to its body?"

"Guy!" I say. "She's just a kid."

"That's no excuse," Guy says. "If you don't point out a child's flaws to them then they will never improve."

He looks down at the girl. "Let me have your stick."

Ashley gives it to him.

"I'll show you how to draw a wolf," Guy says.

He pokes the stick into the mud and tries to draw a circle, it comes out crooked and warped. The tip breaks off.

"Hmmm ..." he says, examining the end of the stick. "This is not a good tool for drawing with. Wait here. I will find some proper art supplies."

Guy gets up and goes to the supply tent, leaving me with Ashley. I see him recruit Apple and a couple other women to dig through their boxes of supplies. When he returns, he has containers of Athena's old tattoo ink. Nobody claimed it after she died. He also has a pair of scissors, a straw, and a couple of empty cardboard boxes.

He sits down and cuts up the cardboard box into squares, then piles them up on the ground by his feet. Ashley goes to pick up one of the pieces of cardboard, and Guy pinches a lock of hair on the back of her head and snips it off with the scissors. The little girl jumps away from the cardboard and feels the back of her head.

Guy stuffs the straw with the lock of Ashley's hair, then he ties the end up tight with some thread from his blue suit, to keep the hair in place. When he looks up at his creation, I see he has just created a paintbrush.

"I guess you have some of grandpa in you, too," I say to Guy.

Guy doesn't comment on that. He opens the containers

of paint and puts a piece of cardboard on his lap.

"Now, pay attention," he tells Ashley. "I'm going to show you how to draw a *real* wolf."

On a stroll outside camp one day, I come across Nova climbing up a tree. She was always climbing up trees when we were young, but now she can get up the branches incredibly fast with her wolf-like body.

She sees me looking at her and invites me up. It takes me much longer to climb as high as she is, but I try to get up as quickly as I can. She doesn't help me when I get up there, just waits patiently on a branch.

"I've been worried about you," I tell her. "You keep avoiding me."

She turns to me and half-smiles. "I'm sorry. I didn't mean to make you feel abandoned."

She puts my hand in her lap.

"I've just been wanting to be alone lately," she says. "I was a different person before you arrived. I had forgotten about a lot of things."

She rests her head on my shoulder. "I'm remembering things. Some things I wish would have stayed forgotten. But there's a lot of good things I'm remembering that have made me happy, especially things about you. I used to have such a crush on you, but I didn't want anyone to know. We used to climb trees like this and just sit in them for hours. I think those were probably the best times of my life."

"I know they were my favorite times," I say. "Mc-Donaldland was a dreary, depressing place after you left."

I wrap two of my arms around her. The scabs on her shoulder are itchy against my skin.

"That night that we made love," Nova says. "Thanks for not letting us go all the way. I wanted to. More than

248

anything. I didn't care about what would happen to me."

"I felt guilty for rejecting you," I say. "I just figured it would have been better if we waited."

She nods. "It's difficult to resist the urge. When I see you walking around the camp, all I want to do is rip your clothes off. Sometimes I want to hurt you for making me feel this way, even though it's not your fault. That's one reason why I've been ignoring you. I'm worried that I won't be able to control myself."

"You're fine now," I tell her.

"I guess so," she says.

As we sit in the tree, holding each other, I notice somebody watching us from afar. It is Pippi, hiding in a tree across the clearing. She is looking at me with an angry red face, as if I've somehow betrayed her.

Nova kisses me on the cheek and then begins to climb out of the tree.

"Where are you going?" I ask.

"I need to get away from you for a while," she says. "I'm starting to get the urge again. We'll talk later."

Once she is on the ground, she cuts through the field, heading in the opposite direction of the camp.

When I climb out of the tree, Pippi comes up behind me and says, "You're not supposed to be out of the camp by yourself. Who knows what might happen to you."

I turn and face her. The scabby claw marks on her face have become black and infected.

"You have to walk back with me," she says.

I agree.

As we walk back, Pippi holds her belly and says, "I'm having a baby."

"What?" I ask.

"Grandma said so," she says.

"You're pregnant?"

She nods her head. "That bitch, Nova, almost caused me to lose it, though, when she cut me so deeply. I think she did it on purpose."

The thought of Pippi carrying my child makes me groan and rub my hands against my face.

"Are you sure you're pregnant? With my child?"

"I can feel it," she says. "I know it's true."

She gets in front of me, stopping me in my path.

"I want you to raise it with me," she says. "They say that in the walled city men and women raise their children together. We can do it, too. Out here in the wasteland."

"I didn't want to have a child with you," I say, backing away from her. "You forced me to have sex with you. You wanted to kill me. You refused to free me even after I helped save your life."

"That was before I became pregnant," she says.

"Pippi," I cross my four arms at her, "you're a self-centered, sadistic, evil Bitch, and I don't want to have anything to do with you."

When I say this, she leaps at me. She grabs me by the throat and lifts me off the ground.

"I can kill you in a second," she says, her red eyebrows curling at me with anger.

I look into her yellow eyes, holding her by her furry wrists.

"Fuck you," I croak out of my crushed larynx.

She squeezes tighter. Then tosses me to the ground.

"If it wasn't for Nova you would want to have this baby with me," she says.

"No, I wouldn't," I say.

"I can smell your body releasing sex hormones whenever I'm around you," she says. "I know your body likes me, even if you don't."

"Huh?" I don't know what the fuck she's talking about. "You're crazy."

"You're denying your instincts to be with me," she says.

I get to my feet and she pushes me back down.

"You're not meant to be with Nova," she says. "If I have to kill her to prove it to you, I will."

She smacks her tail in my face, as she turns to walk away.

Guy and Ashley are sitting by a camp fire, painting pictures with their new art supplies. I sit down next to them. I watch them draw for a while. Guy is painting a picture of a hamburger. He is careful to make sure every single detail is correct.

Guy was always the greatest art student when he was a kid. In art class, you are asked to draw something and are graded on how accurate to real life your drawing is. I didn't like art class. I've always loved to draw, but I like being creative and draw pictures from my imagination. You weren't allowed to use your imagination in art class in McDonaldland. You had to draw what you were told to draw.

When Guy is finished, he holds the image outward and nods proudly at his work.

"What is it?" Ashley says, examining the painting.

"Can't you tell?" Guy says. "It's a Big Mac."

"What's a Big Mac?" the girl asks.

"You've never had a Big Mac?" he asks. "It is only the greatest burger on the McDonald's menu."

"Oh," Ashley says, even though she doesn't have a

251

clue about what he's talking about.

"So, what are you drawing?" Guy asks the girl.

She shows him her picture. It is a painting of a man in a blue suit with blond hair. It is actually quite well done for such a young girl.

"Who is that supposed to be?" he asks.

"You," Ashley says.

"Me?" Guy asks. He takes the cardboard painting from her hand. "Well, I guess it does bear some resemblance to me, but you're missing the most important thing."

Ashley looks up at him. "What?"

Guy holds out his face toward her. Then he strokes his finger across the hair above his lip.

"My mustache, of course," he says.

"It's too hard to draw your mustache," she says.

"But my mustache is the most prominent part of my body," he says. "A drawing of me cannot be complete until the mustache is drawn perfectly."

He curls his mustache along his finger and the little girl laughs.

When Ashley goes back to her painting, I say to Guy, "I need to go into the woods to pick berries for the wine I'm supposed to make. Want to come with me?"

"Certainly," Guy says.

After he stands up, he looks back at Ashley,

"Now, before I get back," he says, "I want you to draw a mustache on my face. If it's not perfect I will have you draw ten more mustaches until you get it just right."

"No," she says. "I don't want to draw ten mustaches."

"Then paint it perfectly the first time," he says.

She nods her head and goes back to painting hands and shoes on the cardboard.

We can't go into the woods without an escort, so Hyena comes with us. I'm not sure what a berry bush looks like, but Grandma assured me they grow out here.

Hyena isn't wearing any clothing. She rarely does, except when she's on raids. Many of the wolf women seem to walk around topless, probably because their fur is too warm for clothes. While walking with her, I notice that the spots in her fur and the blackness of her face don't look to be naturally occurring. It is as if she has dyed her skin and hair to look this way. But her tail, it does look natural. It does look like the tails of hyenas I have seen in books. Perhaps it is possible that she is turning into a hyena. The only one of her kind.

Before she notices I am staring at her, I turn to my brother.

"She seems to have warmed up to you," I tell Guy.

When he gives me a confused face, I say, "Ashley."

"She's a satisfactory kid," Guy says.

"Is that a compliment or an insult?" I ask.

"It is not an insult," he says.

"You probably miss your family," I say.

He grunts in agreement at me, then goes silent for a while. Maybe half an hour passes.

When he breaks the silence, he says, "Molly's dying."

"What?" I ask.

He walks a ways before he explains, trying to get a bit ahead of Hyena so that she doesn't listen in.

"She was diagnosed earlier this year," he says. "Stage 4 Lymphatic Cancer. She has only months to live."

I've never liked Molly, but this is tragic news to me. Guy is never allowed to leave the wolf women. His wife is dying. What are to become of his children? What is to become of Guy knowing that his wife will die, leaving his children all alone? And with the attack on McDonaldland coming, I can see why Guy wants to escape and get back home as soon as possible.

I look at my brother with a sad, apologetic face, but when my eyes meet his I do not see sorrow. He is giving me a look of readiness. He wants us to use this moment to escape.

I look back at Hyena. Her rifle is hanging casually from her hands as she strolls behind us. Her eyes focused on June bugs and grasshoppers. Any type of movement instinctively grabs her attention. Guy waits until she turns her head, her eyes locked on a bumble bee flying over her head, then he kicks her gun out of her hands.

Before she can react, Guy has the rifle pointed at Hyena's gut. She sneers and foams at him. The look on Guy's face seems like he is about to shoot her. The look on Hyena's black face seems like she is trying to figure out a way to rip Guy's head off without being shot.

"He just wants to warn his people about the attack," I tell Hyena. "He doesn't want to shoot you."

She doesn't seem to care, and I'm not too sure Guy doesn't want to shoot her. We slowly back away. Hyena bends her spotted hyena legs, as if ready to pounce. Then my brother and I turn and run away.

Hyena doesn't just let us go. Once we are out of shooting range, she charges toward us. She gets down on all fours and runs like a cheetah, hopping through the air. Soon she is no longer moving on the ground but pouncing from tree to tree.

We run through the woods. Guy points the gun at the trees, as if ready to shoot Hyena if she gets too close.

"Don't shoot her," I say.

He grumbles at me and lowers his weapon.

Hyena disappears. We don't know where she went

until we see her jumping down from a tree ahead of us. She kicks Guy in the face with her clawed feet and he goes down, then retrieves her rifle and hits me in the stomach with the butt of the gun.

She puts her hyena foot onto Guy's chest, the sharpened toenails poking into the skin of his neck. She cackles at us, but doesn't say anything.

Then we hear screaming coming from the woods. Male screams. Hyena picks us off of the ground and then leads us at gunpoint toward the noise.

We hide behind some bushes and see two men running from a giant wolf. When they come into a better view, I realize that I recognize them. It is Robby and one of his Outlander friends from the facility.

The blonde wolf snatches Robby up by the leg and then thrashes him around, trying to break his neck. He shrieks and punches at the wolf's muzzle. As the wolf thrashes, Robby's leg rips off at the pelvis and his body flies over the trees. The wolf swallows his leg and then smells around for the rest of him. Before Robby can be found, the other Outlander catches the wolf's attention and it chases after him.

When we get to Robby's body, he is still alive. The ground is already covered in a pool of blood. He's just about bled to death already. I go to him, sit next to him.

"Daniel!" he cries.

"What happened?"

"The Mayor," he says, struggling to stay conscious. "He found out about our plan. Some of us escaped, but he had the rest of us killed. He's changed the date of the attack. He's attacking McDonaldland today."

Guy's eyes go wide at him.

"He also knows about the Bitches," he says. "He knows they're going to help protect McDonaldland, so he plans to attack them first. He plans to take out the Bitches, then attack McDonaldland."

"But I couldn't convince them to help," I tell him. "The Warriors never were going to join forces with the Fry Guys."

"It doesn't matter," Robby says. "The Outlanders are already on their way. They know where the Bitches' camp is. They'll be attacking any minute."

Before I can ask him anything else, he closes his eyes and his muscles relax. A deep breath escapes from his lungs as he dies. When I look up at Guy and Hyena, they nod their heads. Then we run back to the Warrior camp.

By the time we arrive, it's already too late. The camp looks like a tornado has passed through. We haven't even been gone an hour and the Outlanders have attacked, destroyed the wolf girl army, and moved on. Smoke billows out of burning vehicles and barbequed flesh.

Trees have fallen around the perimeter of the camp. Cars are turned over, smashed into the ground. Bodies litter the landscape. Not a single wolf girl was left standing.

"What could have done this?" Hyena says.

We go through the camp, checking the bodies for pulses. Nothing. The only one moving is Casper. One of her arms is missing. She crawls through the mud toward Grandma's body.

Guy goes straight to the spot where he left Ashley. She lies in the dirt, tattoo ink splattered on her dress, a bullet hole in her chest. She is not moving. The drawing of Guy is in her hands. She didn't even have time to draw the mustache on his face. When my brother sees her, he just stands above her, looking down. He picks up the cardboard drawing of himself and holds it in front of his face so that I don't see the tears.

Some wolf girls begin coming in from the woods, from all sides. A lot of them had escaped the carnage. Like us, there are some who have no idea what happened. When I see Nova, I go to her and wrap my arms around her. Apple and Pippi are the only other wolf girls I recognize.

Krall and Slayer are the last to arrive at the camp. They have smiles on their faces until they see the destruction. Slayer is stopped in her tracks at the sight of her dead friends, but Krall rushes forward to help the wounded. He goes to Casper and Grandma first. Grandma isn't breathing. A shotgun blast has torn her torso to a bloody pulp. Pippi, Nova, and several other wolf girls gather around her, all in complete disbelief. Even Pippi seems ready to weep.

Casper has her one arm wrapped around Grandma's body. She also tries to hug her with her stump, which is blackened as if she had cauterized it herself by sticking it inside of a fire pit after it was severed. Krall tries to give Casper medical attention, but the pierced wolf girl insists he go look after the other wounded.

Talon is found face down in the mud beneath a collapsed tent. She is unconscious, but still breathing. When Krall gets her to her feet, she doesn't seem to recall anything that happened. Krall checks to see if she has a concussion, but she seems to be okay. Hyena goes to her and fills her in on the situation.

The Warriors have been cut down to a third of their original number. Only a few dozen of them remain alive, and many of those are wounded. Some of them are in bad shape. Krall tries to save the ones in critical condition, but many of them are hopeless cases.

The wolf girls look at Talon for guidance. Their leader has fallen and now it is up to her to take her place. They gather around her. They are angry and distressed. They want vengeance.

"This will not go unpunished," Talon says to them. "The Meat must pay for what they have done!"

They stomp their feet and cheer.

"Who wants blood?" she cries to her sisters.

The Warriors raise their fists and bark.

"The Meat are on their way to attack the walled city as we speak," she says. "They think we're out of this fight. They won't even see us coming. Now, who wants to show the Meat how sharp our claws are?"

The Warriors shout and howl.

"We'll tear them apart!" Slayer yells.

"We'll feast on their bones!" Pippi cries.

The Warriors raise their weapons and bark.

"We go now!" Talon yells. "Leave the wounded and dead where they lie! Take only what you need to kill! We will not give up until we taste their blood in our teeth!"

Chapter 17

Hamburglar

The wolf women go for their weapons and check on their vehicles. Only five cars and two motorcycles are still operational. Pippi and Slayer take the bikes. Nova and Apple take one of the vehicles.

Casper refuses to stay with the wounded. She can no longer ride a bike properly with her one arm, so she gets into the back of Apple's vehicle with Nova.

Krall tells Casper, "You can't fight in your condition."

She just sneers at him and says, "There's no way I'm backing out of this." Then she takes her seat next to Nova on the roof of the car.

Slayer pulls her bike up next to Krall.

"You coming?" she asks.

"No," Krall responds. "I've got work to do here."

She rides off.

"She could have at least said goodbye or something," I say to Krall.

"That's the way she is," Krall tells me with a smile, before walking off to the wounded.

Guy takes a shotgun from a fallen Warrior and gets into the back of a truck. At first, the wolf girls in the truck sneer at him. He is not permitted to fight.

"You need all the help you can get," Guy says, the look on his face is just as vengeful as any of the women's.

They don't argue with him.

Following Guy's lead, I take a machine gun and some ammo from the dead and go to Nova's vehicle.

"I'm coming with you," I say to her.

"Stay here," Nova says.

I get into the car anyway, riding shotgun next to Apple. Nova peeks her head down from the roof into my window at me.

"You're just going to be a liability," she says to me.

"If I die I'd rather it be with you," I say.

Then I kiss her upside-down mouth. She accepts the kiss passionately and doesn't seem like she wants to stop. We continue until Talon peeks her head in at Apple.

"Slayer is going to lead the attack," Talon says. "I'll be getting recruits and will meet up with you shortly."

The girls nod at her.

Then the small motorcade rides off, toward the walled city, ready to do battle.

The sun is high in the sky as we hit the road leading to McDonaldland. I can hear Casper and Nova moving around on the roof of the car. There is a small platform up there with a spiked railing around it to keep them from falling off the top. Within the cab, I am alone with Apple. Her yellow Asian eyes focused on the road, getting herself emotionally prepared for what is to come.

To break the awkward silence, I ask, "Why do they call you Apple?"

She looks at me, then looks back at the road.

"I can shoot an apple off of a man's head from a hundred yards away."

"Really?" I ask.

"No." She smiles. "I just really like apples."

I am about to laugh, but hold my smile as I see Pippi riding up alongside the vehicle to stare me down. She is juggling a throwing knife in one free hand, looking up at Nova and then down at me. It's like she is threatening to put the knife into November's head.

"You should be riding with me," Pippi yells.

I break eye contact with her and stare forward. She continues eyeing me until the road thins out and she slows down to bring up the rear of the group.

When we get to the great wall of McDonaldland, the fight between mutants and Fry Guys has already begun. Machinegun fire can be heard echoing through the valley, as hundreds of men scramble on the battlefield near the gates. Dozens of vehicles collide. Red, yellow, and blue suited men fall below the feet of multi-limbed mutants. And in the center of it all, there is an enormous beast with eight limbs nearly as high as the great city wall.

"What the fuck is that?" Apple says when she sees the creature.

It's Kroger the Mighty, the multi-limbed hermaphroditic gargantuan wolf. And riding on top of the beast, I see the giant hamburger head of Mayor McCheese.

The Mayor is riding the creature like an ant on a horse, directing it to tear down the city wall. The Fry Guys are already losing the fight. Whichever men are not taken down by mutants disappear within the massive jaws of Kroger the Mighty.

The great beast slashes at the great wall with its many claws. Although the wall is made of steel, it is able to create large dents and claw marks. The Mayor commands it to crush its weight down on the wall in an attempt to bring it down.

Slayer, on her motorcycle at the head of the pack, raises her weapon. The Warriors get into formation and charge straight into the skirmish, before the mutants notice what is coming up from behind.

The Warriors cut down the mutants that get in their way. With their attention on the Fry Guys, several Outlanders fall before they even realize the small army is attacking at their rear.

Slayer acts as a perfect spearhead. She guns down every mutant in her path, and takes down every Fry Guy as well. Her black fur ruffling in the wind quickly becomes sticky with blood.

As our vehicle enters the combat, Nova takes down mutants with her crossbow and Casper decapitates passing Fry Guys with her saw-toothed sword. I point my gun out the window and fire randomly at the crowd. My stomach becomes queasy as I see the mutants fall. I know some of them are just normal people, like myself, who had become victims of the parasite. Many of them probably don't even want to fight. Perhaps they only do so for fear of what the Mayor might do to them if they disobey.

Pippi speeds past us from behind, throwing knives into two mutants at once. A big smile is on her face. She has never been in a battle this size before, and she seems to be loving every second of it so far.

Ahead, I see Guy firing his shotgun at mutants. Hyena and three other wolf girls are in the back of the truck with him, firing on the Outlanders. None of them in that truck appear to be targeting Fry Guys, as if they do so out of respect for my brother.

Of the Outlanders, I recognize the bald mutant, Captain Kongun, leading the foot soldiers. He has pistols in all six of his hands. Since he has two arms on his chest and two arms on his back, he is able to fire in all directions at once. As of now, he is only fighting the Fry Guys, but once he comes after the Warriors he will be a lethal opponent.

Not long into the battle, Talon comes down from the hills. She is riding atop the giant black alpha wolf toward the gates of McDonaldland. Behind her, a pack of wolves two dozen strong follow suit. They come in all sizes, from those which are as big as cars to those which are as large as buses.

They swoop down the hillside and dive into the battle, flipping mutant trucks and cars. As Talon reaches the center of the field, she leaps from the black wolf and lands in the back of a mutant truck. Swinging both axes, she chops men so powerfully that their limp bodies fly into the air and down under the wheels of passing vehicles.

Many of the wolves go straight for Kroger. They leap up and bite at its many legs, snapping at it like piranhas. When the black wolf digs its fangs deep into one of Kroger's

thighs, the massive beast shrieks and topples downward. It only falls to a seated position, but it still crushes two mutant trucks and one Warrior vehicle as it lands.

With the giant wolves on our side, the Warriors quickly gain the upper hand in the battle. Many of the mutants don't even stand to fight the beasts, they just turn and run away.

As we drive through the chaos, I watch as a brown wolf bites a mutant in half, his four legs still keeping the rest of his body standing upright. Then I see a great blonde wolf, raping a man in the bed of an Outlander truck, with the entire vehicle crushed under the monster's belly.

Outside the window, I watch Pippi as she squeals with joy. She rides her motorcycle under a wolf's legs, then fires her gun into a wounded mutant trying to crawl to safety under an abandoned truck.

The great wall has cracked open a little, but not enough for it to fall. After noticing that the tides of the war have changed, the Mayor directs Kroger away from the wall toward the battle. He points the mammoth at the female wolves, which are mere rabbits in comparison to Kroger. And like a rabbit, Kroger snatches one up in its enormous jaws and thrashes it until its neck breaks. Then the creature goes for another one.

I see a Warrior vehicle ahead burst into flames as it is hit with a Molotov cocktail. It crashes into an abandoned Fry Guy van and explodes. Another Warrior vehicle loses both its gunners, with only a spear-wielding woman left to joust the mutants they pass.

After Kroger kills a third wolf, the smaller beasts back away, growling. The Mayor has the hermaphrodite wolf charge the wolves and the Warriors, to take them down as quickly as possible so that he can get back to tearing down the wall.

We drive in circles around the battlefield, steering clear of the big sisters, taking out mutant after mutant. Nova must be running low on arrows, because she fires only when an enemy is close and she is guaranteed a hit. Casper is malicious with her strikes. All I see is her long saw-like sword come swinging down next to my open window, shredding the men into pieces as we drive by.

Apple focuses on driving, but she also fires a pistol into men whenever she gets a chance or whenever they get too close to her side of the vehicle. I focus on shooting the men in the distance, to weaken the numbers of the group before we get to them.

We pass Talon as we drive. She is standing atop a truck that is turned on its side, pulling an axe out of the driver's giant mutant head. When she notices what has happened to the wolves that she led into battle, she turns her attention to Kroger and Mayor McCheese.

She raises both axes out to her sides and howls. As the hermaphrodite beast charges at the black alpha wolf, Talon runs through the battlefield toward it. The black wolf holds its ground, snarling up at the massive creature. Talon hops high into the air and lands on the black wolf's back.

As Kroger comes forward, Talon runs through the black wolf's fur. She leaps off the alpha's forehead just as Kroger opens its massive jaws, and her axe lands square in the nose of the beast.

Like a mere bug hanging from Kroger's snout, Talon chops at the creature's lips and nostrils. The hermaphrodite backs up, shaking its head in pain, as if it is being stung repeatedly by wasps. The black wolf comes at

Kroger and bites its leg.

Talon continues to chop with her free axe. Kroger kicks the alpha wolf away from it with one of its spare legs, then turns its attention to the irritant on the tip of its nose.

I see Talon looking up at Mayor McCheese, and the Mayor looking down at her. She holds her axe back, aiming it at the man's head. But before she throws, Kroger jerks her off of his snout and then snatches her in the air. In just a single gulp, Talon is gone.

Without their leader, the wolf girls panic. If any of them were to call a retreat it would be Slayer, but she is far ahead of the rest of the group, fighting the Outlanders all by herself.

I load another clip into my gun and continue firing. I realize that most of the Fry Guys have retreated. Many of the mutants are dead, but they are now the dominant force on the battlefield.

From behind, I notice the Warrior truck is no longer moving. It must have tried to retreat, because it is facing away from the battle. They didn't seem to make it far before the driver died.

Guy and Hyena are standing back to back in the bed of the truck, firing their guns into the mutants coming at them. The other three wolf girls in the back are either wounded or dead. As Apple curves toward the gate of McDonaldland, I lose sight of the truck, not sure of the fate of my brother or Hyena.

I suddenly realize our vehicle is the only one left moving. The Fry Guy vehicles were destroyed by the mutants, the mutant vehicles were torn apart by the wolves, and all the rest of the Warrior vehicles are either crashed or out of sight.

Mutants surround us on all sides. They are all on foot and do not fight with guns, but they outnumber us ten to one.

We head toward a group of yellow Fry Guys who are backed against the gate, hoping to join forces with them. But before we make it, a pair of massive legs land in our path. The vehicle crashes into the boulder-sized paw and Apple's face slams into the windshield, knocking her unconscious. Nova flies over the hood and lands inches away from the mammoth's toes.

I get out of the vehicle and run toward Nova. I pull her away as the feet continue to move onward. Another foot kicks the vehicle, flipping it into the air, as Kroger walks toward the gate. I see Casper leaping off of the vehicle as it rolls. The car tumbles, with Apple's unconscious body flopping around inside.

The mutants close in. I stand my ground, protecting my Novey. The Outlanders glare at me, yelling with anger, like I'm a traitor. They threaten to rip me limb from limb. Then I open fire on them, taking a line of them down.

Casper doesn't come to us. Instead, she stays by the vehicle, guarding Apple. The mutants quickly surround her. The weapon she fights with is large enough that she probably needs to use two hands, but with her missing arm this is impossible. She is strong enough to use this large weapon with only one hand, but her strength is wearing thin. Her swings are sluggish as she strikes the mutants. She cuts one in half as she falls to her knees, breathing heavily. Then she leaps up and slashes one through the neck, his head falling backwards like a removed hood.

I fire on mutants and accidentally hit Kroger in the leg. The beast roars and lifts its limb like a thorn is in its paw. I slap gently on Nova's cheek, trying to wake her up. Her crossbow is broken next to her, so she only has her sword left to protect herself.

When I run out of bullets, I switch to the last clip and continue to fire. But this clip must not have been full, because it runs out after I take down only two more mutants.

I look at Casper. She drives her sword deep into a mutant's stomach. So deep that it hits the ground behind him. As she tries to pull the long saw-toothed sword out of the man's gut, another mutant stabs a stake into her back. She catches him with her armpit and breaks his neck with only her stump. After pulling the stake out of her back ribs, she retrieves her sword from the hunk of dead flesh and then falls over. The mutants bear down on her. She slashes her enormous sword at their legs, cutting through all five ankles of the two closest mutants. They go down, screaming in her face.

I don't have any bullets left to back her up, so I just watch as they stab spears and axes down into her. They stab repeatedly, just to make sure she is dead. Then they come for me.

Standing beneath the legs of the massive Kroger, hiding in its shadow, I try to calm myself as the mutants surround us. The only weapon left nearby is Nova's sickle-shaped sword. I pull it from the belt on her waist, and point it at the Outlanders as they approach me. There are seven of them, and only one of me. My only hope is that they will move on after they kill me and assume Nova is already dead.

Before they get to me, someone hollers behind them. The group of mutants stop their pursuit and look back.

"He's mine," says the gurgling cartoonish voice.

The mutants separate and I see who is speaking. It is the Hamburglar. He steps forward with his black cape and black mask, two katana swords (one short and one long) are sheathed at his waist. With most of his enemies dead on the battlefield, he needs an opponent to play with. He has chosen me.

I run at him with the sickle-sword. In an instant, he draws his short katana, blocks my attack, slices my ass as I pass him, then re-sheaths the sword. Just like a master samurai would do. The Hamburglar bows at me, and then giggles like a cartoon bunny. His bulbous face pulses as he licks his teeth. His mouth in a permanent, creepy smile.

This time I wait for him to attack. He inches sideways toward me, and then whips out the long-bladed katana for just an instant. I try to hook my sickle-sword onto his blade to flick it out of his hand, but I miss. He spins around, his cape flashing into my face, and cuts me across the bridge of my nose. Then he re-sheathes his sword.

"You fucking freak," I say to him, blood trickling down my cheeks.

His large head wobbles at me.

I strike again, using all my weight in this attack. He draws a katana, catches the hook of my sword, and it flies out of my hand. He spins and trips me into the dirt. Then he re-sheathes his sword.

"You're no fun," the Hamburglar says, peering down at me with his cartoon eyes.

As he drives the sword down toward my body, a black form flies across my vision, hitting him in the side of the face, throwing him back. It's Nova.

When the other mutants see Nova, they come at her. Unarmed, she kicks one of them in the face, breaking his neck backwards, and punches another so hard in the chest that blood explodes from the sides of his ribs. Claiming this mutant's spear, she turns to three more mutants coming at her. Using the spear like a pool cue, she pierces through the defenses of three mutants. It happens so fast that it looks as if she fired crossbow arrows at them from a machinegun. She swings the spear over her head, cutting another mutant's throat on the way up, and then slashes down on the final mutant through the skull. Only the Hamburglar remains.

The Hamburglar seems impressed with Nova's fighting skills. He bows at her. She gets between him and I, guarding me from the cartoonish mutant. Hamburglar whips out both of his katana and poses in a ninja-like stance, his black cape and red tie blowing in the wind.

Then she charges him with the spear. He twirls his long katana, knocking the blade of her spear back, but she only flips it around and slices at his jugular. He bends back, dodging the tip of the spearhead by centimeters, then he swings the short katana at her. She thrusts her chest outward to block it with a long spike from her metal bikini.

When they separate, Hamburglar rushes her, spinning his katana at her one at a time. She does backflips to avoid him, blocking his attacks with the spear as she flips. He continues rushing forward to slice at her, as she continues backflipping. Then she twists to the side and lunges the spear toward his crotch.

271

Hamburglar cuts the spear in half with his short katana, then swings the other at her face. Instead of blocking, Nova throws the bottom of the spear shaft. It whacks him across the face and he stumbles back.

Nova goes for the saw-toothed sword by Casper's body. The Hamburglar charges her. The enormous saw-toothed sword looks twice the size of Nova's body as she picks it up and swings it at the big-headed freak. He jumps five feet into the air to dodge the attack, giggling with excitement.

As Kroger shifts above us, he blocks out the light, encasing the Hamburglar in shadow. He backs away. Nova swings the sword around her head like a slow deadly windmill and steps toward him. The Hamburglar runs to the side, ducking behind a crushed mutant truck as the sword swoops toward him. The saw-toothed sword cuts the truck's bumper clear in half. Then Nova leaps over the vehicle, flipping through the air with long sword coming down at the Hamburglar's big head like a guillotine.

The Hamburglar blocks with his long katana, but the saw-toothed sword just breaks through it. The sword cuts off the top of his nose and then lands in his shoulder. The Hamburglar does not cry out. He does not even react as if something painful has just happened to him. He just stands there, glaring at Nova with his crooked grin.

With the sword stuck inside of the Hamburglar's shoulder, Nova is defenseless. The Hamburglar throws his short katana at her. She lets go of the sword and jumps back to dodge the blade. It still slices across her stomach as it whizzes by. She cries out and falls to her knees. I run toward her, but she holds her hand out to keep me back.

Hamburglar attempts to free the saw-toothed sword from his shoulder, but it won't budge. He tries walking toward Nova, to finish her off, but the weight of the dragging sword keeps him from moving fast.

Nova stares him in his googley cartoon eyes. He stares

back in her yellow wolf eyes. Then he curls his fingers into a fist, roars, then punches the blade in half. With the top of the sword still stuck inside of him, he retrieves the lower half of the sword. He staggers over to Nova and looms down on her.

"Robble-robble!" the Hamburglar says, as he raises the sword over his head.

A bullet hits Hamburglar in the face. Blood leaks down the curves of his globular head and then he collapses next to November.

I turn and see Pippi, driving her motorcycle up to me, lowering her machinegun down to her handlebar. She gives me a smile.

"I told you that you should have rode with me," Pippi says.

Then she sticks out her tongue and rides away.

I retrieve the sickle-sword and go to Nova. I kneel, holding her wound to stop the bleeding.

"We're still alive," she says, and smiles.

Then I kiss her. We gaze into each other's eyes.

When I let go of her, she looks over my shoulder at something coming toward us. Her face becomes panicked. The next thing I know I'm being lifted into the air, Nova still on the ground looking up at me, stretching her arms out to grab me.

I don't know what is happening until I feel the wet tongue under my hands and the teeth closing around me. I'm inside of Kroger's mouth. When the teeth close, I feel a contraction of wet flesh around me and then I slide down the creature's throat.

Chapter 18

Captain Kongun

I'm surprised to see light within the beast's belly. The light appears to be coming from a Fry Guy flashlight. There is movement everywhere. Some of the movement comes from the flesh walls rippling around me. Other movement comes from the people who are trapped inside of this stomach with me. There is a moaning sound coming from the other side of the cavity.

Kroger is the size of an apartment building, and so his stomach is about the size of an apartment. I'm sitting on something meaty and don't realize what it is until a splash of light fills my area. Below me is a pile of half-digested Fry Guys. Most of them are in pieces. I crawl across the bodies toward the light.

I'm bounced and thrown about as I travel, probably from Kroger running and jumping through the battlefield outside. Limbs move around me as I inch forward. Even though it looks as if these people are still alive, it is actually the stomach muscles shifting them around that are making them appear that way. But I do hear the moaning of at least one person, a male, so I head in his direction.

When I arrive, I see a Fry Guy in a blue uniform with red stripes on his arm. It is the Chief, Duncan Charles, Nova's father. He must have been swallowed by Kroger a while ago, before the Warriors arrived. Beyond him, I hear a whacking sound, coming from the other side of the light. When I crawl closer, I see that it is Talon. She is still alive, attempting to chop her way out of the beast's belly.

"Talon?" I say.

She looks back at me. Then gets back to work. I notice

the flashlight is stuck inside of the guts of a dead Fry Guy near her, pointed upwards to illuminate the cavity. Before I can crawl past the Chief to get to Talon, he grabs me by the arm.

"Help me," he says.

I try to jerk his hand off of me, but he holds onto it like a death grip.

"You're that Togg boy," he says to me. "November's boyfriend."

"Yeah," I say.

"You have to get me out of here," he says. "The Mayor betrayed me. McDonaldland must be saved."

"There's no way I would help you," I say.

"Why not? I am the Chief of the Fry Guys. McDonaldland needs me."

"I know what you did," I tell him. "You were the one who raped Nova, you sick son of a bitch. You had sex with your own daughter and got her thrown out into the wasteland."

He shakes his head at me.

"You don't understand," he says.

"What's there to understand, you fucking pervert?"

"I did it to keep order."

He goes on to explain how the citizens of McDonaldland were angry that their daughters were being sent into the wild after they were being raped. They didn't think it was fair. The Chief promised it was for the good of the community, but they didn't believe him. So he raped his own daughter, claimed it was an unknown assailant, and had her removed from the city. He did all of this to prove that he was willing to make the sacrifice himself, so the citizens should, too.

"That's why you did it?" I yell. "You think that justifies what you did?"

"It had to be done," he says. "Keeping order in McDonaldland is more important than my daughter, and I

276

was right. After she was removed from the city, none of the people ever complained about the policy ever again."

"Why didn't you just change the fucking policy?" I ask. "You should have made exceptions for the girls who were raped."

"But if we made exceptions then people would have sex illegally all the time. All they would have to do was claim they had been raped. I made the best choice available to me."

I rip his hand away from me and back up.

"I loved my daughter," he says. "Raping her for the sake of the people was the hardest choice I have ever made. It haunts me to this day."

An axe lands in his chest. He wheezes and gags before he dies. I look up at Talon.

"You're wasting oxygen," she says. "Help me get us out of here."

I crawl to the hole she has created. She has already cut her way down through the stomach and much of the muscle. We just need to get through the hide.

She hacks with her axes, one at a time. I use the sickle sword to slice at the hole above where Talon hacks. I notice her skin is bright red, like a sunburn. But it is the stomach acid that has caused the redness.

When a slit of light shines through, I know we're home free. I take the sickle and hook it on the outside of the cut, then saw upwards. Talon hacks downwards. Once the wound is open wide enough, Talon tells me to grab onto her back, then she crawls out of the stomach into the open air.

Talon hangs on to the beast's fur as we dangle in midair. I

WARRIOR WOLF WOMEN OF THE WASTELAND

have all four of my arms locked around her. Then she begins climbing up the wolf's coat, toward the top of its back.

When I look around, I see that Kroger has made it past the wall and is now inside of McDonaldland. Below, the battle has also moved into McDonaldland. Fry Guys and citizens of the city take up arms against the mutants. There are also some wolf girls in the fight. Slayer is still on top of her bike, shooting at mutants with a rifle she must have gotten from one of her dead enemies. I also see my brother, Guy, leading a group of Fry Guys against mutant soldiers led by Captain Kongun.

Kroger rampages through the city. Buildings collapse under its eight mighty legs. Talon holds on tight as the structures explode below us, but I nearly lose my grip. If I had only two arms I probably would have fallen to my death just now.

When she reaches the top, we see Mayor McCheese at the head of the hermaphrodite wolf. He is standing near a control platform. A section of the top of Kroger's skull has been removed. Part of its brain is showing, with a large computer board imbedded into the neural tissue.

Talon removes my hands from her torso, then charges across the wolf's back. I follow her, my sword raised high. As we get to the Mayor, he turns around and points one of his shotguns at us. Before he can fire a blast, Talon kicks him in his hamburger face and he goes flying off of the wolf's back to the street below.

Looking down, I see the body of Mayor McCheese on the ground. He jumps instantly to his feet; his enormous head must be cushy enough to protect his brain within. Although he moves with a severe limp, he's able to go right back to fighting, firing his shotgun into the yellow dresses and red suits of the McDonaldland citizens.

Then I see Captain Kongun looking up at me. He sees the Mayor on the ground and sees Talon trying to take over Kroger's controls. He drops his pistols and runs toward one of the beast's legs, leaping at its foot, and then climbing the hair toward us.

I look back at Talon. She can't figure out the controls. She puts her hand down on the wolf's neck and tries to communicate with it in the way that she can communicate with the female wolves. But Kroger remains out of control.

Kongun crawls up the beast like a spider. When he gets up onto the back of the creature, I yell at Talon that we have company. She steps away from the controls.

As she passes me, her axes swinging by her legs, she says, "Figure out a way to stop this thing. I'll take care of this Meat."

While I step carefully to the wolf's head, I look back, watching Talon as she raises her axes to fight.

Captain Kongun pulls the holster from his back containing the row of chainsaws. He shoves each of his hands into the backs of each of the chainsaws, until I can no longer see a single one of his six hands. I only see six chainsaws attached to his wrists.

He lifts his six arms up and when he bends them at the elbow, all six of the saws turn on. They buzz loudly at Talon as she circles him.

She makes the first move, attacking with one of her axes. He blocks with a chainsaw, and she strikes with the other axe. He blocks that, then swings a third chainsaw at her ribs. With her lightning reflexes, she leaps back just in time.

Kongun smiles. "You Bitches might be fast, but you're not fast enough."

He raises all six of his chainsaws out, pointing them in all directions. From above, he must look like an asterisk. Then he spins toward her, the chainsaws moving like helicopter blades. She hacks down at his waist, but Kongun just needs to bend one elbow to block it, leaving her head open to his whirlwind chainsaw attack. She ducks just in time, but loses a braided lock of hair.

"Take this thing down," Talon yells at me, as she notices I'm not doing my job.

I look away to figure out the controls on this beast. It is only a computer keyboard with some levers and switches. I move some levers, but it doesn't seem to do any good. The beast continues rampaging the city no matter what I press.

Looking back, the two fight like clashing cyclones. Kongun moves like a spider, striking and spinning with his many arms. Talon, with her two axes and quick reflexes, is able to block and counter every assault.

I rip the keyboard out and toss it over the side of the wolf's neck. If I'm not able to control him at least nobody else will be. I go to the brain of the wolf and rip out the computer board, wires slip out of its wet flesh, blood gushes out of the holes. Grandpa told me that the brain might be the nerve center of a living being, but much of it doesn't actually feel much pain. With this in mind, I strike at the creature's neural tissue using the sickle-sword. If it can't feel it then hopefully it won't jerk me off of its back. As I cut, I look back to Talon and Kongun.

Kongun has the upper hand. He has too many arms for Talon to avoid. Even if she gets behind him, he is somehow able to block her strikes blindly with the arms on his back. As soon as the Captain finally cuts her, right along the side of her torso, he smiles. Then unleashes a battery of attacks, spinning and slicing in multiple directions. He forces Talon up against the edge of the wolf's back.

Talon drops down into the fur and, with both of her feet, kicks him in his belly. He stumbles backwards, his arms twirling chaotically to catch his balance. Talon swings at his chest, but he is able to block even when off balance. She hooks his wrist behind the chainsaw with the axe head, and pulls down. The chainsaw cuts down on one of the limbs on his chest, amputating it down the middle. The severed chainsaw arm falls and lands by his foot. As Kongun screams, he steps too close to the chainsaw buzzing at his feet, and it cuts through his ankle.

He falls back. Before he hits the fur, Talon brings an axe down into his forehead. He dies instantly, but doesn't fall. The axe is so deep in his skull that he hangs in midair.

His chainsaw arms dangle, and as his face slides off of the blade of the axe, four of the buzzing saws cut into the flesh of the hermaphrodite mammoth.

The beast roars below us and shakes its hide, trying to fling us off. I grab onto the edge of Kroger's skull cap, as Talon hangs onto the fur.

Talon kicks Kongun's body off of the wolf's back, and the creature stops shaking. She gets to her feet and rushes to help me. Together, we chop and slice the beast's brain until its mind finally shuts off. It lets out a whimper and comes crashing down onto a small McDonald's restaurant.

Before we hit the ground, Talon grabs me and leaps from the wolf's back. We land safely away, in a field, surrounded by nu-cows that slither around us like a herd of snails.

When we get back to the fight, there is only one enemy left standing. It is Mayor McCheese. He fires his shotguns at the crowd as they circle him. There are Fry Guys, McDonaldland citizens, wolf girls, and even other mutants, who all want a piece of him. He shouts at them, limping with a broken leg as he fires. Even after he blows a hole through a yellow Fry Guy's chest, they keep coming.

Guy steps out of the crowd and shoots him in the back with a handgun. The Mayor staggers forward. Then he whips around to aim his shotgun at my brother, but before it is fired Guy shoots him in the chest. The Mayor drops his weapon.

Another mutant shoots him. Then Pippi fires a burst of

machinegun bullets into his stomach. He refuses to go down. He picks up a sledge hammer by his feet and limps across the sidewalk. A long tongue dangles from his hamburger bun mouth. As he raises it over his head, Slayer shoots him though a pickle on his face. The Mayor drops the sledgehammer. He drops to his knees.

Then, the citizens and ex-citizens of McDonaldland, with knives and spears and axes, take apart the Mayor's giant hamburger head, to get to the small human brain buried within.

Chapter 19

Apple

After it's all over, the surviving Fry Guys point their weapons at the wolf girls and rebel mutants. The McDonaldland citizens back away.

As she looks down at the barrel of a gun, Talon says, "We just saved your shitty town. The least you could do is let us leave in peace."

The Fry Guys hold their ground. There are about a dozen of them. Most of them are young yellow Fry Guys, just out of training. Blood and charcoal is caked to their skin as they stare down the mutants and wolf girls with crazed looks in their eyes. There are only three mutants and, of the Warriors, only Talon, Pippi, Slayer, and two others remain.

Guy, the only blue-suited Fry Guy in the vicinity, steps forward. He walks into the center of the face-off, standing in Mayor McCheese's head mush. He faces the Fry Guys.

"Lower your weapons," he orders the yellow Fry Guys.

They don't lower their weapons. Too combat-shocked to even comprehend language. Guy has to lower some of their guns for them. The rest follow suit. The mutants and wolf girls lower their weapons as well.

"What is going on around here?" yells a voice from the back of the crowd.

When we turn around, we see five old men in black business suits with red and yellow ties coming down the street toward us with a group of red Fry Guys. I've never seen any of them before, but they appear to be some of the executives of The Blessed McDonald's Corporation. They are in good shape for McDonaldland citizens and I'm surprised how old they are. Even my grandfather never looked that old.

When they arrive, the red Fry Guys immediately separate the citizens from the rest of us. They push them back as far as they can, and surround us as if we are prisoners, including my brother.

"Who's in charge here?" asks the leader of the group, a man with white pointy eyebrows.

Guy steps forward. "I'm Guy Togg, First Lieutenant of the Fry Guy Force."

"Where's Chief Charles?" they ask.

"Dead," I say.

The executive glares at me. When he sees my extra limbs, a look of disgust crosses his face.

"What are these people doing here?" he says, staring down all of the outsiders. "They must be evacuated immediately."

"They helped save the city," Guy says.

"Yes, well that was quite decent of them," says the executive with the white pointy eyebrows, "but we certainly can't allow them to stay, now can we?"

Guy just smoothes his mustache at him.

"I don't have time for this," says the executive. "Corporate Headquarters has been destroyed. The CEO is dead." He sticks his finger in Fry's chest. "As the highest ranking officer, I'm putting you in charge of this. Get these people out of here and barricade the hole in the wall before any more of those wolves get in here."

As he walks away, he looks up at the giant body of Kroger in the middle of the city. He points up at the dead wolf, and says, "And get rid of that thing, too."

Guy salutes them. Then he orders a red Fry Guy to oversee the reconstruction of the city gate and another one to oversee the removal of Kroger. When both Fry Guys look at him as if he is crazy for giving them such enormous tasks after such a grueling battle, he tells them, "You're Fry Guys. You'll figure it out."

As my brother escorts us out of town, passing through my old neighborhood, now in ruins, Pippi walks alongside me with a smile on her face. Killing so many people was like the best sex she has ever experienced in her life. She is so satisfied with her experience that she is glowing.

"Look what I got," Pippi says to me.

She digs in her pocket and pulls out five human eyeballs, each one of them from a unique person. She shows them to me like an excited little boy showing his parents his bug collection.

"You should have gotten one of the Mayor's eyes," I tell her. "Did you see how big they were?"

She grumbles at me and puts the eyes back in her pocket. "These are better," she says.

We walk a ways further in silence. Pippi is practically skipping down the road, smiling at all the destruction like she's a kid looking at toys in a McToy store. She's never been within McDonaldland before, but she seems more excited by the wreckage than the wonders of the civilization.

She turns to me and says, "Nova's going to flip when she sees you're still alive."

My eyes light up. "She's okay?"

She nods. "Yeah, the coward stayed back with the wounded. She says you got gobbled up by that Biggie." She points at Kroger's corpse sticking out from the buildings behind us. "I'm impressed that you and Talon cut your way out of there. I didn't know it was possible."

I nod my head and stop listening to her, impatient to see Nova again. She's going to be so excited to see me.

Outside of McDonaldland, I scan the landscape for my Novey. There are bodies and smoking vehicles covering the battlefield. I see Fry Guys walking through the wreckage, looking for survivors. In the distance, the wounded mutants are driving away in smashed up vehicles that are so damaged they can hardly move.

Then I see a handful of wolf girls by the remains of a truck. I recognize Hyena and Apple. They are sitting in the back of the pickup, licking their wounds and smoking McCigarettes they must have scavenged from Fry Guy bodies. I see Nova's back, covered in so much dirt that I can't make out the strip of fur that goes down her spine. She is tending to one of the fallen Warriors, tying a splint onto her broken leg.

When she turns around, her eyes lock with mine and her mouth drops open with shock. I run up to her and give her a hug.

"You're alive?" she says.

She probably can't tell if she is dreaming or awake.

"I saw you eaten," she says.

I point at Talon. "We escaped."

"Talon's alive, too?"

"We took down Kroger and Mayor McCheese," I say. "We won."

Nova wraps her arms around me and I kiss her cheek.

"I have to help my sisters," she tells me. "But I'm glad you're okay."

I nod at her.

When she's done with the wounded, Nova wanders off. I follow after her.

"Where are you going?" I ask.

287

"To look for my father," she says. "I have some un-finished business with him."

Then she walks away.

"Nova," I say.

She keeps walking.

I run after her and grab her by the arms.

"Nova, he's dead," I say.

"What?" Her eyes widen.

"I saw it myself," I say. "He's gone."

Her eyes water up and she shakes me loose. Then she turns her back and puts her hand in her face. Her long fingers extend all the way past her forehead. For some reason, I become offended when I see her crying over that bastard.

"Nova ..." I approach her and put my hand on her shoulder. "It's okay."

"It's not okay," she says.

"Look," I say. "He was a son of a bitch. Forget about him."

She turns and looks at me with anger. "He was my father!"

I step back.

Then I say, "Nova, I know what he did to you. He told me all about it."

Her expression is at first stunned, then furious. I tell her the story of why her father raped her. I don't think she ever knew. I don't think she ever got an explanation. Perhaps that was the unfinished business she had with him.

"You don't understand," she says, attacking me as if she blames me for everything that happened to her, rather than her father.

"He was a sick fucking asshole," I tell her. "He deserved to die."

She pushes me away from her so hard that I fall down. "Fuck you, Daniel!"

Then she runs away, off into the woods.

288

On the way back to the Warrior camp, I ride with Talon and Apple. Guy stayed with his people. He said he wanted to check on Molly and his kids, then he would catch up with me later. I didn't believe him, but he gave me his word and a man like Guy always honors his word. He said there was somebody back at the camp he had to pay his respects to.

"I can't believe they just turned us away," Apple says. "After all we did for them."

"It's the way it should be," Talon says. "We don't belong with their kind."

When we arrive at the camp, Slayer and Krall run at each other so hard that they nearly knock each other down. She picks him up and spins him around her. Then they embrace.

Nova doesn't even look at me once we get there. Now she is not only distant with me, but completely pissed off. I guess she has the right to be mad at me for what I said about the Chief. No matter what he did to her, he was still her father.

They bury their dead and have a mass funeral. The graves line the campsite, with Grandma's resting mound in the center. Once they were almost two hundred strong, now the Warriors are but nineteen women. During the ceremony, Talon explains that these hunting grounds are their home. They will rest peacefully here. However, she wants to take the surviving Warriors far away, deep into the wasteland. She says there are other civilizations to the south who might accept them, or maybe they will be good targets for future raids. None of the wolf women object.

Krall decides not to go with them. He believes they

will be fine without his skills, but the Outlander camp is in need of medical attention. He says they might even need guidance or leadership, which he can also provide.

I'm surprised that Slayer is not disappointed to see him go. She seems happy for him. Perhaps it is just an act. When they say goodbye, it is awkward. Slayer waves her paw bashfully with a little smile.

As she turns away from him, Krall grabs her by the arm and pulls her close to him. He kisses her deeply, despite the hair and teeth and black dog lips. She is uncomfortable with it at first, but then gives in. She wraps herself around him and kisses him back. Judging by her reaction, I believe it is the only time they have ever kissed. It goes on for a very long time, and instead of looking away all of the wolf girls cheer and howl for them. Slayer practically has to rip herself away from him in order to get herself to stop.

She smiles in a daze as they separate. Krall blows her a kiss and gets into a vehicle. He honks the horn and waves at everyone with three hands as he drives away. I doubt Krall and Slayer will ever see each other again, but they both seem fine with that. They both seem happy to have just spent the time they did together, satisfied with only the memories. Perhaps they know it will never work out and want to depart on a pleasant note.

Later in the day, I find my brother alone in the center of the camp. He stands over Ashley's grave, looking down at the tiny mound of dirt with a flower sticking out of its top.

I come up behind him. He doesn't seem to be standing in mourning. He stands there with his back straight and his head held high, as if he was proud to have known the girl. In his hands, he holds the drawing of himself. He has put it in a frame that he took from his home. Although the drawing was not quite finished—everything was drawn perfectly except for Guy's missing mustache—he still nods his head in approval at the fine work of art.

When he hears my footsteps coming closer, he turns his head to look at me. I notice that he has shaved off his mustache, so that it would match Ashley's drawing of himself. So that her last creation in this world would indeed be complete.

He continues admiring the painting as I approach him.

"I'll be heading back soon," he tells me. "There's a lot of work that needs to get done."

I nod at him.

He says, "With the Chief dead, I'll most likely replace him. I'll at least become Deputy Chief. Things are going to change in McDonaldland. I don't how long it's going to take, but things are going to change."

"I don't suppose they'll let wolf girls and mutants back in any time soon, will they?" I ask.

He grunts. "Maybe someday."

We only spend another ten minutes together before he has to go. I shake his hand, knowing that I'll probably never see him again. After all of this, I've come to understand my brother a little better. Perhaps he has come to understand a little of me.

When he goes, he takes the painting with him. He turns and gives me a salute, as if I were an honored Fry Guy hero. I salute him back. Looking at his clean shaven face, all I can think about is how stupid he looks without his mustache.

The Warriors take down their camp and get ready to move out, far into the wilds of the wasteland. Nova is packing up her tent and supplies, and stuffing them into the back of Apple's car.

I go to her and place my hand on her upper arm.

"I'm sorry about what I said back there," I tell her.

She pauses and then nods her head.

"No, I'm sorry," she says. "You were right. I just overreacted."

"It wasn't fair of me to bring that up," I say.

She returns to packing her belongings. When she is finished, we take a walk in the woods together. We find a tree to climb and sit up there, staring across the landscape. She holds my hand and I put two of my arms around her.

"I don't want you to come with us," she says.

Her hand becomes limp around mine.

"What?" I ask.

She sighs and gathers her thoughts.

"When I saw you eaten by that creature, and I thought you were dead, I was horrified," she says. "It felt like my heart had been ripped out of my chest."

After a pause, she says, "But then I felt a wave of relief. I didn't understand why at first. But then I thought about it, and realized that I was relieved that I wouldn't have to be with you anymore."

I remove my arms from her. A pain wells up from the inside of my guts.

"Don't get me wrong," she continues. "I'm happy you survived. More so than I can explain. But I'm also kind of angry for some reason. I don't really understand why I feel this way. Maybe it's because you remind me of my old life. I just want to forget about my old life."

She hugs me with all her strength and begins to cry. She weeps so much she can hardly speak, as she says, "I just think it would be better if we went separate ways. We have no future together. I'm a Warrior. Someday I will be wolf like my big sisters. I want this to happen. I can't have somebody like you holding me back, preventing me from going all the way, into the wild."

She kisses me and I kiss her back. I don't speak. I

292

can't think of anything to say to her. We climb down from the tree and make love in the woods. Unlike last time, we both let loose. We put all of our passion into it. When Nova comes, she orgasms so powerfully that it causes her to transform three times the amount as any transformation I have seen before. Hair sprouts on her arms and chest. Her face twists and stretches until a muzzle forms. Her muscles bulge and pop all over her body.

After she collapses on top of me, we nuzzle our faces together, holding each other in silence. I hold her tight with all of my limbs, not wanting to let her go.

When she leaves, she doesn't look at me. She just gets up, grabs her clothes, and wanders away naked through the forest. That was her goodbye. No words, no gestures, just an intense physical connection.

"I told you," Talon says, looking at me somberly as the Warriors rev their engines to leave. "We're just not meant to be together."

"I still believe in compromise," I tell her.

"I know you do," she says.

293

Talon says her goodbye and then gets on her motorcycle. She looks back only for a second to hail my bravery with the raising of an axe over her head. Then she rides off, leading the caravan of wolf women out of the woods, to find a new home far away from here.

I slump down on a log by a smoldering campfire, placing my forehead into my hands. Part of me wishes I just would have gone with the Warriors anyway. Even if Nova doesn't want to be with me now, she might change her mind someday. At least I would have some friends, and a purpose. But there is another part of me that knows November will never again be the girl I fell in love with when I was a kid. We've grown too far apart. It's probably best if we go our separate ways. I still think Talon is wrong. Men and women can be together in this world. But for Nova and I, we weren't meant to be.

After a few minutes, I hear an engine roaring through the woods. When I look up, I see a motorcycle entering the camp. Pippi's face gleams at me as she pulls up to the campfire.

"I didn't know you weren't coming with us," she says, getting down off of the bike and turning off the motor.

"I don't belong with the Warriors," I say.

She squats down in front of me, trying to look me in the eyes as I stare into the dirt.

"Huh," she says.

She sits down on the log next to me. "What are you going to do, then?"

I inch away from her.

"I have no idea," I say.

"You're not going to join the Meat, are you?" She asks me this with an angry tone.

"I don't know," I say. "I don't want to."

"Are you going to just stay here, then? All by yourself?"

I shrug. "Maybe."

"Okay," she says, smacking her hands into her lap. "Then I'll stay with you."

She looks at me with a big smile on her face.

"What?"

That was the last thing I wanted to hear her say.

"Well, you're going to get eaten by one of my big sisters if you're all alone. You need me to protect you. And I want you to help me raise my baby."

She holds her stomach at me.

"But you're a Warrior," I say. "You belong with your own kind."

"Yeah, but this is my home," she says. "I lived in these woods my entire life. I'd rather stay than leave with the others."

She puts one of my hands in hers.

"Besides," she says, "this way I don't have to worry about other people messing with my things."

By *other people* she must mean Nova, and by *things* she must mean me.

"So what do you say?" she asks.

"I don't know."

"Come on," she says. "What else are you going to do?"

I find it strange that she is actually trying to persuade me rather than order me to agree.

"Fine," I say. "We'll give it a try."

I'm not sure if I agree because I don't know what else to do, because I don't want to be alone, or because I'm worried about what she'll do to me if I refuse. I decide that it's all of the above.

Epilogue

Pippi's Puppy

Pippi and I move into an old building in an ancient ruined city not too far from McDonaldland. I decide to reinforce the structure the best I can so that it doesn't come crashing down on us someday. At first, being with Pippi is a living hell. She still tells me what to do as if I'm still her property. But after a while I begin to warm up to her. She's not all teeth and claws.

After a few months, new women join our group as they are cast out of McDonaldland. From their stories, not much seems to have changed there. Yet. We also let some mutant men join our camp, but not many of them stay. I hear that Krall is doing well as leader of the Outlanders. He is working on a way to remove the parasites from infected citizens and reverse the effects, but I'm not sure how successful he's been. Perhaps one day the mutations will come to an end, but until then the wasteland continues to fill with outcasts.

Pippi has her baby. We haven't named him yet, but she calls it her *Puppy*. I really hope the name doesn't stick. She wants to have another one soon, so we've already started working on it. We don't have sex very much. I do as Talon recommended and focus more on foreplay than actual penetration. When we're turned on enough, we have a quick burst of sexual intercourse. Sometimes Pippi has an orgasm, sometimes she doesn't. Either way, her transformations are not very drastic.

She doesn't really want to turn any time soon. She says she wants to wait until her children are grown up. Then she wants to become a giant wolf and run wild with her big sisters, hunting and eating plump little men who cross her path. Sometimes she even teases about how she'll eat me when she's a big wolf. I don't know if she's serious or not, but I wouldn't doubt it.

A year ago, I ran into a black wolf in the woods. It was larger than a car, but not quite as big as a bus. The beast didn't growl or attack. It gazed at me not with a hungry stare, but one of longing. It crept slowly up to me, sniffed me, and then licked me across the face.

When I looked into its enormous eyes, I swear that I could see Nova looking back at me. With all she had been through, it seemed likely that she would want to turn as soon as possible, leave her memories behind and embrace the wilderness absolutely.

She couldn't possibly have remembered me in that state, but there definitely seemed to have been some kind of recognition. A familiar smell, perhaps. An instinct.

The wolf nuzzled its enormous black head against mine, breathing heavily and wagging its tail. It closed its eyes. I closed mine, and hugged its large fluffy neck, imagining it to be Nova. I inhaled the smell of her hair, imagining the time I held her in my arms when we were young, on our picnic overlooking farm country.

After a few minutes, the wolf squished its nose against my chest like it was giving me a quick kiss. Then the wolf turned and dashed away, looking back only once. I haven't seen that particular wolf since.

Eventually, our group becomes large enough to be called the Warriors of the Wild once more. A woman with strength of leadership takes charge of the group. She is wise and filled with courage, but Pippi still likes to pretend she is in charge.

Pippi isn't the best mom. She likes to ditch her Puppy in the crib—which I built out of McDonald's straws—and go off into the woods by herself, catching animals with her own teeth. I'm happy I stayed with Pippi, for the kid's sake. She has another one on the way, but that hasn't made her slow down for a second.

Some days I wonder what it would have been like if it would have worked between Nova and I. I wonder if I would have been happier. Perhaps. But I like my life with Pippi. There's something about her that just fills me with spirit. I can't quite figure out what.

She's a hairy, dirty, smelly, dog-faced, flea-ridden, sadistic, evil, self-centered, arrogant, demanding, annoying, immature, bossy, needy, murderous, cold-hearted, psychotic bitch who drives me insane every second of every day, but for some reason I have grown to love her more than anything in the world, and there's no one I'd rather be with.

THE END

ABOUT THE AUTHOR

Carlton Mellick III is one of the leading authors in the new *Bizarro* genre uprising. Since 2001, his surreal counterculture novels have drawn an international cult following despite the fact that they have been shunned by most libraries and corporate bookstores. He lives in Portland, OR, the bizarro fiction mecca.

Visit him online at **www.carltonmellick.com**

Bizarro books

CATALOG   SPRING 2010

Bizarro Books publishes under the following imprints:

www.rawdogscreamingpress.com

www.eraserheadpress.com

www.afterbirthbooks.com

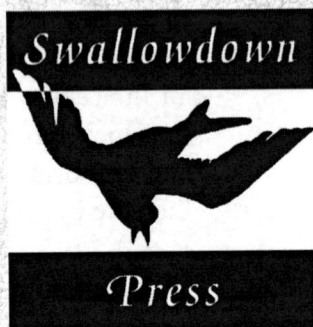

www.swallowdownpress.com

For all your Bizarro needs visit:

WWW.BIZARROCENTRAL.COM

Introduce yourselves to the bizarro genre and all of its authors with the Bizarro Starter Kit series. Each volume features short novels and short stories by ten of the leading bizarro authors, designed to give you a perfect sampling of the genre for only $5 plus shipping.

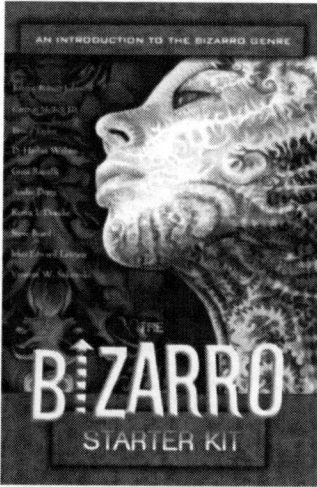

BB-0X1
"The Bizarro Starter Kit" (Orange)

Featuring D. Harlan Wilson, Carlton Mellick III, Jeremy Robert Johnson, Kevin L Donihe, Gina Ranalli, Andre Duza, Vincent W. Sakowski, Steve Beard, John Edward Lawson, and Bruce Taylor.

236 pages $5

BB-0X2
"The Bizarro Starter Kit" (Blue)

Featuring Ray Fracalossy, Jeremy C. Shipp, Jordan Krall, Mykle Hansen, Andersen Prunty, Eckhard Gerdes, Bradley Sands, Steve Aylett, Christian TeBordo, and Tony Rauch.

244 pages $5

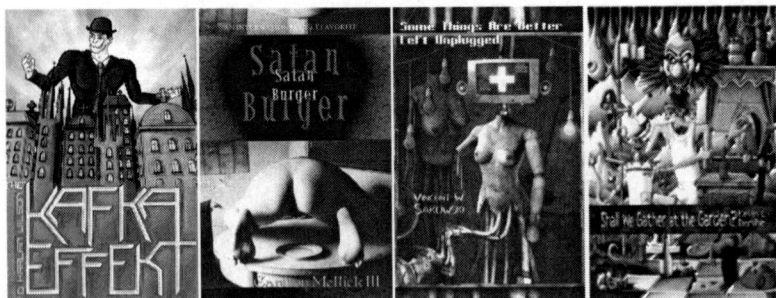

BB-001 "The Kafka Effekt" D. Harlan Wilson - A collection of forty-four irreal short stories loosely written in the vein of Franz Kafka, with more than a pinch of William S. Burroughs sprinkled on top. **211 pages** **$14**

BB-002 "Satan Burger" Carlton Mellick III - The cult novel that put Carlton Mellick III on the map ... Six punks get jobs at a fast food restaurant owned by the devil in a city violently overpopulated by surreal alien cultures. **236 pages** **$14**

BB-003 "Some Things Are Better Left Unplugged" Vincent Sakwoski - Join The Man and his Nemesis, the obese tabby, for a nightmare roller coaster ride into this postmodern fantasy. **152 pages** **$10**

BB-004 "Shall We Gather At the Garden?" Kevin L Donihe - Donihe's Debut novel. Midgets take over the world, The Church of Lionel Richie vs. The Church of the Byrds, plant porn and more! **244 pages** **$14**

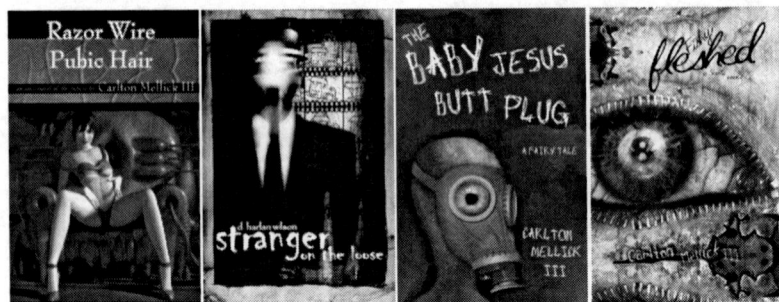

BB-005 "Razor Wire Pubic Hair" Carlton Mellick III - A genderless humandildo is purchased by a razor dominatrix and brought into her nightmarish world of bizarre sex and mutilation. **176 pages** **$11**

BB-006 "Stranger on the Loose" D. Harlan Wilson - The fiction of Wilson's 2nd collection is planted in the soil of normalcy, but what grows out of that soil is a dark, witty, otherworldly jungle... **228 pages** **$14**

BB-007 "The Baby Jesus Butt Plug" Carlton Mellick III - Using clones of the Baby Jesus for anal sex will be the hip sex fetish of the future. **92 pages** **$10**

BB-008 "Fishyfleshed" Carlton Mellick III - The world of the past is an illogical flatland lacking in dimension and color, a sick-scape of crispy squid people wandering the desert for no apparent reason. **260 pages** **$14**

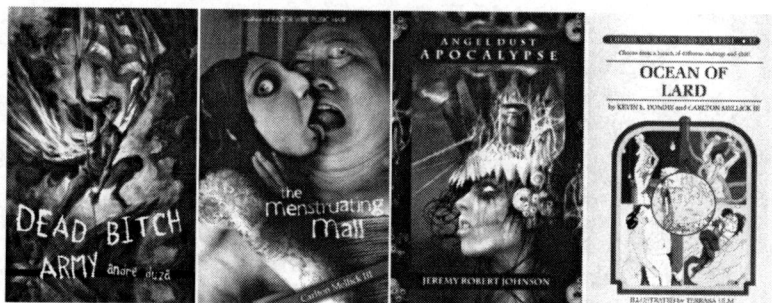

BB-009 **"Dead Bitch Army" Andre Duza** - Step into a world filled with racist teenagers, cannibals, 100 warped Uncle Sams, automobiles with razor-sharp teeth, living graffiti, and a pissed-off zombie bitch out for revenge. **344 pages $16**

BB-010 **"The Menstruating Mall" Carlton Mellick III** - "The Breakfast Club meets Chopping Mall as directed by David Lynch." - Brian Keene **212 pages $12**

BB-011 **"Angel Dust Apocalypse" Jeremy Robert Johnson** - Meth-heads, man-made monsters, and murderous Neo-Nazis. "Seriously amazing short stories..." - Chuck Palahniuk, author of Fight Club **184 pages $11**

BB-012 **"Ocean of Lard" Kevin L Donihe / Carlton Mellick III** - A parody of those old Choose Your Own Adventure kid's books about some very odd pirates sailing on a sea made of animal fat. **176 pages $12**

BB-013 **"Last Burn in Hell" John Edward Lawson** - From his lurid angst-affair with a lesbian music diva to his ascendance as unlikely pop icon the one constant for Kenrick Brimley, official state prison gigolo, is he's got no clue what he's doing. **172 pages $14**

BB-014 **"Tangerinephant" Kevin Dole 2** - TV-obsessed aliens have abducted Michael Tangerinephant in this bizarro combination of science fiction, satire, and surrealism. **164 pages $11**

BB-015 **"Foop!" Chris Genoa** - Strange happenings are going on at Dactyl, Inc, the world's first and only time travel tourism company. "A surreal pie in the face!" - Christopher Moore **300 pages $14**

BB-016 **"Spider Pie" Alyssa Sturgill** - A one-way trip down a rabbit hole inhabited by sexual deviants and friendly monsters, fairytale beginnings and hideous endings. **104 pages $11**

BB-017 "The Unauthorized Woman" Efrem Emerson - Enter the world of the inner freak, a landscape populated by the pre-dead and morticioners, by cockroaches and 300-lb robots. **104 pages $11**

BB-018 "Fugue XXIX" Forrest Aguirre - Tales from the fringe of speculative literary fiction where innovative minds dream up the future's uncharted territories while mining forgotten treasures of the past. **220 pages $16**

BB-019 "Pocket Full of Loose Razorblades" John Edward Lawson - A collection of dark bizarro stories. From a giant rectum to a foot-fungus factory to a girl with a biforked tongue. **190 pages $13**

BB-020 "Punk Land" Carlton Mellick III - In the punk version of Heaven, the anarchist utopia is threatened by corporate fascism and only Goblin, Mortician's sperm, and a blue-mohawked female assassin named Shark Girl can stop them. **284 pages $15**

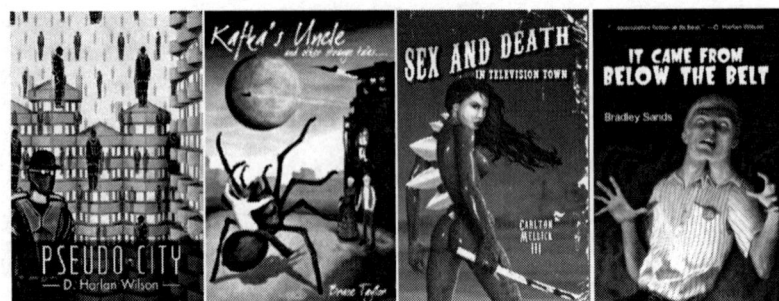

BB-021 "Pseudo-City" D. Harlan Wilson - Pseudo-City exposes what waits in the bathroom stall, under the manhole cover and in the corporate boardroom, all in a way that can only be described as mind-bogglingly irreal. **220 pages $16**

BB-022 "Kafka's Uncle and Other Strange Tales" Bruce Taylor - Anslenot and his giant tarantula (tormentor? fri-end?) wander a desecrated world in this novel and collection of stories from Mr. Magic Realism Himself. **348 pages $17**

BB-023 "Sex and Death In Television Town" Carlton Mellick III - In the old west, a gang of hermaphrodite gunslingers take refuge from a demon plague in Telos: a town where its citizens have televisions instead of heads. **184 pages $12**

BB-024 "It Came From Below The Belt" Bradley Sands - What can Grover Goldstein do when his severed, sentient penis forces him to return to high school and help it win the presidential election? **204 pages $13**

BB-025 "Sick: An Anthology of Illness" John Lawson, editor - These Sick stories are horrendous and hilarious dissections of creative minds on the scalpel's edge. **296 pages $16**

BB-026 "Tempting Disaster" John Lawson, editor - A shocking and alluring anthology from the fringe that examines our culture's obsession with taboos. **260 pages $16**

BB-027 "Siren Promised" Jeremy Robert Johnson - Nominated for the Bram Stoker Award. A potent mix of bad drugs, bad dreams, brutal bad guys, and surreal/incredible art by Alan M. Clark. **190 pages $13**

BB-028 "Chemical Gardens" Gina Ranalli - Ro and punk band Green is the Enemy find Kreepkins, a surfer-dude warlock, a vengeful demon, and a Metal Priestess in their way as they try to escape an underground nightmare. **188 pages $13**

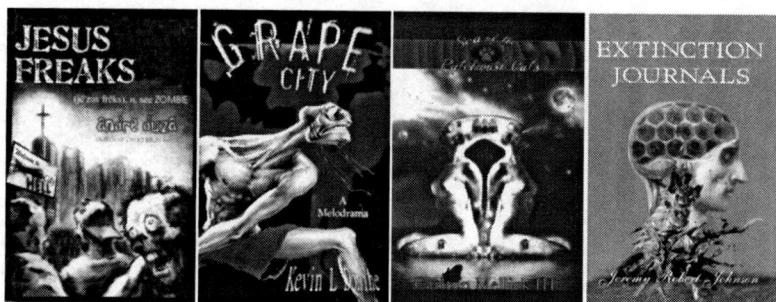

BB-029 "Jesus Freaks" Andre Duza - For God so loved the world that he gave his only two begotten sons... and a few million zombies. **400 pages $16**

BB-030 "Grape City" Kevin L. Donihe - More Donihe-style comedic bizarro about a demon named Charles who is forced to work a minimum wage job on Earth after Hell goes out of business. **108 pages $10**

BB-031"Sea of the Patchwork Cats" Carlton Mellick III - A quiet dreamlike tale set in the ashes of the human race. For Mellick enthusiasts who also adore The Twilight Zone. **112 pages $10**

BB-032 "Extinction Journals" Jeremy Robert Johnson - An uncanny voyage across a newly nuclear America where one man must confront the problems associated with loneliness, insane dieties, radiation, love, and an ever-evolving cockroach suit with a mind of its own. **104 pages $10**

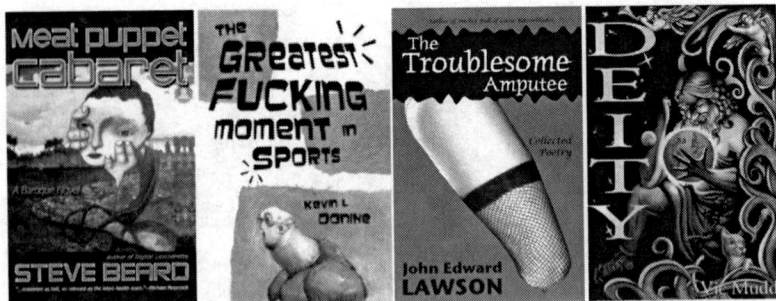

BB-033 **"Meat Puppet Cabaret" Steve Beard** - At last! The secret connection between Jack the Ripper and Princess Diana's death revealed! **240 pages $16 / $30**

BB-034 **"The Greatest Fucking Moment in Sports" Kevin L. Donihe** - In the tradition of the surreal anti-sitcom Get A Life comes a tale of triumph and agape love from the master of comedic bizarro. **108 pages $10**

BB-035 **"The Troublesome Amputee" John Edward Lawson** - Disturbing verse from a man who truly believes nothing is sacred and intends to prove it. **104 pages $9**

BB-036 **"Deity" Vic Mudd** - God (who doesn't like to be called "God") comes down to a typical, suburban, Ohio family for a little vacation—but it doesn't turn out to be as relaxing as He had hoped it would be... **168 pages $12**

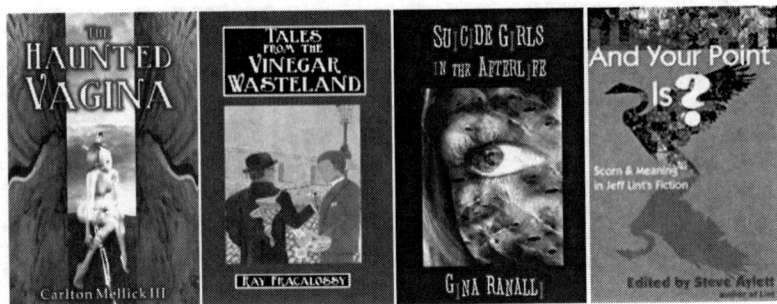

BB-037 **"The Haunted Vagina" Carlton Mellick III** - It's difficult to love a woman whose vagina is a gateway to the world of the dead. **132 pages $10**

BB-038 **"Tales from the Vinegar Wasteland" Ray Fracalossy** - Witness: a man is slowly losing his face, a neighbor who periodically screams out for no apparent reason, and a house with a room that doesn't actually exist. **240 pages $14**

BB-039 **"Suicide Girls in the Afterlife" Gina Ranalli** - After Pogue commits suicide, she unexpectedly finds herself an unwilling "guest" at a hotel in the Afterlife, where she meets a group of bizarre characters, including a goth Satan, a hippie Jesus, and an alien-human hybrid. **100 pages $9**

BB-040 **"And Your Point Is?" Steve Aylett** - In this follow-up to LINT multiple authors provide critical commentary and essays about Jeff Lint's mind-bending literature. **104 pages $11**

BB-041 "Not Quite One of the Boys" Vincent Sakowski - While drug-dealer Maxi drinks with Dante in purgatory, God and Satan play a little tri-level chess and do a little bargaining over his business partner, Vinnie, who is still left on earth. **220 pages $14**

BB-042 "Teeth and Tongue Landscape" Carlton Mellick III - On a planet made out of meat, a socially-obsessive monophobic man tries to find his place amongst the strange creatures and communities that he comes across. **110 pages $10**

BB-043 "War Slut" Carlton Mellick III - Part "1984," part "Waiting for Godot," and part action horror video game adaptation of John Carpenter's "The Thing." **116 pages $10**

BB-044 "All Encompassing Trip" Nicole Del Sesto - In a world where coffee is no longer available, the only television shows are reality TV re-runs, and the animals are talking back, Nikki, Amber and a singing Coyote in a do-rag are out to restore the light **308 pages $15**

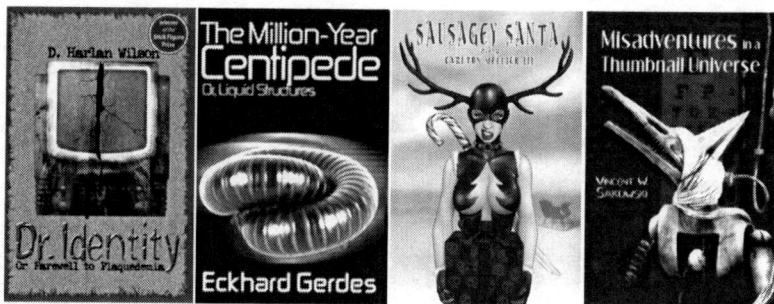

BB-045 "Dr. Identity" D. Harlan Wilson - Follow the Dystopian Duo on a killing spree of epic proportions through the irreal postcapitalist city of Bliptown where time ticks sideways, artificial Bug-Eyed Monsters punish citizens for consumer-capitalist lethargy, and ultraviolence is as essential as a daily multivitamin. **208 pages $15**

BB-046 "The Million-Year Centipede" Eckhard Gerdes - Wakelin, frontman for 'The Hinge,' wrote a poem so prophetic that to ignore it dooms a person to drown in blood. **130 pages $12**

BB-047 "Sausagey Santa" Carlton Mellick III - A bizarro Christmas tale featuring Santa as a piratey mutant with a body made of sausages. 124 pages $10

BB-048 "Misadventures in a Thumbnail Universe" Vincent Sakowski - Dive deep into the surreal and satirical realms of neo-classical Blender Fiction, filled with television shoes and flesh-filled skies. **120 pages $10**

BB-049 "Vacation" Jeremy C. Shipp - Blueblood Bernard Johnson leaved his boring life behind to go on The Vacation, a year-long corporate sponsored odyssey. But instead of seeing the world, Bernard is captured by terrorists, becomes a key figure in secret drug wars, and, worse, doesn't once miss his secure American Dream. **160 pages $14**

BB-051 "13 Thorns" Gina Ranalli - Thirteen tales of twisted, bizarro horror. **240 pages $13**

BB-050 "Discouraging at Best" John Edward Lawson - A collection where the absurdity of the mundane expands exponentially creating a tidal wave that sweeps reason away. For those who enjoy satire, bizarro, or a good old-fashioned slap to the senses. **208 pages $15**

BB-052 "Better Ways of Being Dead" Christian TeBordo - In this class, the students have to keep one palm down on the table at all times, and listen to lectures about a panda who speaks Chinese. **216 pages $14**

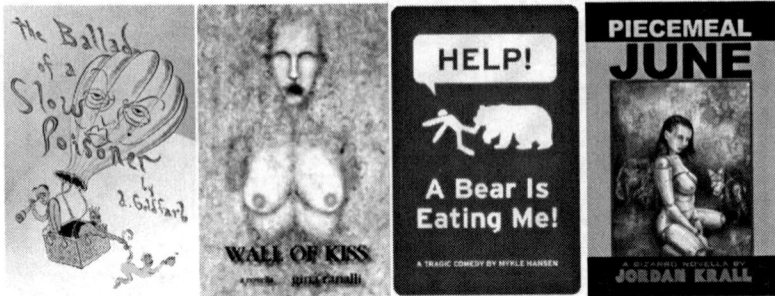

BB-053 "Ballad of a Slow Poisoner" Andrew Goldfarb Millford Mutterwurst sat down on a Tuesday to take his afternoon tea, and made the unpleasant discovery that his elbows were becoming flatter. **128 pages $10**

BB-054 "Wall of Kiss" Gina Ranalli - A woman... A wall... Sometimes love blooms in the strangest of places. **108 pages $9**

BB-055 "HELP! A Bear is Eating Me" Mykle Hansen - The bizarro, heartwarming, magical tale of poor planning, hubris and severe blood loss... **150 pages $11**

BB-056 "Piecemeal June" Jordan Krall - A man falls in love with a living sex doll, but with love comes danger when her creator comes after her with crab-squid assassins. **90 pages $9**

BB-057 "Laredo" Tony Rauch - Dreamlike, surreal stories by Tony Rauch. **180 pages $12**

BB-058 "The Overwhelming Urge" Andersen Prunty - A collection of bizarro tales by Andersen Prunty. **150 pages $11**

BB-059 "Adolf in Wonderland" Carlton Mellick III - A dreamlike adventure that takes a young descendant of Adolf Hitler's design and sends him down the rabbit hole into a world of imperfection and disorder. **180 pages $11**

BB-060 "Super Cell Anemia" Duncan B. Barlow - "Unrelentingly bizarre and mysterious, unsettling in all the right ways..." - Brian Evenson. **180 pages $12**

BB-061 "Ultra Fuckers" Carlton Mellick III - Absurdist suburban horror about a couple who enter an upper middle class gated community but can't find their way out. **108 pages $9**

BB-062 "House of Houses" Kevin L. Donihe - An odd man wants to marry his house. Unfortunately, all of the houses in the world collapse at the same time in the Great House Holocaust. Now he must travel to House Heaven to find his departed fiancee. **172 pages $11**

BB-063 "Necro Sex Machine" Andre Duza - The Dead Bicth returns in this follow-up to the bizarro zombie epic Dead Bitch Army. **400 pages $16**

BB-064 "Squid Pulp Blues" Jordan Krall - In these three bizarro-noir novellas, the reader is thrown into a world of murderers, drugs made from squid parts, deformed gun-toting veterans, and a mischievous apocalyptic donkey. **204 pages $12**

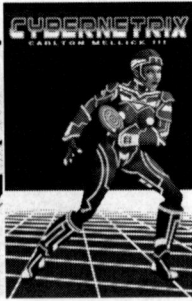

BB-065 "Jack and Mr. Grin" Andersen Prunty - "When Mr. Grin calls you can hear a smile in his voice. Not a warm and friendly smile, but the kind that seizes your spine in fear. You don't need to pay your phone bill to hear it. That smile is in every line of Prunty's prose." - Tom Bradley. **208 pages $12**

BB-066 "Cybernetrix" Carlton Mellick III - What would you do if your normal everyday world was slowly mutating into the video game world from Tron? **212 pages $12**

BB-067 "Lemur" Tom Bradley - Spencer Sproul is a would-be serial-killing bus boy who can't manage to murder, injure, or even scare anybody. However, there are other ways to do damage to far more people and do it legally... **120 pages $12**

BB-068 "Cocoon of Terror" Jason Earls - Decapitated corpses...a sculpture of terror...Zelian's masterpiece, his Cocoon of Terror, will trigger a supernatural disaster for everyone on Earth. **196 pages $14**

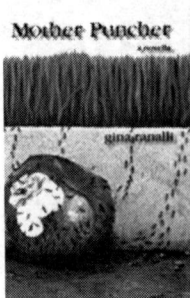

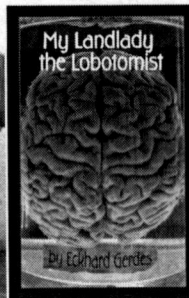

BB-069 "Mother Puncher" Gina Ranalli - The world has become tragically over-populated and now the government strongly opposes procreation. Ed is employed by the government as a mother-puncher. He doesn't relish his job, but he knows it has to be done and he knows he's the best one to do it. **120 pages $9**

BB-070 "My Landlady the Lobotomist" Eckhard Gerdes - The brains of past tenants line the shelves of my boarding house, soaking in a mysterious elixir. One more slip-up and the landlady might just add my frontal lobe to her collection. **116 pages $12**

BB-071 "CPR for Dummies" Mickey Z. - This hilarious freakshow at the world's end is the fragmented, sobering debut novel by acclaimed nonfiction author Mickey Z. **216 pages $14**

BB-072 "Zerostrata" Andersen Prunty - Hansel Nothing lives in a tree house, suffers from memory loss, has a very eccentric family, and falls in love with a woman who runs naked through the woods every night. **144 pages $11**

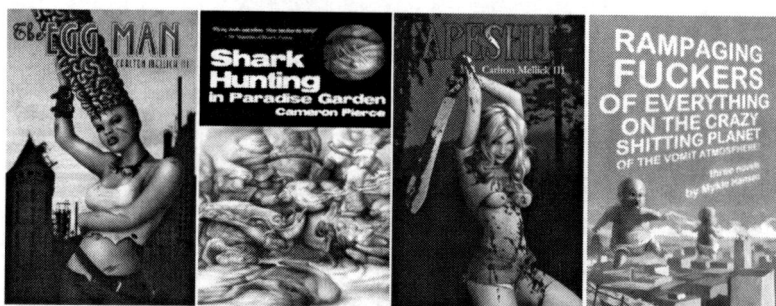

BB-073 "The Egg Man" Carlton Mellick III - It is a world where humans reproduce like insects. Children are the property of corporations, and having an enormous ten-foot brain implanted into your skull is a grotesque sexual fetish. Mellick's industrial urban dystopia is one of his darkest and grittiest to date. **184 pages $11**

BB-074 "Shark Hunting in Paradise Garden" Cameron Pierce - A group of strange humanoid religious fanatics travel back in time to the Garden of Eden to discover it is invested with hundreds of giant flying maneating sharks. **150 pages $10**

BB-075 "Apeshit" Carlton Mellick III - Friday the 13th meets Visitor Q. Six hipster teens go to a cabin in the woods inhabited by a deformed killer. An incredibly fucked-up parody of B-horror movies with a bizarro slant. **192 pages $12**

BB-076 "Rampaging Fuckers of Everything on the Crazy Shitting Planet of the Vomit At smosphere" Mykle Hansen - 3 bizarro satires. Monster Cocks, Journey to the Center of Agnes Cuddlebottom, and Crazy Shitting Planet. **228 pages $12**

BB-077 "The Kissing Bug" Daniel Scott Buck - In the tradition of Roald Dahl, Tim Burton, and Edward Gorey, comes this bizarro anti-war children's story about a bohemian conenose kissing bug who falls in love with a human woman. **116 pages $10**

BB-078 "MachoPoni" Lotus Rose - It's My Little Pony... *Bizarro* style! A long time ago Poniworld was split in two. On one side of the Jagged Line is the Pastel Kingdom, a magical land of music, parties, and positivity. On the other side of the Jagged Line is Dark Kingdom inhabited by an army of undead ponies. **148 pages $11**

BB-079 "The Faggiest Vampire" Carlton Mellick III - A Roald Dahl-esque children's story about two faggy vampires who partake in a mustache competition to find out which one is truly the faggiest. **104 pages $10**

BB-080 "Sky Tongues" Gina Ranalli - The autobiography of Sky Tongues, the biracial hermaphrodite actress with tongues for fingers. Follow her strange life story as she rises from freak to fame. **204 pages $12**

ORDER FORM

TITLES	QTY	PRICE	TOTAL

Please make checks and moneyorders payable to ROSE O'KEEFE / BIZARRO BOOKS in U.S. funds only. Please don't send bad checks! Allow 2-6 weeks for delivery. International orders may take longer. If you'd like to pay online via PAYPAL.COM, send payments to publisher@eraserheadpress.com.

SHIPPING: US ORDERS - $2 for the first book, $1 for each additional book. For priority shipping, add an additional $4. INT'L ORDERS - $5 for the first book, $3 for each additional book. Add an additional $5 per book for global priority shipping.

Send payment to:

BIZARRO BOOKS
   C/O Rose O'Keefe
   205 NE Bryant
   Portland, OR 97211

Address		
City	State	Zip
Email	Phone	

Lightning Source UK Ltd.
Milton Keynes UK
UKOW05f1930071013

218638UK00020B/1869/P